W9-CDK-415

cover story

cover story

a novel

SUSAN RIGETTI

wm
WILLIAM MORROW
An Imprint of HarperCollins*Publishers*

This is a work of fiction. Names, characters, places, and incidents are products of the author's imagination or are used fictitiously and are not to be construed as real. Any resemblance to actual events, locales, organizations, or persons, living or dead, is entirely coincidental.

For information, address HarperCollins Publishers, 195 Broadway, New York, NY 10007.

HarperCollins books may be purchased for educational, business, or sales promotional use. For information, please email the Special Markets Department at SPsales@harpercollins.com.

FIRST EDITION

Designed by Bonni Leon-Berman

Library of Congress Cataloging-in-Publication Data has been applied for.

ISBN 978-0-06-307205-3

22 23 24 25 26 LSC 10 9 8 7 6 5 4 3 2 1

For Chad, Seymour, and Boaz

cover story

PART 1

the intern

FEDERAL BUREAU OF INVESTIGATION

DATE OF TRANSCRIPTION: 3/15/2017

CAROLINA J. KOPP, an editor at *ELLE* magazine, a subsidiary of Hearst Magazine Media, Inc., was contacted at her employment at 300 West 57th Street, New York, New York, after calling the NYFBI office and requesting a meeting. Kopp was advised as to the nature of this investigation and provided the following information.

KOPP stated that CAT WOLFF has worked as a freelance journalist at *ELLE* magazine since 2016. She advised that CAT WOLFF was given the title of "contributing editor" in January 2017, after CAT WOLFF stated that *Marie Claire* magazine had made her an offer of employment.

KOPP stated that at a party in February 2017, she spoke with Sapna Kumari, an editor at *Marie Claire* magazine. Kopp provided that during this conversation she mentioned CAT WOLFF to Kumari and learned that *Marie Claire* never made an offer of employment to CAT WOLFF and that, furthermore, CAT WOLFF had never worked at *Marie Claire* in any capacity.

KOPP advised that after this incident, she looked into the background and social media presence of CAT WOLFF. She stated that she found the Instagram account of CAT WOLFF to be followed by what she believes to be bot accounts. She advised that CAT WOLFF provided The Plaza Hotel as her address. She provided that CAT WOLFF is paid $1,500 each month by *ELLE* and that CAT WOLFF had stated that her position as contributing editor at *ELLE* is her sole employment and only source of income.

KOPP provided that *ELLE* had been unable to confirm the identity of CAT WOLFF. Kopp stated that when she looked at a routine background check *ELLE* had run in January 2017, it reported the full name of CAT WOLFF as "Inge Catherine Wolff." Kopp further advised that according to public records research obtained by *ELLE*'s human resources department, Inge Catherine Wolff currently resides in Buenos Aires, Argentina, and not at The Plaza Hotel.

INVESTIGATION ON: 3/15/2017

At: NEW YORK, NEW YORK

By: SPECIAL AGENT JENÉE PARKER

LORA E. RICCI

400 Broome Street
New York, NY 10013
March 17, 2017

ELLE

Attn: Human Resources
300 West 57th St.
New York, NY 10019

Dear Internship Coordinator,

I would like to apply for a summer 2017 internship at *ELLE*.

I'm currently a student at NYU, where I'm pursuing a double major in English and journalism.

I have been a loyal reader of *ELLE* for over a decade. Growing up in Allentown, Pennsylvania, my life was far from glamorous, but magazines like *ELLE* showed me what was possible, showed me what my life could be. When I was in middle school, I'd go to the library and read the latest issues of *ELLE* and other fashion magazines from cover to cover. In high school, I used the money I earned babysitting and working at Target to become a subscriber to these same magazines, and they've been arriving at my doorstep ever since.

ELLE has the perfect combination of everything that impacts the lives of young women: fashion, beauty, books, and thoughtful essays on politics and current events that have changed the way I see the world around me. My dream is to become a magazine editor after I graduate from college, and being an intern at *ELLE* would bring me one step closer to achieving this goal.

I think I would be a strong addition to the team. I'm organized, extremely hardworking, and reliable. I'm passionate about fashion, beauty, and pop culture, and I read about these topics obsessively so that I'm always up-to-date on current trends. I have a lot of experience doing research, fact-checking, and writing long-form pieces in my college classes and short articles for my school newspaper.

My résumé is enclosed. I'm so excited about the possibility of working at *ELLE* this summer, and I can't wait to hear back from you.

Sincerely,

Lora Elizabeth Ricci

Lora Elizabeth Ricci
400 Broome Street | New York, NY 10013

OBJECTIVE
To obtain an internship at *ELLE*.

EDUCATION

New York University
Majors: English and Journalism
Degree: Pursuing a Bachelor of Arts Degree
Fall 2016-Present

Penn State Lehigh Valley
Major: English
GPA: 3.7
Degree: None (Transferred to NYU)
Fall 2014-Spring 2016

Bucks County Community College
Major: Liberal Arts
Degree: None (Transferred to Penn State)
GPA: 4.0
Fall 2013-Spring 2014

William Allen High School
Allentown, PA
GPA: 4.0
Graduated Spring 2013

WORK EXPERIENCE

Target
Cashier, 2011–2016

The Centurion
Staff Reporter, 2013–2014

Allentown Public Library
Volunteer, 2011–2013

SKILLS
Microsoft Word, Microsoft Excel, WordPress, CPR certification

Lora,

Your Dad and I are so proud of you.

Can't wait to hear all about your big New York City fashion magazine adventures.

Love,

Momma

P.S. Knock 'em dead, kiddo—Dad

The Diary of Lora Ricci

May 14, 2017

~~Dear Diary,~~

~~Dear Journal,~~

~~Dear,~~

~~Hi~~

Tomorrow is my first day at *ELLE*.

ELLE.

I've been dreaming of this day for so many years and I can't believe it's finally happening.

For as long as I can remember, I've had one major goal in life: become the editor in chief of a fashion magazine. I wanted to be Anna Wintour or Miranda Priestly (the *real* hero of *The Devil Wears Prada*), and was determined to get any job I could at any fashion magazine, and then work my ass off and rise through the ranks until I was the obvious choice to lead the publication. I could picture myself walking into a glass-walled conference room in a Manhattan skyscraper, wearing a dress right off the runway, and deciding which articles would go into the next issue, which celebrity would be the next cover star. Over the years, the specific dress (and shoes) in my fantasy changed a hundred times, but everything else stayed the same.

For years this was my only dream. And then I discovered contemporary fiction.

In school, we only read the classics. I liked them, don't get me wrong, but I didn't *love* them. They didn't make me feel anything. They didn't speak to me. But then I started reading contemporary novels and short stories written by women. Every time I read one, I'd think to myself, *Now this is what a book is supposed to be.* Soon I was obsessed, constantly searching for something that would make me feel that way again. I'd stay up late at night after finishing my homework, searching the internet for new (old) books to read, then order them through the library the next day. I was addicted. I couldn't stop. Donna Tartt. Margaret Atwood. Zadie Smith. Lorrie Moore. Helen DeWitt. Jenny Offill. Joan Didion. I loved them all.

There was this ache deep in my heart that only these books could fill, and their pages held secrets that only these women could tell me. *Tell me about myself,* I'd pray to each book before I opened it. *Tell me what my life can be. Tell me what it's like to be a woman in the world.* Eventually, I started to ask myself which secrets I knew that I could tell, which stories of mine would inspire stories in others.

And so a new dream came together: I would work at a fashion magazine *and* be a novelist *and* be a short-story writer. I was going to be all of these things, just like my goddess hero Zadie Smith, if Zadie was Zadie but also ran *Vogue* or *ELLE.*

I want to be all of these things. Hell, I *am* going to be all of these things, because here I am, about to actually work at *ELLE.* I'm still not even sure I believe it. This is going to change everything for me. Yeah, I know I won't be picking out covers or writing features or anything like that right off the bat, but so what? The only thing that matters is that I'm *in.* I have my foot in the door. I have the opportunity to work my ass off, learn everything I can, get hired for a full-time position, rise through the ranks, and prove to myself and to the whole world that I can do this.

I'm going to take everything I learn at the magazine and use it to become a better writer. And I'm going to spend all my extra time and energy writing my short stories and trying to figure out how to write a novel. I'm not going to waste a single moment.

That's why I'm starting this diary. First, it's another way for me to practice my writing. After all, if I can't write coherently about my own life, what good will I be at writing about fictional lives? Second, I want to hold myself accountable. I'm going to document what I'm learning and what I'm writing, and keep checking in with myself as often as I can to make sure I'm on track to realize my dreams. (And let's be real: after last year's grades, this might be my only chance.)

I still haven't told Mom and Dad about any of it. Not about the grades, the scholarship, the *I can't register for classes because I have no money to pay for them*—none of it. I wanted to tell them when they were here, but I couldn't. They're so excited for me. They never had the chance to go to college, and they're so impressed by everything I do. "You have no idea how proud you make me and your father," Mom told me before they left. "You're in the big leagues now, kiddo," Dad said.

They drove all the way up to the city to help me move out of my dorm and into my new apartment, and I was sick to my stomach with guilt the whole time. I kept wanting to tell them that they didn't understand, that they wouldn't be proud of me if they knew the truth. Every little brain cell in my head was screaming, *You've never kept a secret from them, you tell them everything, how can you possibly lie to them now?* And still, I lied: "Oh yeah, Mom, I'm totally going to register for classes, I just haven't had time, you know how busy I am."

Daughter of the year right here. Ugh.

On a happier note, I *really* love my new apartment. I've always wanted to live in Brooklyn, so this is basically another dream come true. It wasn't easy to find something I could afford this close to Prospect Park. I almost didn't find anything at all. But then, at the last minute, I joined a summer housing email list and found three other NYU students who had just signed a lease on a one-bedroom in a big Park Slope brownstone and needed a fourth roommate. They'd managed to cram two twin-size bunk beds into the bedroom (I'm stuck in one of the bottom bunks, lol).

The apartment has a lot of "character." There's only one bathroom and it has this weird avocado-green toilet, bathtub, and sink. And I'm pretty sure that the kitchen used to be a coat closet or something like that: there's a fridge, stove, sink, and tiny dishwasher, all squeezed next to one another in a line, but there's only like a foot of space between the appliances and the wall they face. Mom brought me a bunch of groceries from home, and when I tried to put them away, I found out that the fridge door only opens like six inches before it hits the wall.

Honestly, though? It's perfect. I love it.

But I can't let myself get carried away. I have to work my ass off and make a good impression so that I have a fighting chance of someday becoming an editor or writer. This may be the last opportunity I get.

Internship Goals:

1. Work your ass off.
2. Do high-quality work.
3. No slacking. Don't procrastinate.
4. Learn as much as you can.
5. Network. Get to know people, make sure they know YOU.

6. Try to impact things that go into the magazine.
7. Write at least one article.
8. In your free time, write a novel or short stories.

Tomorrow is your first day at *ELLE*.
Don't screw it up, Lora.
Do. Not. Screw. This. Up.

The Diary of Lora Ricci

May 15, 2017

Well, I officially survived my first day.

I woke up at six in the morning and was immediately hit by the cold, hard reality of sharing one bathroom with three other women when I found myself standing in line for the bathroom (and yes, I was last). There wasn't any hot water left by the time I got in the shower, so I took the quickest, coldest shower of my life.

Even though I'd picked out my "first day" outfit like a month ago, it took me forever to decide what to wear—everything I'd picked seemed wrong. I scrapped my original choice and, after like ten changes, finally settled on a black pencil skirt, black ankle boots, a sleeveless white top, and a blazer.

By that point, I was running out of time, so I had to rush my hair and makeup and skip my plans to eat breakfast at home (I ended up grabbing a bagel and coffee on the way to the Seventh Avenue station). I didn't even read my book or listen to any podcasts on the ride—I couldn't think about anything except the fact that it was my first day.

I got off the train at Fifty-Seventh Street, and I swear to god my heart skipped a beat when I saw Hearst Tower looming over Eighth Avenue. I'd never been inside the building before, and it turned out to be even more incredible than I'd imagined. When I walked through the doors and found myself standing inside this huge, expansive lobby with three escalators and an artificial waterfall, it all hit me: *Holy shit, I work at a magazine.* Working in this building will set the tone for how I approach my life right now: I'm going to take the internship seriously and I'm going to take *myself* seriously.

I rode one of the escalators up to the "real" first floor, where, after getting completely lost for a few minutes, I finally found the elevators. Waiting for the elevator took *forever* (I'm not kidding—I must have been standing there waiting for like eight or nine minutes). I was worried the elevators were broken and I'd be late, but the other people who were waiting didn't seem to care. I couldn't help but wonder where each of them worked, couldn't help but wonder if I'd ever read anything they'd written or edited.

The elevator finally arrived, and everyone crowded inside. By the time we got to the twenty-fourth floor, there were only two other women in the elevator with me. When the doors opened, we stepped out and there it was: the *ELLE* office. One of the women walked up to the glass door, badged in, and opened the door for me and the other woman. Before I could say thank you, they had already walked away and I was standing there in the lobby, wondering what I should do next.

There were three other women in the lobby, staring at their phones. They all seemed to be around my age, and were ten thousand times more stylish than me. For a brief moment, I felt so self-conscious, painfully aware that I looked like a complete nerd standing next to a group of fashion models. To make myself feel better, I told myself that they probably *were* models, and then I focused on the task at hand. I couldn't remember what on earth I was supposed to do. Was someone supposed to meet me? Was I supposed to go to a conference room? I pulled out my phone and started searching through my emails. Suddenly, I heard the sound of footsteps and looked up to see a woman in jeans, a white T-shirt, and pink heels walk into the lobby.

"Interns?" she asked with a smile.

The three other women looked up at her at the same time I did.

"Welcome!" the woman said, her voice warm and confident. "My name is Carolina Kopp, and I'm the deputy editor here at *ELLE*. We're so happy to have you here, and I hope you're all ready to jump in and get to work."

She turned around and left just as quickly as she'd arrived. The other interns and I all stared at each other, the confusion evident on our faces as we each asked ourselves the same question: *Are we supposed to follow her?* And then we heard Carolina's voice echo from down the hallway: "Our first stop is the fashion closet." We scrambled after her.

When we reached the fashion closet, my heart nearly stopped in my chest. The fashion closet is the heart and soul of any fashion magazine, and *ELLE*'s was just so impossibly wonderful. It was packed with racks and racks of designer clothing hot off the runway, and the whole place was so busy. People were grabbing things off the racks as others were putting things back on. A model was standing in the middle wearing an evening gown as a photographer walked around her in circles and a seamstress sewed something onto the hem of the dress. I think I could have happily lived and died in that room. I never wanted to leave.

Carolina sized us up pretty quickly. "You, you, and you," she said, pointing at the other three interns, "will be working here." Two of the interns smiled at each other—I think they're friends—and the other one sighed in relief.

"And you," Carolina said, turning to me. "I have something

else for you." With that, she left the room. I took one more look at the fashion closet, then hurried after her.

We walked through a series of busy hallways, passing other *ELLE* employees, seemingly endless rows of cubicles, the bathrooms, and the enormous kitchen. Finally, we reached a door. Carolina stopped and put her hand on the doorknob. "And *this* is where you'll be working: the beauty closet."

She opened the door, revealing a small closet lined with IKEA-white shelves that were stuffed to the brim. I walked inside. "Welcome to *ELLE*!" she said. Then she shut the door, leaving me alone in the closet.

I walked over to a corner, where there was a small desk, chair, and iMac. I put my bag on top of the desk and took a look around. In the middle of the room, on the gray carpet floor, was an enormous stack of unopened packages and shopping bags. I looked through several of the bags and found a bunch of brand-new makeup inside. The shelves that lined the walls were filled with all sorts of makeup, skin-care, and hair products. Everything appeared to be organized by type and then in alphabetical order by brand. There were several brands I'd never heard of before and others that I was familiar with from magazine ads and browsing around Sephora, like Dior, Urban Decay, and Shiseido.

I wasn't entirely sure what I was supposed to do, and disappointment was starting to set in. I couldn't help but wish I'd been assigned to the fashion closet, and wondered if I'd screwed myself over by showing up in clothes from Target and H&M. But let's be real: What choice did I have?

I soon met Haley, the assistant beauty editor. She explained how the closet works: products come in, either sent by PR people at beauty companies or requested by the beauty editors, and then the intern (me) keeps everything organized so that the beauty editors can easily find whatever they need. "Packages are just coming in *constantly,* like *all the time,*" she said, "so any time something comes in, just put it in the right place or find a new place for it, and label it." For today, she said, my job was to open up the packages and bags on the floor and put everything away.

When lunchtime rolled around, I met up with the other interns and we headed downstairs to the Hearst cafeteria, CAFE57. The two interns who seemed to be friends are Maggie and Katrine, who both go to Columbia. This is Maggie's second year interning at *ELLE* (she worked in the beauty closet last year); she said she loves it here and is hoping to get an editorial assistant job—at *ELLE* or elsewhere—later this year.

Katrine complained the whole time we were eating because she wore heels on her first day and was sent out on a "run." I learned that runs are when the editors send the fashion interns to pick up clothes from a store and bring them back for a shoot or for the editors to look at. Anyway, Katrine found herself walking around the city in three-inch heels; she said that by the time she was finishing her second run, she had to take off her shoes and walk in bare feet because her feet hurt so much.

As Katrine covered her blisters with Band-Aids, Maggie shook her head. "Rookie mistake," Maggie said. "Never, *ever,* I mean *like never* wear shoes you can't walk around in for hours."

Piper, the third intern, was pretty quiet the whole time. I could tell she listened closely to everything we were talking about, but the only things I remember her saying were "I'm Piper," and "Yeah, it's so cool here."

After lunch, I went back to the beauty closet. Haley stopped by again and showed me how to use the intern email account to contact beauty companies. She then pointed to the several thousand unread emails and asked me to read and respond to as many as I could. By six P.M., I was exhausted and my brain was completely melted.

I'm back at the apartment now. Only one of my roommates is also back from work. As soon as I finish this diary entry, we're going to make dinner together and watch a show on one of our laptops.

My internship is only Monday, Wednesday, and Friday, so I have tomorrow off. You know what that means, Lora: Tomorrow, you have to write. I mean it. No excuses!!!

From: Olesya Dorokhova
To: Nikolay Dorokhov
Subject: (no subject)
Date: May 18, 2017

Kolya—

With every passing day, I grow more frustrated. I pace around my hotel room like a caged animal, spending all my time and energy planning my escape. I used to love this suite and everything it symbolized, everything it meant. What was once my sanctuary is now my prison.

It breaks me that I will return to Nizhny the same way I left: poor, defeated, and on the run. I will come back home—that I promise you. But even if I wanted to return tomorrow, I could not. They allow me to fly around the states using my various passports, but I am certain that the moment I try to board an international flight, I will be arrested.

The moment I give them any suspicion that I am on the run, they will put me in handcuffs, drag me in front of a judge, and force me to spend the rest of my life in prison. I can't let that happen—I would rather die. My exit plan must be foolproof. It must be so good, and so perfectly executed, that nobody will realize what has happened until I am on a flight to Moscow.

They are closing in on me, Kolya, I can feel it. I saw an FBI agent at the office a few days ago, and then again at The Plaza this morning. I am certain that they follow me, that they listen to my every conversation, that they have discovered every place I live and work, that they know every single one of my names. But they are waiting, aren't they? If they truly had anything, wouldn't they have arrested me by now?

There can only be one conclusion: they do not have enough—not yet.

Just like me, they are waiting. I am waiting to find my final, missing perfect puzzle piece; they are waiting for me to make a mistake.

I will not make a mistake.

—Olesya

From: Nikolay Dorokhov
To: Olesya Dorokhova
Subject: Re:
Date: May 19, 2017

i know you will try to come back with money and i worry you will fuck it up

really, who cares if you are poor when you come back? nobody

we have survived worse haha

From: Olesya Dorokhova
To: Nikolay Dorokhov
Subject: Re: Re:
Date: May 19, 2017

Kolya—

It's not about the money. Really, it's not.

—Olesya

From: Nikolay Dorokhov
To: Olesya Dorokhova
Subject: Re: Re: Re:
Date: May 19, 2017

then what

what is it about

what have you even been doing all this time

From: Olesya Dorokhova
To: Nikolay Dorokhov
Subject: Re: Re: Re: Re:
Date: May 20, 2017

Kolya—

It's about everything I've done. The books. The articles. The companies. All of it.

I will never be recognized for any of it.

I do more in a year than most people do in a lifetime—and for what? For nothing. Absolutely nothing. Do you know how that feels? To have done everything people said you could never do, to have achieved your wildest dreams, and be forced to walk away knowing that nobody will ever understand what you have accomplished?

—Olesya

From: Nikolay Dorokhov
To: Olesya Dorokhova
Subject: Re: Re: Re: Re: Re:
Date: May 20, 2017

just be careful, ok?

better for you to be here in russia than in rikers

The Diary of Lora Ricci

May 20, 2017

When I went in to work Wednesday morning, I found another big pile of packages and bags waiting for me. Before I unpacked and organized anything, I checked the intern email account and saw that the inbox was filled with messages from beauty companies asking if our editors wanted any of their new products. I Slacked Haley, who said that Laura Graham (the beauty director) would Slack me if she needed anything.

And then, right on cue, Laura messaged me and asked me to bring swatches of the new Dior lipsticks to her desk. I ran over to the pile of packages and, thankfully, found one from Dior. I quickly opened the box and found a dozen lipsticks inside. And then it hit me: I had no idea what I was doing.

So I googled.

"How to swatch lipstick" brought up photos of women putting the lipsticks on the insides of their forearms to compare the colors. Okay, that made sense: that was how I swatched my own eyeshadow. Maybe the teenage beauty junkie way of swatching wasn't that different from the fancy fashion magazine method. I opened up one of the lipsticks and smeared it on my left wrist. Then I opened another one and smeared it next to the previous smear. And then another one.

After I'd swatched them all, I looked down at my arm and started to feel weird. This couldn't be right. Why the hell would Laura want to look at the lipsticks on my arm?

Dammit.

Another Google search: "How to swatch lipstick for magazine editor." Not helpful.

Think, Lora, think!

I looked around the closet, panicking, hoping to find a clue—any clue—as to what the hell I was supposed to be doing. And then I saw it, tacked to the bulletin board above the iMac: a piece of paper with patches of bright colors. Upon further examination, it turned out to have swatches of nail polish, not lipstick, but I hoped and prayed that the format was the same.

Final Google search: "How to swatch lipstick on paper." I breathed a huge sigh of relief when I saw the image results. BOOM: carefully wipe the lipstick on paper, write the name of the color right next to it. Repeat until you've swatched every color. *Oh my god. Of course.*

I did this as quickly as I could, then walked/ran over to the cubicles where the beauty editors sat, discreetly trying to rub the lipstick off my arm with a tissue. I gingerly walked around, trying to figure out who Laura was and what she looked like. (Why don't they just label each cubicle with the name of its inhabitant??)

I eventually found Haley, but didn't recognize the woman sitting in the cubicle beside her, so I took a deep breath, prayed that the woman was Laura, and walked right up to her.

"Hi, Laura!" I squeaked, trying to sound confident and completely failing.

She looked up and gave me an awkward smile. "Um, I'm Meghana. Laura sits on the *other* side of Haley." She pointed to an empty cubicle. I cringed and apologized, then walked over to Laura's desk. I put the swatches beside her keyboard and returned to my little closet as quickly as possible.

After I opened and organized the remaining packages, I walked to the fashion closet to find the other interns and join them for lunch. This time, I brought my own lunch from home (a peanut butter and jelly sandwich). I was glad to find I wasn't the only one who had packed a lunch: while Katrine and Piper stood in line at the sushi bar, Maggie sat down next to me at the table and pulled chips and a sandwich out of her bag. "Oh my god," Maggie said, looking at the line of people ordering food. "I'd be *so* broke if I bought lunch every day."

When the others returned with their food, we talked about what we were working on. I told them about the packages and they told me about their runs. I was surprised (and kind of sad) to find out that they're not allowed to try on any of the clothes. "You'd be fired . . . on . . . the . . . spot," Piper said.

Later that afternoon, I had coffee with Haley in the cafeteria, and we talked about my interests and the various opportunities I would have during my internship. I told her my dream of being a magazine editor and writing books on the side. She said I'll be invited to some of the big staff meetings and that there might be opportunities to write book reviews and help with research, fact-checking, and proofreading, but emphasized that I should really focus all my energy on my tasks in the beauty closet. I was a little bummed out after the meeting, but whatever—keep your head down, work your ass off, yada yada yada.

Friday was more of the same, but then, in the afternoon, I finally met Laura. She popped into the closet, introduced herself, told me that today was Meghana's birthday, handed me her corporate credit card, and asked me to pick up cupcakes from a bakery down the street. As soon as I got back, cupcakes in tow, Haley asked me to take the birthday card around the office and make sure everyone signed it. That took up the rest of my day. It was a nice break from the closet, and I loved meeting the other editors.

I've been trying to figure out what to write on Tuesdays and Thursdays—my "off days," when I don't go to work. I'm torn between a novel and short stories. I don't yet have an idea for a novel, but I was thinking I could write some stories about fashion magazines since I'm surrounded by so many interesting people at work.

So, on Tuesday, I half-heartedly tried to write a short story, but there wasn't anywhere to sit down and work in the apartment, so that went nowhere. On Thursday, however, I found the perfect coffee shop to write in—it's quiet, relatively empty, and they don't seem to care if you sit there all day but only order a small iced coffee. It's a thirty-five-minute walk from the apartment, but that's okay—I need the exercise. I was actually productive and came up with an outline for a short story. I'm not sure if the story is going to be any good, but at least it's a start. Words on paper—that's all that matters.

THE NEW YORK TIMES | BOOKS

After Four Quiet Years, Daphne Rooney Finally Wrote Her Third Book. What Took So Long?

By Jeanine Fox

May 20, 2017

Like most novelists, Daphne Rooney writes alone. "I try to distance myself from the expectations and pressures that come from having success," she says. After her first book, "Marigold," she worked for three years on her second novel, "Wythe," which spent two weeks on the hardcover fiction best seller list. Rooney says she "struggled to find enough loneliness" to write her third novel, "The Hawk," which debuted at number nine on the hardcover fiction list and is still on the list, eight weeks after publication.

The reclusive author, who resides on the Upper East Side, says she almost didn't write "The Hawk." She was afraid, she explained, that she would end up writing something that she knew other people wanted rather than writing what she wanted to write. "Though, in the end, it turned out to be both," she says.

As for the plot of her latest novel, Rooney isn't afraid to admit that she took a different path with "The Hawk," and says that the choice was deliberate. "In my earlier novels, I was writing because I was entertained by these stories in my head and I wanted to share them with the world. When I sat down to write a new novel, I decided that I wanted it to be more than just entertaining and well written—I wanted it to push the boundaries of what a novel could be."

Jeanine Fox is a contributing writer at The Times.

The Diary of Lora Ricci

May 22, 2017

Cons of working in the beauty closet:

- It's not the fashion closet
- I'm the only beauty closet intern and I work all by myself
- I'm only one week in and I'm already lonely
- The endless packages (I'm basically Sisyphus—every time I'm done unpacking and organizing stuff from a box, a new one arrives and I have to do the whole thing over again)

Pros of working in the beauty closet:

- Learning more about beauty products
- It's peaceful and quiet
- I have more responsibility and autonomy *because* I'm the only intern
- I have my own "office"
- I'm still working at *ELLE,* which is the most important thing!!!

Jenée Parker | 05–24–2017 8:39 AM
Are you still working at the US Attorney's Office?

Amanda Harris | 05–24–2017 8:42 AM
Yeah

Amanda Harris | 05–24–2017 8:43 AM
What's up?

Jenée Parker | 05–24–2017 8:46 AM
I have a new case you might find interesting

Amanda Harris | 05–24–2017 8:57 AM
?

Jenée Parker | 05–24–2017 9:00 AM
Bank fraud, wire fraud

Amanda Harris | 05–24–2017 9:01 AM
How big?

Jenée Parker | 05–24–2017 9:03 AM
Not sure yet

Amanda Harris | 05–24–2017 9:05 AM
Do we have a name?

Jenée Parker | 05–24–2017 9:07 AM
An alias: Cat Wolff

Amanda Harris | 05–24–2017 9:14 AM
Let's talk

Amanda Harris | 05–24–2017 9:15 AM
Call me when you can

The Diary of Lora Ricci

May 26, 2017

This morning, I joined Piper for one of her runs and we went to The Row to pick up some clothes for a shoot. The store was beautiful—so sparse and intimate and clean, like an art gallery. While Piper waited for the clothes, I explored the first floor, then walked up a curved marble staircase to the second floor, where I looked through the collections and wished that I had enough money to buy everything (or even just *one* thing).

I'm more than a little jealous of Piper and the other fashion interns, who get to do this every day. They're in the middle of the action—they're *part of it,* not stuck on the sidelines like me. Sometimes, on days like today, I'm afraid I'm always going to be on the outside, always going to almost-but-not-quite fit in. I'm beginning to feel like *ELLE* isn't that much different from NYU.

I almost let my guard down and said something over lunch, but instead I said the opposite of what I actually meant. "I don't know how you guys do it," I said, biting into my peanut butter and jelly sandwich (which was a little soggy and gross after sitting in my bag all morning). "I would be so tired if I had to go on runs all day long."

"All I do is runs," Katrine said, grimacing. "Like *literally,* all I ever do is go on runs."

Piper smiled. "I like runs," she said. "It feels so cool to walk into a store and be like, 'I'm here from *ELLE.*'"

"It's shit work *for sure,* but you gotta do the shit work if you're going to get *anywhere* in this business," Maggie added. "The editors are impressed by interns who, when they're asked to do something, do it, and then ask, 'and what else do you need?'"

"It's like, ask not what the magazine can do for you, ask what *you* can do for the magazine," Piper said.

Katrine rolled her eyes. "Whatever," she mumbled.

Katrine is a real character. She's tall, has dark shoulder-length hair, always wears bright purple eyeshadow, and exudes this high level of confidence and energy. She knows a lot about beauty, fashion, journalism, print media—you name it, she knows something about it and has met all the big names working in it.

I think Katrine and I are very close in age—she's a rising senior at Columbia—but this is her third magazine internship. Last year, she interned at *InStyle,* where she met stars like Jessica Alba, Priyanka Chopra, and Kerry Washington. Her Instagram is full of selfies with celebrities, and her profile picture is of her and Jessica Alba (who she says is "old-school"). I was wondering how Katrine knew so much and had all these opportunities, and said as much to Piper while we were on our run. "Duh, her mom is an editor at *Vogue,*" Piper said, as if she couldn't believe I didn't know.

Piper's cool aloofness is the opposite of Katrine's frantic energy. Her hair is platinum blonde (almost white), and she has a very cool minimalist style, both in beauty and in fashion. As for makeup, she wears a single bold line of neon eyeliner and that's it. She doesn't do anything with her eyebrows, and they're just *barely* there. Everyone is always complimenting her eyebrows and saying how much they love them (myself included).

I'm not sure where Piper goes to school. I googled her and found out that she has a "street looks" fashion blog and her dad runs a hedge fund. She doesn't talk about herself or her life very much. She just lets Katrine and Maggie pick the topic of conversation and goes along with whatever they decide is interesting.

Maggie's mom works in marketing (or sales? idk) at Louis Vuitton, and her dad is a photographer. She knows and likes everyone and everyone knows and likes her. When we go to lunch, the editors we walk by always smile at her and say hello. I think she already graduated from Columbia, but I'm not 100 percent sure. She's applying for assistant positions this summer, but it's so hard because nobody is hiring. I can't imagine her *not* getting a job, since I'm sure she is going to have really awesome references from everyone here, but it's kind of scary that even *she* doesn't have an offer when she has so much experience. If Maggie can't get a job, is there any hope for the rest of us? (And by "the rest of us," I mean, uh, *me*.)

After lunch, I helped Haley set up a PR happy hour in one of the conference rooms. It wasn't even for beauty stuff—it was for a tequila company that was buying an ad in one of the upcoming issues. Almost everyone in the office stopped by for a margarita and then had to go home early because they were too tipsy to keep working.

The final thing I did for the day was mail out a bunch of copies of our June issue to various people. Haley gave me a long list of names and addresses and I sat there filling out cards that said things like "Hope you love our newest issue! xoxo, *ELLE*," which was a bit hard to do after three margaritas. There were a bunch of extra copies left over—Haley said I could keep them and share them with the other interns.

I was having such a good day until Mom called on my way

home. I ignored her call. I couldn't talk to her. I can't talk to her. Not yet.

I've been having so much fun that I'd actually forgotten all about the whole mess with school. Then I got Mom's call and BOOM—it all came flooding back. Now I'm a goddamn mess all over again and the anxiety is killing me. I don't think I'll be able to sleep tonight. I don't know how I'm going to fix this mess. I don't even know if it's fixable.

katrine baker 👚👗💅✨ nbd just hanging out in the fashion closet 💕💃 #fashioncloset #intern #internship #elle #fashion #beauty #ellemagazine #journalist #nyc #newyork #fashioninternsofinstagram

The Diary of Lora Ricci

May 31, 2017

Haley stopped by the closet this morning and asked me to transcribe an interview for the September issue. Remembering my conversation with the other interns about how we should take on any and all extra work, I said I could definitely do it even though I didn't really have enough time. I skipped lunch, finished up everything else on my to-do list, and finally sat down to do the transcription at like four thirty in the afternoon.

While I was in the middle of the interview, I heard laughter coming from outside the closet. It was so loud that even when I turned the volume all the way up on my headphones, I could still hear it. At first, I tried to ignore the noise, but after around fifteen minutes or so, I walked out of the closet and down the hallway to see what was going on.

As soon as I rounded the corner and reached the sea of cubicles, I saw a group of people gathered around a woman with dark blonde hair who was wearing a black silk pajama-like pantsuit. They were all completely captivated by her, and, after a few moments, so was I. Her voice was so loud and clear and distinct that it seemed like she was standing right in front of me, talking to me and only me. I was caught off guard by the deepness of her voice (it sounded kind of masculine and raspy, like she used to be a smoker) and the ambiguity of her accent (I *think* it's German, but it also sounds vaguely Russian). She sounded like a German Scarlett Johansson.

At first, German Scarlett's head was turned the other way so that I couldn't see her face. I took a few steps toward her, and at that very moment, she said something that made everyone around her crack up. She threw her head back as she laughed, and I saw her face. She was absolutely gorgeous, without a doubt, but there was something about her that was beautiful in a way that I'd never noticed about anyone else. It wasn't just that her eyes were stunning, it was how she moved them, how every blink, every glance seemed to carry some kind of significance. And it wasn't just that her lips were beautiful, it was the way they moved when she spoke and the way they looked when she laughed. I was lost, completely mesmerized by her, and then she looked at me. I swear it felt like time itself stopped. She was still talking, but our eyes were locked and I couldn't hear a single thing she said. I couldn't hear anything at all.

And then she looked away. The spell was broken. I took a step back, my ears ringing, and walked back to the closet. I sat down at my desk and tried to work, but there was nothing left in my head except *her.*

I don't even know who she is.

I was sitting there, dazed, trying to figure out what had just happened, and when I looked at my watch, I saw it was almost seven (I should have left two hours earlier!). I packed up my things and turned off the lights in the closet. I was about to leave, but I had missed lunch earlier, so I decided to swing by the fashion closet and see if any of the other interns were still there.

When I peeked my head in, it was gloriously messy as usual, packed with racks and racks of the most beautiful clothes I'd ever seen. The only person there was a tall woman with dark brown hair, who was standing in front of one of the racks and carefully comparing several tops. I knew who she was the moment I saw her: Alexa Bell, *ELLE*'s famous fashion director.

I was about to leave, hoping that she hadn't noticed me (believe me, I was in no state to meet her), but then her voice rang out, loud and clear. "Can I help you?"

"I was just looking for the other interns," I said.

"They left a while ago," she said.

"Oh, okay. Thank you." I quickly turned to leave before I said anything embarrassing.

"Wait," Alexa said. "I'm stuck on something and I could use another pair of eyes. Could you take a look?"

There was no way in hell I was going to say no, so I nodded and walked over to where she was standing. There were a few mood boards propped up against the wall, covered with drawings and photographs and clippings from other magazines.

"There's something missing," she said. She pulled a few silk tops from the racks and held them up to each other, then tried to pair them with a selection of pants and skirts. After a moment, she sighed in frustration, then put them all back on the racks. "They're not right."

I thought of German Scarlett, and of her pajama-like suit. "What if one of the tops came with matching pants? Silk pants, like in the same exact material as the top."

Alexa thought for another moment, then pulled a white silk top from the rack and looked at it carefully. She nodded her head. "Yes, yes. Perfect." She pulled a pen from behind her ear and sketched something out on a notepad. Then she looked up at me. "It's late. You going home?"

I offered to stay and help, but she said she'd be heading out soon, so I left the office and headed back to Brooklyn. The whole train ride home, I should have been fizzing with the excitement of meeting Alexa. I'd just met one of my role models, one of the most powerful women in fashion, the woman who could make or break my career. But I couldn't get German Scarlett out of my head. I still can't.

From: Jenée Parker (FBI)
To: Carolina Kopp
Subject: Internship
Date: June 1, 2017

Hi Carolina:

As discussed, we'd like to have one of our special agents work undercover at *ELLE* for a short period of time (a few weeks to a few months, depending). My guess is that an internship position would be ideal.

Please call me so we can set this up.

All the best,

Jenée
SA Jenée Parker

The Diary of Lora Ricci

June 2, 2017

I couldn't stop thinking about German Scarlett. So today, at lunch, I decided to mention her, hoping Katrine or Maggie would know who she was. And they did.

"Oh, that's Cat Wolff," Katrine said.

"Definitely Cat," Maggie added. "God, I *hate* her."

"Who?" I asked. I'd never heard that name in my life.

"Cat Wolff," Katrine repeated. "You know, the Austrian heiress."

I did not know. I shook my head.

"Her dad is, like, a billionaire," Katrine explained, "and he runs this huge clean energy business thing in Europe. Like, solar, wind, rain, I think. You know? Like 'natural' energy. Like Goop for energy. Yeah, he's like . . . the Gwyneth Paltrow of, like, electricity . . ."

"But what's she doing here?" I asked, interrupting her.

"She's the absolute fucking worst," Maggie said under her breath.

Piper's eyes grew wide, but she didn't say a word.

Katrine shrugged. "I don't know, I think she's a contributing editor or something," she said. "I'm not sure what her deal is, but according to the rumors I've heard from . . . let's just say, from some of the higher-ups here . . . she's trying to figure out what to do with her life. You know, make her own way in the world and make a name for herself and whatnot. I've heard she might start her own fashion label or her own magazine, or maybe even buy *ELLE* altogether. And she can definitely afford it. Like, last week, I was talking to Padma, the features intern over at *Cosmo,* and she said that—"

Maggie sat up straight. "Look," she said, interrupting Katrine, "Cat exploits interns, okay? I'm not kidding. I worked for her last summer, when I was in the beauty closet, and I did all the research for her articles. All of it. I worked my ass off. And what did I get for it? Nothing. She didn't give me any credit."

Before I could ask Maggie to elaborate, Katrine jumped in. "Speaking of articles, what are you all going to pitch? To the editors?" She must have seen the confused, blank look on my face, because she quickly clarified: "Before the big meeting on Wednesday."

Pitches? To the editors? Big meeting on Wednesday? What???!!!

I should have asked for more details, but instead I did the dumbest possible thing and lied, pretending I knew what she was referring to. "Oh yeah, definitely. I have a bunch of ideas, but I'm not sure which one will be perfect yet. What about you guys?" I listened as the others discussed the pieces they wanted to write. Book reviews, lists of best new designers, the new women of Hollywood . . .

I spent the rest of the day trying to brainstorm ideas for pitches, and I couldn't come up with anything good. There's nothing in my head. NOTHING. GAH. I've been reading this magazine for years and I can't think of a single idea that the editors might be excited about. The only things that pop into my head are fiction stories. Stories about women who work at magazines. Stories about dates gone wrong. Stories about dates gone right. *Stories.*

From: Carolina Kopp
To: Jenée Parker (FBI)
Subject: Re: Internship
Date: June 5, 2017

Hello Jenée,

I tried to call but your office said you were out.

I agree that an internship would be ideal. It works for me and can be easily arranged. Only the editor in chief and I would know. We don't currently have a features intern, and anyone in that position could easily work in close proximity to Cat Wolff.

I'll be in my office all day today. Please call me at your earliest convenience.

Best Regards,

Carolina Kopp
Deputy Editor, *ELLE*

The Diary of Lora Ricci

June 7, 2017

Today we had the big Wednesday meeting, which turned out to be a staff meeting to close out the September issue and continue working on the October and November ones. The whole masthead was there, and the elle.com teams were there, too.

Maya Jacobs, *ELLE*'s editor in chief, kicked off the meeting and jumped right into a final review of the front-of-book stuff and our September cover star (Alicia Vikander). Then she started talking about what the other magazines were planning for their fall and winter issues, speculating about what they had lined up, and asked if any of us knew anything about their covers (we didn't). A few minutes later, she pulled up the Instagram accounts of the editors of other women's magazines and was analyzing their recent photos, looking for clues. ("Genevieve," she barked at her assistant, "pull up the Instagrams!")

While Maya was breaking down the photos ("What's she wearing? Someone needs to go find out. What's that in the background? Is that Prada? Wait, where did those shoes come from? Who's sitting on her lap this time?"), I looked around the room to see who else was here, and spotted Cat Wolff sitting at the conference table.

After about forty-five minutes, Maya turned the meeting over to Carolina, who went into the details of the rest of the issue. I learned a lot about the magazine just from listening to her, and I made sure to take notes. Things like: every issue is planned at least four or five months in advance, and then closed two months before it's published; each issue has a theme (women in music, women in Hollywood, sustainability, etc.), and *ELLE* sells ads based on that theme.

Speaking of ads, one of the things we covered in the meeting was that Maybelline wanted a right-page ad, and as part of the ad agreement, they wanted us to put an article about lipstick on the left page, directly across from their ad. Every advertiser wants either a right page or a two-page spread.

Toward the end of the meeting, Carolina moved the discussion to the October and November issues, which were three features short, and asked if anyone wanted to pitch something they'd been working on.

Cat raised her hand. "We've been doing these fantastic features on women in tech startups, especially female investors in the tech space," Cat said. "I think we should do a similar sort of thing about women who are starting companies in the fashion space. I'd been thinking of doing it for January or February, but I think October or November could also work."

Maya nodded. "I like this, I like this," she said.

"I've met a few women, mostly fashion designers or ex-models, who are looking into starting their own companies in Silicon Valley. They're casting off the old ways of running labels and adopting the startup mentality instead. It's really fascinating, and I think it could honestly be very inspiring for our readers," Cat said.

Carolina took some notes, then looked up at Cat. "You should have one of the interns help you with that."

"That would be great," Cat agreed.

Carolina then moved on to other topics. She brought up new beauty trends and floated the possibility of doing a perfume feature. Maya agreed and mentioned ad considerations, then asked, "Laura, what do you think?"

I was looking down at my notebook, taking notes, not really using my brain, and thought she meant me. I felt like time slowed for a moment, and this desperate little voice in my head shouted, *OMG, Lora, this is your chance! Go for it! Seize the goddamn day!* And so, without thinking, I stood up and said, "Yeah, I think that would be so cool. I can start reaching out to all the companies and getting samples of their new fragrances."

My heart stopped when I heard the room go completely silent. I looked around. Haley had this horrified look on her face and was shaking her head and mouthing, *No, no, no!* Genevieve was trying to fight back her laughter. I could feel my face burning and knew my cheeks had turned bright red.

"Not *you,*" Maya said, glaring at me. "I'm sorry, but I don't know who you are." She looked at Laura Graham, who was sitting only a few feet away from me. "Laura?"

"I love it," Laura said, then (mercifully), without missing a beat, quickly launched into an ad-strategy discussion with Maya and Carolina.

I was so fucking embarrassed I wanted to crawl into a hole and die. I couldn't look at anyone for the rest of the meeting. Why on earth did I think she meant *me*???!!!

As soon as the meeting was over, I got out of the conference room as quickly as I could. That hallway had never felt so long. I must have passed fifty people, and I couldn't look at a single one of them. I knew that the second I looked anyone in the eye, I'd burst into tears and make an even bigger fool of myself.

After what felt like an eternity, I finally reached the beauty closet. I shut the door, burst into tears, and curled up in a ball on the floor. It all hit me at once, everything I was carrying: the humiliation of the meeting, the loss of my scholarship, how I'd nearly failed out of NYU, the way that I felt completely and utterly lost and alone. I was crying so hard I didn't even hear the door open and close.

"Lora, right?"

I took my glasses off, then wiped the tears from my eyes with the hem of my shirt and squinted at the door. To my complete surprise, standing there, only a few feet away from me, was a very blurry Cat Wolff. "I can come back later if that's better," she offered.

"No, it's okay, I'll be fine," I said. I took a few deep breaths, trying to calm myself down and stop my shoulders from shaking.

While I was trying to stop sobbing, Cat walked over to the shelves. "Let's see," she said softly, pulling things out of the bins and boxes. "Mascara, eyeliner, some concealer, a bit of foundation, and . . . makeup wipes. Where are the makeup wipes?"

I pointed to one of the cabinets. "In there, second shelf from the top."

She opened the cabinet and dug around until she found them. "Aha!"

Then she walked over to me and got down on her knees so that we were face-to-face. Our eyes met, and I swear that there wasn't a shred of pity, or judgment, or criticism in the way she looked at me. No, what I saw in her eyes was a strangely calm sort of solidarity. And, in that moment, I felt so much less alone.

"Here," Cat said. "Hold your bangs up." She lifted my long bangs up over my forehead onto the top of my head and put my hand firmly on top of them.

She worked quickly, carefully patting foundation on my face with her fingertips, dabbing concealer around, and gently lining my eyes.

"Look up," she said softly.

I felt the mascara wand lightly brush my eyelashes as I gazed at the ceiling.

She took my hand off my head, fixed my bangs, then stood up and stepped away. "Good as new," she said triumphantly.

I looked over at the floor-length mirror to my left. We looked similar in a way, she and I. It might have been something about the angle or the eye makeup or the fact that I couldn't see very well without my glasses—I'm not sure—but in that moment, it made me feel a little better about myself.

I put my glasses back on and got back on my feet. "I'm so sorry," I began. "God, this is all so humiliating, I can't believe—"

She interrupted me with a gentle hug. "Don't let it get to you. The truth is, I'm sure quite a few people in that room are secretly relieved they didn't make the same mistake. And the rest of them, well, they're just wondering if Maya noticed what they were wearing."

"You think?"

"Oh, I *know*." She laughed. "I'll let you in on one of life's little secrets: most people are so caught up in their own internal drama and so worried about their own problems, they rarely pay attention to anyone or anything else for very long."

This made me smile. I knew she was right. I mean, hell, *I'm* one of those people. "Thanks."

She laughed again as she walked over to the shelves. "I didn't come in here to fix your makeup, believe it or not. I actually wanted to ask you for a favor."

"Me?"

"Yes, you. Do you remember that article I mentioned in the meeting? About the startups?"

I nodded.

"It's going to be so much work, you know, pulling all that information together." She looked at me, hopeful. "I could really use your help."

I thought about it for a moment. I really wanted to help her, but I was already leaving work at seven at night and could barely keep up with my work as it was. I'd been stupidly taking the other interns' advice seriously and taking on every random task that surfaced: running errands, filming beauty videos, posting those videos on Facebook, organizing all the book mail, etc. "I wish I could, but I'm completely swamped. I'm the only beauty intern. You should check with the fashion interns—there are three of them."

"Of course," she said. "I totally understand. Well, thanks for considering." She turned around and walked toward the door.

Then it hit me: What on earth was I doing? Here was a contributing editor, standing in front of me and asking me if I wanted to work with her on a feature—a feature!—and I didn't even have to come up with the idea myself. This was the universe giving me a second chance (or was it the third? Fourth? Fifth? I've lost count at this point). Saying no was the stupidest possible thing I could do.

"Wait!" I shouted.

She turned around and raised her eyebrows.

"I'm free on Tuesdays and Thursdays."

She smiled. "I'll send a car for you first thing tomorrow morning. Email me your address. I'm in the system."

And with that, she closed the door.

What a strange day.

From: Cat Wolff
To: ELLE HR
Subject: Interns
Date: June 7, 2017

HR:

I'm working on a large feature for the October issue and will need an intern to help with research (Carolina Kopp's suggestion, btw). Could you please send me more information about each intern (e.g., résumés, cover letters, w9 forms)?

Cat Wolff

From: ELLE HR
To: Cat Wolff
Subject: Re: Interns
Date: June 7, 2017

Hi Cat,

After discussing this, we feel it would be better if you reached out to the intern or interns you would like to work with instead. Perhaps get to know them over coffee or something like that . . .

Best,

Ellen McKay
Human Resources, *ELLE*

From: Cat Wolff
To: Lora Ricci
Subject: Working Together
Date: June 7, 2017

Lora:

HR has informed me that, in order for us to work together, they will need updated copies of your cover letter, resume, w-9 form, driver's license, and passport. Please bring these items tomorrow and I will pass them along to HR.

Thanks, and see you tomorrow!

Cat Wolff

From: Lora Ricci
To: Cat Wolff
Subject: Re: Working Together
Date: June 7, 2017

Hi Cat!

Will do!!

Looking forward to tomorrow!!!

Best,

Lora

The Diary of Lora Ricci

June 8, 2017

This morning, I stepped out of my building to find a black SUV waiting outside my door. The driver rolled down his window as I walked down the stairs toward the car. "Miss Ricci?" he asked. I nodded. "My name is Bob. Ms. Wolff sent me over to pick you up."

Even though Cat had said she'd send a car, I almost didn't get in. For a few moments, I stood there on the sidewalk as *Dateline* specials flashed through my mind. If I got in that SUV, would I be kidnapped and trafficked or something? But then I heard Katrine's voice in my head: *"Her dad is, like, a billionaire, and he runs this huge clean energy business thing in Europe. Like, solar, wind, rain..."*

I got in.

Bob didn't say a single word. It was kind of jarring. I don't think I've ever gotten into a cab or Lyft and not had the driver talk at me the entire time. I looked out the window, watching as the city flew by. He drove through Brooklyn, over the Brooklyn Bridge, up the FDR, and dropped me off right on Fifth Avenue—at the entrance to The Plaza Hotel.

Bob stepped out and walked around the car to open my door. I paused, and he noticed my hesitation. "Room 2040," he said.

I stepped out of the car and looked up. Every inch of the building was glamorous, old-world, *Great Gatsby* New York. When I looked back down at the entrance, a woman wearing a suit smiled at me and directed me toward one of the revolving doors. "Welcome to The Plaza," she said.

I'd never been inside The Plaza—or, frankly, any fancy hotel—before, and the lobby was even more elegant than I'd expected from my years of rewatching *Home Alone 2*. I walked around slowly, trying to take everything in. There were so many people eating and drinking at the bar and checking in at the front desk, and there were tons of tourists who were staring at every inch of the building just like I was. "Twenty-forty, twenty-forty," I whispered under my breath, trying not to forget Cat's room number.

I kept walking until I found the elevator bank, then pressed the "up" button. Before I knew it, I was in one of the gilded elevators with half a dozen other people. "Which floor?" someone asked me. "Twenty," I replied.

I wondered what it would be like to work with Cat. Maybe I would finally get to write something. Maybe I would get to share a byline, and the editors would be so impressed that they'd ask me to write my own article. I started to daydream about meeting a celebrity in the lobby of a fancy hotel, just like The Plaza, and interviewing her for our cover story.

I was jolted back to reality when the elevator stopped at the twentieth floor, and I got out. Compared to the high, chandeliered ceilings of the lobby, the low hallway ceiling felt almost oppressive. *Twenty-forty, twenty-forty,* I thought as I walked down the long, empty hallway, passing a long row of rooms, until, at last, at the very end, I found Cat's penthouse suite.

I knocked. After awkwardly waiting for several minutes, I knocked again. Then I laughed at myself when I noticed a doorbell, and pressed it. A few moments later, the door opened with a loud click, and Cat appeared. With her hair up in a ponytail and dressed in gray cashmere sweatpants and a sweatshirt, she looked more casual than I'd ever seen her before, yet she was still somehow as enigmatic and elegant in a sweat suit as she was in a dress. "Welcome to my humble home," she said. "Come in, come in!"

I stepped inside and leaned down to take off my shoes as she closed the door behind me. When I stood up, I found my reflection staring back at me in a gilded mirror. Cat then led me down a hallway that had beautiful hardwood floors. On our left, we passed an enormous bedroom (Cat's, I assumed), followed by a powder room ("There's a bathroom, if you need to use it," she said).

The hallway led to a large living room that, with its two chandeliers, marble fireplace, velvet couch, and gold-trimmed everything, can only be accurately described as "opulent." In one corner of the room was a staircase, though I couldn't tell where it led. Directly to our right was a large dining table, covered with a laptop and notebooks and a big pile of what appeared to be printouts of online articles.

"Here," Cat said, pointing to an empty chair at one end of the table, "take a seat. Make yourself at home. I'll grab you some breakfast." And with that, she walked over to a long, kitchen-like row of cabinets and returned with a French press of coffee and a platter of fruit and pastries.

I slid onto a velvet-upholstered dining chair and put my computer and notebook on the table. While I was getting settled, Cat poured me a cup of coffee and made up a plate of food for me. "How do you like your coffee? Black? Cream? Sugar?"

"Black," I said. She poured me a cup and set it on the table.

"This is a *really nice* place," I said, awestruck, though "really nice" was an understatement. Cat's hotel room was *gorgeous*. It was the way I imagined all high-end New York City apartments looked, the way my future New York City apartment looked in my daydreams about being a successful author and the editor in chief of *Harper's Bazaar*. Actually, no, it was even more beautiful and luxurious and incredible and perfect than *any* of the apartments of my daydreams—it was the kind of place you see at the top of the page when you browse the listings on Zillow or Sotheby's and sort by "Price High to Low." I ran the tips of my fingers along the gilded edge of the table.

"Isn't it wonderful? I can't imagine living anywhere else," she said. As I ate, she explained that she had originally intended to stay in New York for only a few months. "I was living in our family residence in Vienna. A truly lovely place, honestly, but it wasn't the sort of house you could ever call home. My father bought it after my mother died, and I moved there to be closer to my little brother, but the whole experience was frustrating and alienating. Everything reminded me of my mother. She was Russian, and had lived in Leningrad before meeting and marrying my father, but she *loved* Vienna. It was heaven to her. Everywhere I went, I saw or heard something that brought back too many memories. I couldn't go a day without crying. I had to leave."

This explains her accent, I thought. *The German, the Russian . . .*

Here, she paused. She took a sip of her coffee and looked toward the window beyond the staircase. Then she looked down at her hands. "Eventually, I explained everything to my father, and he encouraged me to travel. I went to Buenos Aires, Tokyo, Morocco. I spent a year in London. And then I came to New York. My father booked me a smaller suite here at first, since I thought I was only staying for a few weeks at the very most. And then, when I fell in love with the city and decided I never wanted to leave, I moved into this one. Now it feels like home. As close to home as I've ever had since I lost my mother, anyway."

"You don't feel weird living in a hotel?" I asked.

"Oh god, no. I absolutely love it. I never have to leave unless I want to. Everything I want is here, only a phone call away. And can you imagine a more lovely apartment? Or a better location?"

"I've never seen anything like it," I admitted. Then I laughed. "I share a one-bedroom in Brooklyn with three other girls. We sleep in bunk beds."

Cat laughed, her eyes sparkling. "That actually sounds like fun. Like a dorm, right?" Immediately after she said that, her eyes went dark, and her smile faded. "At least, that's what I would imagine it would be like, living in a dorm. I never did. It always sounded like a lot of fun, though."

I wasn't sure what she meant. Maybe when she went to college, her father paid for her to stay in a hotel or apartment all by herself? I wanted to ask, but she looked so sad that I didn't want to pry. I knew the look on her face all too well—it's the same one I have whenever I feel nostalgic for a life I've never had.

I changed the subject.

"What did you do before *ELLE*?" I asked.

"A little bit of everything. I didn't know what I wanted to do at the time, so I did the only reasonable thing I could think of: I got to know people. I met everyone who was anyone in the arts, in finance, in fashion, in journalism. I went to every party, every gallery opening, every fashion show, every book launch. I didn't have to work, so I simply didn't work. But it wasn't that I didn't *want* to work. I wanted to find work that I loved, that I found fulfilling."

"And you found that at *ELLE*?"

She laughed again. "No, not exactly. Now don't get me wrong, I love the work. I love writing, but writing about fashion isn't exactly my dream."

"What *is* your dream?"

She blushed. "It's . . . No, no, I can't tell you, you'll think it's silly."

I promised I wouldn't.

"I want to write fiction," she admitted.

Before I could tell her that we had very similar dreams, she abruptly shifted the conversation to the piece she was working on for *ELLE*. She said that she needed me to help her figure out how certain fashion startups were founded and financed and how that financing worked. "My goal is that women will read the profiles of these incredible entrepreneurs and not just be inspired to go and start their own companies but will also have a guide for how to actually do it."

And with that, we got to work. She had compiled a spreadsheet of all the fashion startups she could find, so that's where I started. I dug into each company's history, finding out as much as I could about their product lines, investors, business plans, and financing. We barely moved from the table the rest of the morning. When lunchtime rolled around, she placed a room service order, and we ate at the table while we worked.

That afternoon, I started learning about venture capital. Basically, when someone wants to start a company and they aren't already rich, they have to get money through investors and/or loans. Loans need to be paid back, but investments are usually cash given in exchange for stock in the company—*a lot of cash.* Hundreds of thousands of dollars. Millions. Billions.

I also found out about these things called "startup accelerators." One of the venture capitalists I spoke to over the phone said that people go through an accelerator when their companies are just getting started, when they don't really know what they're doing, and/or when they don't have any investor connections. The most famous accelerator is Y Combinator ("YC" for short) in San Francisco. Companies like Dropbox and Reddit got their start at YC. I couldn't find any fashion companies that went through YC, but it seemed like a good place to route potential fashion startups.

I was having so much fun researching all this—something *real,* something that's going to be printed in a magazine—that I lost track of time. Before I knew it, the sun was beginning to set. Cat said she was running late for a dinner uptown and that Bob would drive me home.

On the ride home, I checked my phone and saw that Mom had left a voicemail. I couldn't bring myself to listen to it. I still haven't called her back or replied to her text from last week. God, what if NYU called her and told her I lost my scholarship??

From: Olesya Dorokhova
To: Nikolay Dorokhov
Subject: (no subject)
Date: June 8, 2017

Kolya—

Can you look into this girl's background for me? I need an assistant to help me with some stuff for the magazine, and she seems like the least dangerous option. I want to make sure she's not an undercover agent, that her father's not a cop, etc.

—Olesya

Attachment: lora-ricci-employment-docs-SCAN.pdf

From: Nikolay Dorokhov
To: Olesya Dorokhova
Subject: Re:
Date: June 9, 2017

yes

give me a week

i will find out

From: Olesya Dorokhova
To: Nikolay Dorokhov
Subject: Re: Re:
Date: June 10, 2017

Kolya—

Thanks. I won't spend any more time with her until I hear back from you. I have another project to work on in the meantime.

—Olesya

From: Cat Wolff
To: Lora Ricci
Subject: Question
Date: June 11, 2017

Lora:

Great work the other day.

Can you send me the email address for that "y combinator" thing you were telling me about?

Cat Wolff

From: Lora Ricci
To: Cat Wolff
Subject: Re: Question
Date: June 11, 2017

Hi Cat!

Thank you so much. I had so much fun researching that stuff. Happy to help anytime!!

The email address for Y Combinator is on the "Accelerators" tab of the updated spreadsheet. I think that's the email address we should give to women who want to start fashion companies.

Best,

Lora

From: Cat Wolff
To: Y Combinator
Subject: Apply to Y Combinator
Date: June 12, 2017

My team and I are working on an AI-powered fashion app called "ClosetAI." The app lets people upload photos of the clothes and shoes and accessories in their closet, then gives them custom recommendations for outfits they should wear that day based on the local temperature, weather, and latest trends. It also gives them recommendations for clothing to buy that will fit in with the rest of their closet, eliminating the one-off pieces we all tend to buy and then never wear.

I think ClosetAI would be a perfect fit for your next batch of companies. How much do you typically invest?

Let me know your thoughts.

Cat Wolff

From: Jenée Parker (FBI)
To: Carolina Kopp
Subject: New intern
Date: June 12, 2017

Hi Carolina:

Just a reminder that Aisha Jackson will be reporting for the first day of her internship at 10 am today.

All the best,

Jenée

SA Jenée Parker

From: Nikolay Dorokhov
To: Olesya Dorokhova
Subject: Re: Re: Re:
Date: June 16, 2017

she's good

i made you a little dossier on her

total nobody from pennsylvania, wrote for her student paper, no family in law enforcement, only social media account is instagram where she just posts photos of buildings in her neighborhood like a tourist, none taken with any friends

seems safe to me

Attachment: lrdossier.pdf

The Diary of Lora Ricci

June 17, 2017

An absolutely ridiculous heat wave hit the city this week. It was so unbelievably and unlivably hot outside that I was pretty sure I would die if I stood out there for more than a few minutes. Our apartment doesn't have air-conditioning, so going inside didn't help much. On Tuesday, it was actually 100 degrees. ONE HUNDRED DEGREES. I was drenched in sweat and completely miserable. I don't know how anyone lives here in the summer unless they're working in an air-conditioned office seven days a week. I was hoping that I'd be able to work with Cat in her hotel suite, but . . .

I thought things went so well with Cat that day we worked together, but I didn't hear back from her for over a week. She hasn't been in the office, and our last interaction was an email about one of the startup accelerators. And then . . . nothing. I was panicking that I'd done something wrong or messed something up, so I was relieved when she called me up last night and asked me if I want to work with her again next week.

It's hard to believe I've been at *ELLE* for an entire month—the time has really flown by. I have the beauty closet pretty much under control, even though there's always new stuff to do and not enough time to do everything the editors need. One really valuable skill I'm learning here is how to prioritize. Oh, and how to be okay with not getting everything done. I'm feeling more comfortable and confident now. Yes, I might not have the same background, or connections, or wardrobe as the other interns, but I can do the work and I can do it well. Maybe there's hope for me yet . . .

Speaking of the others, there's a new intern, Aisha, who just joined. As a features intern, she really has the greatest kind of internship: she gets to *write*. I haven't hung out with her yet, since she's been busy getting all up to speed with the editors in her department, but she sounds pretty cool. Maggie and Katrine spent some time with her yesterday, and they said she's smart and laid-back. I spotted her from across the room in one of our department meetings last week, and noticed that she was dressed a lot like me (Target and H&M, baby!) and not like the other interns, who are always wearing designer clothes.

It's funny, *everyone* here dresses amazingly. But the biggest difference between the interns and the editors is this: the interns are always wearing trendy things, while the editors' outfits are trend agnostic. You could pick an editor's outfit at random and wear it any time in the past twenty years, and you wouldn't look out of place at all—something that is very much *not* true for the intern outfits.

Maggie, Katrine, and Piper always wear expensive clothing and never, ever wear the same thing twice. They told me that they raid their mothers' closets—must be nice to have a mom who has a huge closet filled with size-zero Dolce & Gabbana dresses and size 37.5 Manolos (lol, I'm not bitter or jealous at all, see?). Sometimes, at lunch, they pull out old issues of *ELLE* for inspiration and plan what they'll wear next. And, believe me, they go *all out.* Ridiculously expensive jewelry, fur-trimmed boots in the summer, cropped shirts, leather pants and skirts, and hats (hats!). I can identify them from the other side of the office *just* by seeing what they're wearing.

Several of the editors, like Maya and Alexa, are always dressed impeccably and elegantly, and I've never, ever seen them wear the same thing twice. But the rest of the editors (including Carolina) are far more casual. They never *appear* to wear the same thing twice, but in reality they're just really good at putting together unique combinations of the same pieces.

Meghana told me that almost all the editors have Rent the Runway subscriptions and borrow—not buy—their statement and trend pieces (including bags). She also said that all the higher-ranking editors go to Drybar a few times a week to get their hair done instead of doing it themselves, which is why they always look so polished (I asked her if she does this, since she always looks really gorgeous, but she told me she doesn't make enough to afford this . . . yet).

The funny thing is that my budget has limited me to inexpensive clothes so I look more like a low-ranking editor than an intern. Alas.

From: Y Combinator
To: Cat Wolff
Subject: Re: Apply to Y Combinator
Date: June 19, 2017

Hi Cat,

Please apply here: https://www.ycombinator.com/apply/

The application deadline for our winter 2018 batch is October 3rd.

We invest $120k in exchange for 7% equity in your company.

—YC

From: Cat Wolff
To: Y Combinator
Subject: Re: Re: Apply to Y Combinator
Date: June 19, 2017

Is that $120,000 in cash?

Cat Wolff

From: Y Combinator
To: Cat Wolff
Subject: Re: Re: Re: Apply to Y Combinator
Date: June 19, 2017

Hi Cat,

Yes.

—YC

From: Cat Wolff
To: Y Combinator
Subject: Re: Re: Re: Re: Apply to Y Combinator
Date: June 19, 2017

Would I be able to get it in Bitcoin?

Cat Wolff

From: Y Combinator
To: Cat Wolff
Subject: Re: Re: Re: Re: Re: Apply to Y Combinator
Date: June 19, 2017

No.

—YC

The Diary of Lora Ricci

June 23, 2017

I worked more with Cat this week.

On Tuesday and Thursday, Bob came to pick me up in the morning and took me home at night. Cat and I made some great progress on her startup founders feature. On Tuesday, I explained what I'd learned about venture capital and we discussed how to communicate the information in the piece. She had lots of questions she needed the answers to, things like *Do they give you cold hard cash? What happens if the startup shuts down–do they have to give the money back or do they get to keep it?*

Not going to lie, it felt really cool to call up these venture capital firms and accelerators and say, "Hi, this is Lora Ricci from *ELLE* magazine. I'm doing some research and fact-checking for a piece in one of our upcoming issues . . ."

It blew my mind when one of the venture capitalists I spoke to told me that most startups fail; investors in startups, the VC explained, expect that most of the companies they invest in will close down and that most of the money they invest will go down the drain. "All we need," she said, "is for a few of the companies to succeed: one big, successful investment pays for all the failures and returns an obscene profit." When I told Cat, this fact blew her mind, too.

On Thursday, Cat said something that I haven't been able to stop thinking about.

While we were eating lunch in the Palm Court, somehow the conversation shifted to the other interns. "You know, I really admire you," she said.

"Why?" I asked.

"The chances of having a successful career in fashion journalism are so slim, but you don't let that dissuade you. You know the odds aren't in your favor, but you're giving it your best shot anyway. The other interns have wealth, status, connections, trust funds. I mean, even *I* have those things—they're practically table stakes for a career in journalism. Most people in your situation wouldn't even bother, but you're still giving it your all. I admire that. I wish I had your kind of courage."

I think she meant this as a compliment, but it freaked me out and gave me a panic attack last night when I got home. The thing is, she's totally right. I mean, look at the other interns. They all have money. They probably all have trust funds. They probably all have amazing grades. I'm from the middle of nowhere. My mom works in a grocery store deli, and my dad fixes cars. I had to go to community college and state school in order to get into NYU and then I got the worst GPA of my life my first year there. I bet Katrine has a 4.0 at Columbia. How can I possibly compete? I can't!

And the worst thing is, I can't get it out of my head that maybe I'm just a charity case for NYU . . . and for *ELLE,* too. Ever since I got into NYU, I've been telling myself that I *earned* it, that I worked my ass off to prove that I'm just as good as anyone else, and that by getting into NYU, I proved that I am. But what if I'm not? What if they just brought me in as a, like, socioeconomic diversity student? (Does such a thing even exist?) And I told myself the same thing about getting an internship at *ELLE*—that I'd earned it, that I deserved to be there. But what if it was all a mistake? What then????

If I'm being honest with myself, I know I don't fit in. I'm

not like the other NYU students. I'm not like the other *ELLE* interns. Maybe I don't have a future in this industry. Maybe I don't have a future in this city. Maybe I'm going to end up just like my parents.

What the hell am I doing?

I don't even have a backup plan! If college doesn't work out, then what? If writing doesn't work out, then what?

Nothing!

I have nothing!

THE PLAZA HOTEL

Dear Ms. Wolff,

Unfortunately, it appears that your credit card has been declined. I'm not quite sure how this happened, as we usually run the card beforehand to ensure it is valid. We need an updated card on file at all times to cover any incidentals. Could you please stop by the front desk? The balance on your account, due immediately, is $34,748.51.

Warmly,

John

THE PLAZA HOTEL

John

I must have missed you. I stopped by the front desk this morning, but you weren't there. I'm terribly sorry about the card. It looks like my bank thought the charge was fraudulent and canceled the card as a precautionary measure. They are sending me a new one, but it may take several days to arrive. Would you mind if I paid you by check? I apologize for any inconvenience.

Cat Wolff

THE PLAZA HOTEL

Dear Ms. Wolff,

Of course, I completely understand, and it is no trouble at all. A check is fine. Please bring it to the front desk at your earliest convenience.

Warmly,

John

AMERICAN EXPRESS
El Paso, TX 79998

ClosetAI
Attn: Cat Wolff
The Plaza Hotel
1 Central Park South #2040
New York, NY 10019

June 25, 2017

AMERICAN EXPRESS
Blue Business® Plus Credit Card ending in #54321

Welcome, ClosetAI!

We're pleased to tell you that you've been approved for a Blue Business® Plus Credit Card! Congratulations, and thank you for beginning your relationship with American Express.

Set up your online business account today and enjoy the benefits of your card the moment it arrives. You should expect your card to arrive in 2 to 3 business days.

The Diary of Lora Ricci

June 29, 2017

After three weeks of intense research, Cat and I finally started writing today. We scheduled interviews with a bunch of women who are starting fashion companies, but those interviews won't be taking place until late July and early August. In the meantime, we're putting together a "how to start your own fashion company" guide to run alongside the interviews.

This morning, Bob was waiting outside with the Escalade. When I arrived at The Plaza, Cat was sitting at the table eating breakfast, deep in thought, but she snapped out of it as soon as she saw me and we quickly got to work. She had all our research notes open on her laptop, and, as she read them to me, I wrote up a summary of what she said. Then she'd stop and work on something else while I edited and consolidated and made everything make sense. We fell into a good rhythm: she'd tell me the overall point we wanted to make, and then I'd write the actual words and fill in all the details. We thought it would take us at least a week to finish, but we made so much progress that we were done by the early afternoon.

We read the guide out loud a few times from start to finish, just to make sure there weren't any glaringly obvious mistakes. Cat pushed the coffee table out of the way, climbed up on the velvet couch, held her laptop, cleared her throat, and read the article to me while I paced in circles around the room. I caught some mistakes (should be "which," not "that"), and then she hopped down and handed me the laptop. Still pacing around in circles, I read the piece to her while she rested on the couch. She closed her eyes, focusing on the words and correcting anything that seemed off.

As soon as we were satisfied, Cat took her laptop back to the table and wrote an email to Carolina. I hovered around her like a bee, barely able to contain my excitement. I almost jumped when she whirled around and handed me the computer. "Here, read this email," she said, "and make sure it looks good."

I read through it slowly. It was perfect. I handed the laptop back to her, and she pressed "send."

Cat closed the computer and we looked at each other. "We should go to the Champagne Bar and celebrate," she announced triumphantly. She walked down the hallway and disappeared into her bedroom, shutting the door behind her. I wasn't sure what to do, so I put on my flats and packed up my bag, then sat down on the couch to wait.

A few minutes later, she returned. She'd changed out of her cashmere sweat suit and into a long, flowy black dress and immaculately clean white tennis shoes. "Ready?" she said, smiling. I stood up and put my bag over my shoulder.

"We're just going downstairs," she said, raising her eyebrows. "You can leave your things here."

"Oh, okay." I walked back over to the table and set my bag on one of the dining chairs. She picked up the phone and called the front desk. "Hello . . . could you please send housekeeping up to my room . . . yes . . . yes . . . Wolff . . . Suite 2040 . . . yes . . . all right . . . thank you."

After she put down the phone, she walked to the front door. I was about to follow her when suddenly I noticed a hundred-dollar bill on the arm of the couch. "Wait!" I shouted. "You dropped this!"

She came back down the hallway and smiled when she saw me holding the money. I handed her the bill, but, to my astonishment, she put it right back on the couch. "It's a tip for the housekeeper."

When we got down to the first floor, we went to a bar that was basically part of the lobby. It was a little busy, but we were able to get a table next to a window. Cat ordered a cheese plate and champagne flights (something I truly hadn't known existed until that moment).

We toasted our article, and I told Cat how excited I was that it was going to be published. Cat explained, though, that even if Carolina liked it, it wasn't a done deal. "Most pieces never see the light of day, even after an editor green-lights the pitch. Next time we go to a pitch meeting, write down the number of pieces that are pitched and the number that are approved, then follow up a few months later. You'll be shocked at how many pieces are killed somewhere along the way."

I was about to ask questions about the process, but Cat changed the subject and we started talking about the TV shows we were bingeing. We were in the middle of a conversation about Nicole Kidman's character in *Big Little Lies* when my phone began to buzz. I tried to ignore it, but whoever was calling me was not going to give up. I glanced at the screen. Mom. Again. But this time, instead of leaving a voicemail, she started texting me.

"I'm so sorry, I just need to check this real quick," I apologized to Cat. I looked at the texts: Why aren't you answering my calls? The school called and said you haven't registered for classes or applied for financial aid. What's going on, Lora?

I could feel my face turning bright red. I sighed in frustration as I sent Mom a quick reply: Can't talk now. Am in important meeting. Everything's okay. Busy with internship. School is mixed up about classes—will call them tomorrow. Love you!

"Boyfriend?" Cat asked.

I shook my head.

"Girlfriend?"

I shook my head again. "No. It's my mom."

"It's all right if you need to take the call," she said with a bit of concern in her voice.

"No, no," I insisted. "There's really no point. I wouldn't even know what to say to her."

"I get it," she said with a shrug. "Family is complicated."

I looked down at my drink and felt a wave of emotions rise inside me. I tried to swallow them back down, afraid I'd burst into tears and make a complete idiot of myself. I looked up at Cat, and her eyes met mine. I remembered how she'd opened up to me the first day we worked together, how she'd told me about her late mother and her journey to New York. And I'm not sure how much time had passed since we'd started drinking, but, by this point, I was a bit drunk—drunk enough that my secrets started tumbling out of my mouth.

I told her everything.

Everything.

I told her about how I wanted to be Zadie Smith. How I spent all my free time hoping that I would someday be an editor at a fashion magazine and write novels and short stories on the side.

I told her about my grades. How I'd been a straight-A student until I transferred to NYU. How when I arrived in New York, I found myself totally out of my league and completely overwhelmed by my classes. Everyone seemed to know exactly what they were doing and exactly who they were—everyone except for me. I didn't feel like I belonged. I *didn't* belong. I didn't feel smart enough. I *wasn't* smart enough. My GPA at the end of the first semester was 2.1. At the end of my second semester, my GPA was 1.8.

She listened as I told her how I'd learned, at the end of my second semester, that I'd lost my scholarship. How a financial aid officer sat me down in his office and explained that my low GPA meant I was no longer eligible for the scholarship and now had to come up with the difference—in cash—if I wanted to return in the fall. How I didn't have the money. How I was never going to have the money.

"Wait. So you have to come up with thirty-five thousand dollars in a few weeks if you want to have any hope of going back to school?" she asked, her eyes wide with horror. "How the hell are you supposed to do that?"

I admitted that I didn't know. I told her that I hadn't registered for classes and kept fantasizing about running away somewhere—anywhere—and hiding from the world until I figured out what to do. I told her how I couldn't bear to tell my parents the truth, and how I'd mistakenly believed that interning at *ELLE* would somehow magically fix everything. The truth was that I didn't know how to fix my life, that I wanted to throw it all away and start over again.

I began to cry.

"I just keep pushing it out of my mind, ignoring it, pretending it's not a problem and that it will all magically resolve itself," I said, wiping the tears from my face, "but I know that the second I tell my parents, it'll be real, and I'll have to face it. I'll have to face the fact that I'm a failure, that I'll never graduate from NYU, that I'll never be a writer. So instead, I lie. I lie, and

I lie again and again and again and I just keep lying to everyone around me because I can't tell anyone the truth."

I looked up at her. Just like the time she fixed my makeup in the beauty closet, there was genuine solidarity and something like determination written all over her face. Not pity, not sympathy, but a look that said, *You are not alone in this.* "This is why the world is so fucked up," she said. "It's not fair. It's so not fair, Lora. The truth is, the world isn't built for people like you and me. We don't fit inside these perfect boxes; we don't match everyone's preconceived ideas of who and what a writer is supposed to be. And the funny thing is, if people just gave us a chance, if they stopped forcing us to fit into their stupid little boxes and just let us be who we are, we'd give them the best writing they'd read in years."

I wasn't sure what she meant. I'm still not sure. "What should we do?" I asked.

"I think," she said, choosing her words carefully, "that we have to learn to be comfortable outside the boxes. We have to find ways around the system. We have to break the rules, and we absolutely cannot feel bad about breaking them, not even for a moment. It's the only way we can make it. It's the only way we'll ever have a shot. It's the only way we can survive."

I was about to ask her to elaborate, to ask her what rules I needed to break in order to go back to school, but before I could, her whole demeanor changed. I think that, in that moment, she had let her guard down and allowed herself to be vulnerable. It was like she had taken off her armor, showed me that she was a human underneath all of that wealth and status and beauty, and then freaked out and put the armor back on before I could hurt her. She put her glass down and looked at her watch. "We'd better get going," she said. She waved the waiter over, charged our bill to her room, and then together we headed back upstairs so I could grab my bag.

I was surprised when she came back down to the lobby with me. Bob was waiting outside, as usual, but this time, Cat wanted to join us. "I need to meet a few people in Brooklyn," she explained as she hopped into the back seat with me. The drive over the bridge quickly flew by, and before I knew it, the SUV had pulled up in front of my building. Cat hadn't said a word to me the entire ride.

Just as I was getting out, Cat stopped me. "Hey, Lora," she said. "Let's keep working together."

"Okay," I said as I hopped out, a little surprised. Bob closed the door and walked back to the driver's side.

Cat rolled down the window and stuck her head out. "We make a good team, you and me."

I laughed, feeling relieved. "Yeah, we really do, don't we?" I called, as the SUV drove away.

I watched as she stuck her head out even farther and blew me a kiss. "Good night!" she shouted.

Now I'm back in my bed and I'm exhausted but relieved. Everything about NYU and my grades and the scholarship and my parents—it's all been hanging over me, haunting me, threatening to ruin my life at any moment. I hadn't told a single soul about any of it. I couldn't. Not until tonight. And now it's almost as if by finally spilling my guts out to someone and coming clean about my situation, it has lost some of its terror. If Cat still wants to work with me, even after she knows all of my secrets and all of my lies, maybe everything isn't lost. Maybe everything is going to be okay. Maybe I'll find a way to break the rules and chase my dreams outside the boxes.

From: Olesya Dorokhova
To: Nikolay Dorokhov
Subject: (no subject)
Date: July 1, 2017

Kolya—

There's nobody here I can trust. Except maybe the intern, which is mostly because she is so naïve and gullible. The office is no longer safe, so I'm trying to avoid going in unless I really have to. I'm certain someone from the FBI is there, I just don't know who it is yet. I would quit, but I need to hang on just a little while longer. Just until I get this next thing set up.

Speaking of which, I need help with a project. Can you find four or five ex-models (around 30–35 years old) and get them photographed outside? The backgrounds have to be blurred so that there's nothing identifiable. Make sure it's a diverse group.

I'll send you the names and company details I made up for them, and then I need you to make websites for their "startups."

I need this as soon as you can get it done.

—Olesya

From: Nikolay Dorokhov
To: Olesya Dorokhova
Subject: Re:
Date: July 2, 2017

ok i will do

do i even want to know what this is for lol

are you at least leaving the hotel

you are so paranoid

get outside, get some fresh air

clear your head

The Diary of Lora Ricci

July 8, 2017

The Fourth of July came and went without much excitement. Mom and Dad usually do a big barbecue at our house every year, and Nana and Papa and all the neighbors come over and we eat and play games and have fun and go see the fireworks at night. I almost rented a car and drove down there, but I couldn't bring myself to. It's easy for me to lie to Mom over text, but I knew I wouldn't be able to lie to her in person.

In sad work news: the "guide" part of our feature got killed. Carolina didn't like it. She said it didn't belong in a magazine like *ELLE*. The good news, however, is that the interview part of our feature is still on. Carolina wanted to kill that, too, but Cat lied to her and said that we'd already gotten the photos and finished the interviews and that we just needed to transcribe the interviews and the piece would be ready to go. Carolina *still* wanted to kill it, but Maya, who was also on the call, was intrigued and wanted to read the interviews, so she vetoed Carolina's veto. I feel weird about Cat lying, but I understand why she did it. I mean, Carolina was killing our feature *for no reason at all*.

After the call was over, we went downstairs to the Palm Court for lunch. We barely spoke for an entire hour, and then out of nowhere Cat started laughing. "Guess I'd better interview and photograph some startup founders," she said. I asked if we'd still be working together. She said she might need some help transcribing the interviews, and she'd let me know when they were ready.

I miss spending so much time with Cat, though it is nice to be writing my own stuff on my days off. I went back to the outline for that short story I started earlier this summer, and wrote the whole thing. I'm really happy with how it turned out, and I felt excited enough about it that I wrote another story that same day.

Work was fun this week, too—more fun than usual. I helped Laura and Meghana set up a Drybar PR party, and then, on Friday, I found myself sitting next to Cat on the rooftop patio of a nearby hotel, watching a curling iron demonstration. We both had drinks and weren't really paying attention to the demo; I could tell Cat was bored by the whole event—either that or she had something else on her mind.

I was about to ask her what she was thinking about, when she turned to me and said, "I can't stop thinking about your situation. I found myself lying awake last night, wondering how we were going to get you thirty-five thousand dollars in cash. I thought, *Maybe I could pawn some of my jewelry,* and I actually got up and walked to my jewelry case. I was so mad at myself for not having more expensive jewelry. Everything in there came to, like, five thousand dollars, max. I even thought of calling my father and begging him for the money, but then I remembered what happened last time I asked for cash." She sighed and looked at me, exasperated. "I don't know what we're going to do!"

What <u>*we're*</u> *going to do??* I hadn't realized how much she cared. (Maybe, in all of this depressing mess, I've somehow made a friend?) I told her I had applied for a loan but had been denied because I didn't have enough credit history.

She grimaced. "Ugh, I know exactly how that feels," she said.

"I've applied for loans and had them denied. They always come back and say, 'Why isn't your father cosigning this loan? He's the one with all the money.' As if I'd be applying for a loan if my father was willing to give me money!"

"Oh my god, yes," I said, almost shouting. "The bank said I might be able to get the loan but that my parents would need to cosign. I was like, *Yeah, that's my whole problem—I can't tell my parents!*"

"And you only have, what, like two weeks before you have to come up with the money? It's impossible!"

I know she was trying to help, but talking about it made my stomach twist into a knot. I started to feel like I was going to have a panic attack. I looked down at my yellow-and-gray Drybar-themed cocktail for a moment, then changed the subject. "Let me know when you're ready to work on those interviews, or any other features you want to write. I don't even need a byline. I just like working together."

I bit my lip as soon as the words came out of my mouth. *I don't even need a byline.* Yeah, right. I would give my left arm for a byline in *ELLE*. Why did I even say that?

"I definitely will," she said, kindly allowing me to change the subject. "Even though Carolina killed it, I thought you did a wonderful job with the startups piece. Actually, you know, I'd love to read more of your writing. What else do you like to write? Have you written any fiction?"

I told her about the short stories I'd written this summer and made it clear that none of my stories were all that good. "They're mediocre at best. I ramble too much."

"I'm sure they're better than you think. Send them to me," she said.

Just then, Meghana walked over and sat next to Cat. They started talking about the best salons in the city, and I just sat there with my drink, staring into space, feeling like an outsider again, thinking about how shitty my whole situation was. It doesn't matter how much I try, I feel like I'm always on the sidelines. Will I ever fit in?

I only have a few weeks left before fall classes start.

I don't have any money.

I don't know what I'm going to do.

I don't have anywhere to go.

I'm running out of time.

katrine baker katrine baker, drybar model #intern
#internship #drybar #not_an_ad #elle #fashion #beauty
#ellemagazine #journalist #nyc #newyork #hair #blowout

From: Cat Wolff
To: Lora Ricci
Subject: (no subject)
Date: July 10, 2017

Lora:

The other night, you mentioned you had written some short stories. I'd love to read them. Send them my way?

Cat Wolff

From: Lora Ricci
To: Cat Wolff
Subject: Re:
Date: July 10, 2017

Hi Cat!

I hope I didn't oversell them—they are pretty bad. But here you go! I've attached two of them. Please don't judge me too harshly. Like I told you, I'm not really a good writer. Not yet, anyway.

Best,

Lora

Attachments: horsegirlshortstory1FINALFINAL.doc, fashionshortstory3ALMOSTFINALDRAFTFINAL2.doc

From: Cat Wolff
To: Lora Ricci
Subject: Re: Re:
Date: July 10, 2017

Lora:

Here, we'll make it even. Attached are two short stories I wrote earlier this summer. I'd love to hear your thoughts.

Cat Wolff

Attachments: catwolffshort1.doc, catwolffshort2.doc

THE PLAZA HOTEL

Dear Ms. Wolff,

The check you left at the front desk has been returned and is marked "insufficient funds." Your bill is now $47,822.59. The total balance is due, in full, immediately.

Warmly,

John

THE PLAZA HOTEL

John:

I'm terribly sorry. I asked my father to transfer the money to my U.S. account. Apparently, he forgot. He is wiring the money to my account now.

In the meantime, my new AMEX card has arrived. I'll bring it to the front desk tomorrow morning. In case I don't see you, please look for a payment from an AMEX ending in #4321.

Cat Wolff

The Diary of Lora Ricci

July 13, 2017

We haven't had an intern lunch in a little while because we've all been so busy, but today we got the gang back together and finally all caught up:

- Maggie is interviewing at *InStyle* and is pretty sure she'll get the assistant job (go Maggie!!). Oh, and Alexa asked her to pick out a scarf for a shoot, and Maggie was super psyched but kept complaining about how it's not fair that they don't let interns do *more* things like that.
- Katrine is still Katrine, bubbly and excited and a total know-it-all; she got a water bottle with a giant rose quartz crystal inside it. She said it balances her pH and helps her keep an open heart. Okay, lol . . .
- Piper mentioned that she'd gotten to help with a mood board. I think her exact words were: "I helped make a mood board." And that's all she said the whole lunch.

Yesterday there was a big photoshoot in Chelsea. It was the most fun I've had at *ELLE* so far. A bunch of us went with the editors and got to stay on set all day. Before the models arrived, we stood in for them so that the photographers could make sure the lights and backgrounds were perfect; the photographer would tell us how to pose, and we'd do it (I even got to wear a Derek Lam jacket that the model wore for the real shoot later!).

The rest of the day was less glamorous but just as exciting—I ran around doing various errands and making sure that everyone had what they needed. At the end of the day, I stuck around to pack everything up, then took it all back to the office and helped unpack everything back into the fashion closet.

I wish I could explain the rush of being at the shoot. There was this tangible, infectious energy in the air—everyone was at their happiest and most energized. The models were such professionals—you should have seen how businesslike they were, how they knew exactly what to do. Inspired by them, I tried to be all business and stay super serious the whole time, but whenever I was by myself, I couldn't help but smile so wide I thought I was going to crack my face in half. By the time I went home, my cheeks were actually sore from smiling.

It really was the best day.

In other news, a few days ago Cat asked me to send her some short stories I'd written. I almost told her that reading them would be a complete waste of her time, but then I took a step back and thought about it a little more. She seems pretty interested in working together, she knows about my problems with school, and there doesn't seem to be any point in hiding things from her—even my dumb little short stories.

I really do feel like I can tell her the truth and that we're starting to become friends. And she believes in me and my writing. She's a realist—I think she really *gets* how the world works and knows how to find her way in it. I wish I were more like her. She's like a better version of me, the version of me that would exist if I'd been born with money.

Ultimately, I feel like Cat is the only person I've *really* been getting close to. I was hoping that I would become good friends with my roommates, but they all have their own lives and jobs and boyfriends and social circles, and I'm never really invited to anything. I'm closer to the other interns than to my roommates, though I haven't spent time with them outside the office yet.

I went for a long walk through Prospect Park, trying to figure out what to do. And then I decided that there was no point in me being afraid. If my stories are awful, Cat will just tell me they're awful and we'll move on. I'll live. It's not like my life can get *that* much worse, right?

So I sent them.

To my surprise, she replied by sending me some of her own stories. I read them the moment they hit my inbox.

Truthfully? I have mixed feelings about them.

First, the good: Her ideas are amazing. The plots are fascinating. The characters (or, really, who I think the characters are supposed to be) are amazing. If I had read descriptions of what each story was about, I would have expected them to be some of the best short stories I've ever read. I'm not kidding—they are really good (or could be . . .).

And now the bad: Her pacing is terrible—it's all over the place. She can't write scenes. The dialogue is wooden and unnatural. The characters have no real or unique voices. These are damning faults, because they make the stories almost unreadable.

So, basically, the stories are perfect in theory, but her execution is pretty terrible.

I've never really shared my fiction writing with anyone else, so I'm feeling anxious about Cat reading it. I haven't heard from her since I sent my stories, and I don't think I should say anything about her stories until she says something about mine.

Jenée Parker | 07–14–2017 8:07 AM
Our undercover agent says CW isn't going to the office

Amanda Harris | 07–14–2017 8:08 AM
Do you think she knows she's being followed?

Jenée Parker | 07–14–2017 8:10 AM
Unclear

Jenée Parker | 07–14–2017 8:10 AM
Apparently she usually comes in 3–5 days/week

Amanda Harris | 07–14–2017 8:12 AM
Can we move her to the hotel?

Jenée Parker | 07–14–2017 8:13 AM
Our agent?

Amanda Harris | 07–14–2017 8:14 AM
Yes

Jenée Parker | 07–14–2017 8:16 AM
Definitely. They haven't interacted at all.

Jenée Parker | 07–14–2017 8:17 AM
Her "internship" ends in two weeks

Jenée Parker | 07–14–2017 8:17 AM
Unless anything changes with CW, we'll move her to the plaza then

Amanda Harris | 07–14–2017 8:20 AM
Perfect

The Diary of Lora Ricci

July 18, 2017

Still no word from Cat.

Dammit.

Maybe my writing really *is* that bad.

From: Y Combinator
To: Cat Wolff
Subject: Your Y Combinator Application
Date: July 20, 2017

Thank you for your application.

Unfortunately, your startup isn't a good fit for the next Y Combinator batch. Please understand that this is not a reflection of your promise as a founder or the potential of your startup. Thousands of companies apply for each Y Combinator batch, and we can only select a small number of those.

Many of the companies and founders we rejected will go on to become creative successful startups. And many of them apply to the next YC batch and are accepted.

We encourage you to apply for the next batch. We don't count it against you if you were rejected before—in fact, we think it shows determination.

Best of luck.

—YC

From: Cat Wolff
To: Y Combinator
Subject: Re: Your Y Combinator Application
Date: July 24, 2017

Is it possible for me to apply to the same batch with a different startup idea?

Cat Wolff

From: Y Combinator
To: Cat Wolff
Subject: Re: Re: Your Y Combinator Application
Date: July 24, 2017

No. However, you can wait and apply again next year. Quite a few startups are funded after applying several times.

—YC

Cat Wolff 1:46 PM
Katrine, could you please assist me with transcribing several interviews?

Katrine Baker 1:47 PM
when do u need them done by

Cat Wolff 2:03 PM
I have one that needs to be done today and I'll have another one ready Friday.

Katrine Baker 2:16 PM
yeah cool ok i can do this one im helping alexa friday tho

Cat Wolff 2:17 PM
Thanks. And that's perfectly alright. I'll ask Aisha to help with the next one.

Katrine Baker 2:23 PM
k cool

The Diary of Lora Ricci

July 26, 2017

Today, for the first time in a *very* long time, I feel hopeful. Actually, genuinely, truly hopeful. Like maybe there's a chance I'll be okay. Like maybe there's a chance I can still be a writer and have the life I want and accomplish everything I've set out to do. And it's all thanks to Cat. Cat, my knight in shining black silk pantsuit armor.

I'm getting ahead of myself. I'm so tired and I just want to get right to the point and celebrate. But I'll start from the beginning...

Okay, so, I hadn't heard anything from Cat in a while, and the anxiety was eating me alive. Had she read the stories? Did she hate them?

I haven't been sleeping much in general. But last night my insomnia was so bad I didn't sleep at all. I was up the whole night and didn't know what to do with myself, so I decided to just go in to the office early. I was in the beauty closet a little after six. Genevieve (Maya's assistant) and I were the only ones there.

I walked back and forth through the halls in a sleepless daze, seeing the office in ways I'd never noticed before. The art department was especially cool, with big mock-ups of the cover and various pages everywhere. With no one there yet, it felt like being in a museum, like I was walking through an exhibit at the Smithsonian called "Fashion Magazines in the Digital Age."

Around nine, people started meandering in, so I ceased my aimless wandering and headed back to the closet. My brain was too fried from lack of sleep to focus on anything important, but luckily there were plenty of simple tasks that I'd been putting off, like organizing new products, throwing out old makeup, and replying to PR emails ("Yes, we would love a sample of your new eyeshadow stick," "No, we have enough dry shampoos, thank you").

A little while later, I heard someone walk into the closet. I looked up, hopeful, expecting to see Cat's enigmatic face staring back at me. But no, it was just Haley. My heart sank. "Laura and Meghana are thinking of doing a sunscreen editorial for the fall or winter," she said. "Can you find some that work really well under makeup?"

I nodded, brain-dead, then walked over to the shelf like a zombie, pulled out a tray of sunscreens, and started looking through them. I wondered if I'd have to test the sunscreens myself or if one of the beauty editors would do it. I analyzed every word I could remember of Haley's request so I wouldn't screw up. *She didn't say "find some sunscreen,"* I thought to myself, *she said "find some that work under makeup."* Okay, I would test them myself. That would keep me distracted enough, at least for a few hours.

As I was sitting there talking to myself about sunscreen, I didn't hear Cat come in.

"Do you have a minute?" she asked quietly.

Surprised, I looked up to find her standing there, leaning against the door frame. But before I could answer, she turned around and walked away.

I pulled myself to my feet, my hands and arms covered in white smears of sunscreen. By the time I caught up with her, she was halfway across the office, and I wasn't sure where she was going. We walked past a conference room, and she grabbed my hand. "Let's go in here," Cat said as she pulled me inside. She shut the door behind us. "Sorry, I'm trying to stay under the radar," she explained.

I asked her if she needed help with the fashion startup founder interviews. She waved her hands in the air as if she were waving away the question itself. "No, no, no," she said. "I'll have another intern do that."

The rejection stung. She leaned against the edge of a conference table in the middle of the room. "So, what did you think?" she asked.

I was so lost. "What?"

"About my stories. What did you think?"

A million thoughts rushed through my head all at once. My eyes darted around the room as I tried to figure out what to say and how to get the hell out of there. *I should have slept last night, dammit. Why didn't I sleep last night? Why didn't she ask me earlier? What took her so long . . .*

"Come on, Lora," she begged, "just be honest with me. If I thought my stories were amazing, I wouldn't have sent them to you. My agent would have sent them out and they would have been published by now. Here, how about this—I'll get it out of the way: they're awful. There! Now it's your turn! Go!"

She stared at me intently, her eyebrows arched.

The words just started tumbling out of my mouth. "Actually, they're really, really good. Your ideas, the characters, the plots—those things, I *loved.* But . . ." I paused and looked up at her.

"But . . . ?"

"Well, you have all these amazing ideas, but I feel like the stories themselves need . . . work. Your scenes feel forced. The dialogue is really hard to follow." *Oh shit. My filter. I forgot that when I don't sleep I forget to filter my thoughts.* I stopped there, my lips tightly sealed.

Much to my surprise, instead of being offended or getting defensive, she smiled. The armor was off. "This is exactly why I sent them to you."

Then she sat down on the conference table and sighed. "I wish I could write like you," she said wistfully.

Well, believe me when I tell you that was literally the last thing in the world I expected to hear. "What?" I asked, genuinely shocked.

"You're an *extraordinary* writer. Your characters are so rich, and the dialogue is so compelling. I'm pretty sure I could pull out random lines of dialogue and know exactly which character they belong to, because each character's voice is so unique to who they are. They feel like real, living, breathing people. Your plots are just not that interesting, though. Thematically, it all feels pointless. You can write, you just need something to write *about*."

She stood up and started pacing around the room. "You know, it's so crazy. I keep thinking about how unfair your situation is. It would be awful even if you weren't a great writer, but you *are* a great writer, and you're in this impossible position, where you can't go to school and finish your degree and you basically have to give up your dreams. And you just don't have the connections to get noticed. It's completely unfair and unjust. Honestly, Lora, I know you're going to be a famous writer someday, if only someone would give you a chance to show the world how amazing you really are."

I tried to find something to say, but I was too stunned to

speak. Where could I even go from there? It was hands down the best thing anyone has ever said to me. I'm burning it into my memory forever so I never, ever forget it.

All I could manage was to thank her. Then, after a moment, I told her about how I had called NYU and begged them to help, to give me an extra loan, to do anything they could to help me stay in school—and that they told me there was nothing they could do.

She walked up to me, reached for my hands, and our eyes met. Then, wearing the biggest smile I've ever seen, she said, "Lora, I have a plan."

And, oh my god, she figured it out. She really did. She figured out how to save me. How to fix all my problems. I'm going to be okay. God, it's so perfect. (It's almost too perfect?) I'm so tired and my brain is so fried and I need to go to sleep now. I'll write down all the details later, I promise. For now, sleep. Finally. Sleep.

Katrine Baker | 3:38 PM
lmao aisha we can hear u laughing all the way from over here

Aisha Jackson | 3:39 PM
This interview is something else, lol

Katrine Baker | 3:39 PM
the cat and sophie one?

Aisha Jackson | 3:40 PM
Yeah haha

Katrine Baker | 3:42 PM
they're pretty ridiculous not gonna lie 🤣

Aisha Jackson | 3:42 PM
Do you transcribe a lot of these?

Katrine Baker | 3:43 PM
i did 1 for her a few days ago

Aisha Jackson | 3:44 PM
Are they all completely nuts?

Katrine Baker | 3:45 PM
lol yeah they make no sense. they also hurt my ears like how cat speaks in that really low voice and then sophie's voice is so high 🤣

Katrine Baker | 3:46 PM
it's so extreme. sometimes I joke to myself that it is like the same person doing both of the voices lol

Katrine Baker | 3:53 PM
u still there?

Katrine Baker | 4:01 PM
aisha?

Jenée Parker | 07–29–2017 10:02 AM

We have another alias for CW

Amanda Harris | 07–29–2017 10:04 AM

Who else is she?

Jenée Parker | 07–29–2017 10:05 AM

"Sophie Bisset"

Jenée Parker | 07–29–2017 10:05 AM

A French fashion designer

Amanda Harris | 07–29–2017 10:10 AM

Do we know anything about the real Sophie?

Jenée Parker | 07–29–2017 10:11 AM

Not yet

The Diary of Lora Ricci

July 30, 2017

Cat and I met up at The Plaza today to figure out the rest of the details of ~~her~~ our plan. The more we talked about it, the more real it felt, and the more I started to realize exactly what we were about to do. It's not official yet—I can still back out if I want to or need to. I'm still mulling it all over.

Time to make a list . . .

PROS OF CAT'S PLAN:

- Don't have to worry about scholarship
- Don't have to tell parents about bad grades and loss of said scholarship (unless I really want to)
- Won't have to move back in with Mom and Dad and work at Target again
- Will be a real writer
- Will have path to becoming a novelist
- Will have agent (I think? Unclear)

CONS OF CAT'S PLAN:

- All my eggs in Cat's basket
- Will have to keep lying to Mom and Dad
- Closing the door on NYU, maybe forever
- Not sure how much money I will be making (hopefully more than Target?)
- Not sure where I will be living/working

katrine baker trying on these bright red #fendi boots with #aishajacksonneedstogetoninstagram #internship #elle #fashion #beauty #workworkwork workwork #journalism #interns #ellemagazine #shoes

Aisha Jackson | 11:09 AM
Katrine, could you please take down that photo you posted on Instagram? Thanks.

Katrine Baker | 11:11 AM
what photo i have like a million

Aisha Jackson | 11:12 AM
The photo I'm in, from Monday. The one of us in the shoe closet. That one.

Katrine Baker | 11:15 AM
no way, u look really pretty and i want to keep it to document our good times together ❤

Aisha Jackson | 11:16 AM
Katrine, please take it down now. I'm not okay with having my photo on a public Instagram account.

Aisha Jackson | 11:18 AM
Katrine, I'm serious, please take it down right now

Aisha Jackson | 11:25 AM
Holy shit, Katrine, please don't ignore me about this. PLEASE TAKE IT DOWN.

Aisha Jackson | 11:31 AM
Where are you? If you're going to ignore my Slack messages, we should talk in person.

Katrine Baker | 11:32 AM
im in the closet

Aisha Jackson | 11:33 AM
I'll be right there. Don't go anywhere. We need to talk about this.

From: Katrine Baker
To: Maggie Jiang, Piper Fenton
Subject: wtf
Date: August 2, 2017

wtf why did aisha completely lose her shit about the post?? like, it's just an insta photo calm the fuck down

---

From: Maggie Jiang
To: Katrine Baker
CC: Piper Fenton
Subject: Re: wtf
Date: August 2, 2017

I know, she was so rude about it

She didn't have to get all pissed at you in front of everyone

Like, of course you would delete it if she asked you nicely!

She's always avoiding photos too, it's like she doesn't want to be seen with us

Like, come on, we're not THAT embarrassing lol

From: Piper Fenton
To: Maggie Jiang
CC: Katrine Baker
Subject: Re: Re: wtf
Date: August 2, 2017

yeah wow

The Diary of Lora Ricci

August 5, 2017

I'm going to rent a car and drive back home next weekend and tell Mom and Dad about the plan. I know that they'll support me. I know that they'll understand how important it is for me to follow my dreams. I haven't made up my mind if I'm going to tell them about the grades and scholarship or not, but if they argue with me and we get in a huge fight or something, then I'll just get it off my chest and tell them everything. And *then* they will really understand.

Whew.

Okay.

Here we go.

From: Nikolay Dorokhov
To Olesya Dorokhova
Subject: (no subject)
Date: August 6, 2017

the websites are up

here are the photos

Attachment: photos.zip

From: Olesya Dorokhova
To: Nikolay Dorokhov
Subject: Re:
Date: August 7, 2017

Kolya—

Thank you, these are perfect.

I need to buy Instagram followers. где?

—Olesya

From: Nikolay Dorokhov
To Olesya Dorokhova
Subject: Re: Re:
Date: August 8, 2017

my friend sergey from school, this is his website: *followmenow*

he only accepts bitcoin. very secure, very private. no one will ever know.

tell him I sent you

why do you need this?

From: Olesya Dorokhova
To: Nikolay Dorokhov
Subject: Re: Re: Re:
Date: August 8, 2017

Kolya—

I'm bringing Sophie out of retirement.

—Olesya

From: Olesya Dorokhova
To: FollowMeNow
Subject: Purchase Followers
Date: August 9, 2017

Sergey—

I would like to purchase two million (2,000,000) followers for my Instagram

(My brother Nikolay referred me to you—he says hello.)

—Olesya

From: FollowMeNow
To: Olesya Dorokhova
Subject: Re: Purchase Followers
Date: August 10, 2017

Regards Miss Dorokhova

I would be happy to assist you today. FollowMeNow adds followers slowly to Instagram. All followers are real and verified. No bots. Pay in bitcoin only. Pay fifteen bitcoin to wallet linked below. Followers seen in 30–60 days.

Thank you for your preference in this business.

From: Coinbase
To: Olesya Dorokhova
Subject: Your Bitcoin Purchase
Date: August 10, 2017

Congratulations!

You purchased 15 Bitcoins (BTC) for $50,719.20 USD. Those funds are now available in your account.

Thank you for your purchase.

From: Hertz
To: Lora Ricci
Subject: My Hertz Reservation
Date: August 10, 2017

Your Itinerary

Pickup Location

Brooklyn—Park Slope

Pickup Time

Sat, Aug 12, 2017 at 06:30 PM

Return Location

Brooklyn—Park Slope

Return Time

Mon, Aug 14, 2017 at 10:00 AM

Your Age

20–24

Your Vehicle

Ford Fusion Hybrid (or similar)

What You Pay Now: 307.79 USD

What You Pay At Counter: 46.73 USD

Total: 354.52 USD

The Diary of Lora Ricci

August 11, 2017

I can't believe my internship is over. I'm going to miss *ELLE* so much. Working here has been such an amazing experience, and I can't believe how much I learned in just a few months. I'm still working with Cat on a few things. She's been working on an interview with this French designer, Sophie Bisset, who is starting a fashion company in Silicon Valley. It's the main interview for the feature she's writing, and she asked me if I could help her with research, so I've been spending all my free time at her place working on it. We're almost done—I think we'll be able to finish it before I leave tomorrow.

The editors threw us a goodbye party today. They surprised us with cupcakes and balloons and speeches thanking us for spending our summer at *ELLE*. Some of the editors made a fake *ELLE* cover for Maggie with her face on it and with all the things they loved about her, like "Writes the Best SEO." She worked there for a year and a half, and she got the job she interviewed for at *InStyle* and will start that in a few weeks (I'm so, so happy for her!).

Katrine and Piper are going back to school. I tried to avoid talking about school and classes and post-internship plans with them. Every time the topic came up, I turned to Katrine and asked her what *she* was planning to do. She was always more than happy to tell us about her classes, her MFA applications, and the thesis she's going to write in the spring.

Tomorrow night, we're having our own little goodbye party in Bushwick. It's going to be a long and busy day. I'm going to work at Cat's all day, then I'll go to Park Slope to pick up my rental car, then I have to drive to Bushwick for the party, then, after the party, I have to drive to all the way to my parents' house in Allentown.

I keep getting cold feet about the drive down, but I *have* to tell Mom and Dad in person. I at least owe that to them. I need to show them that I'm okay and explain that everything is going to work out.

I'm going to leave my backpack with all my stuff at Cat's while I'm gone and just bring my wallet and phone because I don't want anyone to break into the car when I'm at the party in Bushwick. My roommate Kenia left her bag with her work laptop in her car and someone broke into it and stole all her stuff—she had to replace the laptop *with her own money*. What a nightmare.

So, dearest diary, I'll catch you up on everything when I return to Cat's on Monday.

Maggie Jiang | 08–13–2017 3:16 AM
omg lora are you sure you're ok to drive?

Lora Ricci | 08–13–2017 3:18 AM
lol yes i didn't even drink that much

Lora Ricci | 08–13–2017 3:18 AM
katrine was the wild one 😂

Maggie Jiang | 08–13–2017 3:19 AM
hahahahahahaha omg sooooo true

Lora Ricci | 08–13–2017 3:20 AM
can't believe our internships are over 😭

Maggie Jiang | 08–13–2017 3:21 AM
i know ugh i already miss you so much wtf

Lora Ricci | 08–13–2017 3:22 AM
same ❤

Maggie Jiang | 08–13–2017 3:23 AM
drive safe text me when you get there

Lora Ricci | 08–13–2017 3:24 AM
ok will do

TOM AND CAROL RICCI
Allentown, PA 18104

The College of Arts & Science
New York University
32 Waverly Place
New York, NY 10003

August 16, 2017

To Whom It May Concern:

We regret to inform you that our daughter, Lora Elizabeth Ricci, will not be returning to NYU for the fall 2017 semester. We are shocked and greatly saddened, and we request that you hold a spot for her, just in case things change and she is able to return. She was an English and journalism double major, and she so loved the classes she took last school year—they were all she ever talked about.

We hope that she can go back to school, and we would give anything in the world to see her graduate. In all honesty, though, we don't know if that will ever happen.

Sincerely,

Tom and Carol Ricci

From: Olesya Dorokhova
To: Nikolay Dorokhov
Subject: (no subject)
Date: August 23, 2017

Kolya—

I found my missing puzzle piece.

—Olesya

PART 2

the one-trick pony

The Diary of Lora Ricci

August 24, 2017

Dear Diary,

I did it.

I told my parents.

After I met up with the other interns in Brooklyn—first at a Skee-Ball place and then a karaoke bar, where we sang our hearts out until it closed—I finally left for my parents' house at around three in the morning. I didn't get there until after five and was so tired, I immediately crawled into my old bed and fell asleep.

When I woke up, Mom had brunch on the table. I decided to get it over with and tell my parents (almost) everything, right then and there. They were confused at first. *What do you mean you're not going back to school? Did you get kicked out? Did something happen? What do you mean you're dropping out?* I didn't—couldn't—bring myself to tell them about the grades or the scholarship. Instead, I framed it all like I was a tech nerd dropping out of college to move to Silicon Valley and start the next Facebook: I was writing a book with someone else, we were going to sell it, I was just skipping ahead a year or two or five or ten and becoming a writer *now* instead of waiting.

Mom was quiet for a little while, but Dad kept asking questions. *So you have a book deal?* No. *So you have an agent?* No, but Cat does. *So Cat has written a book before?* I don't think so but I'm not 100 percent sure.

All of a sudden, Mom burst into tears and started yelling at me. "Why are you doing this? Why are you dropping out?

Why are you throwing away the opportunity of a lifetime? You have one year left, just one year of school, and then you can graduate—why would you throw that all away? Why would you throw away your dreams? Are you in trouble, Lora? Are you on drugs? Are you pregnant?"

"What? No, of course I'm not," I said, trying to reassure her as I fought back tears. "This is just an amazing opportunity for me. Like I said, it's what every aspiring writer wishes they could do many years after they graduate—I just get to do it *now,* instead of five years from now."

Dad jumped in. "Do you *really* have to drop out? Can't you just take a semester off and see how it goes? I'm sure we can work something out with the school."

"No," I said, shaking my head. "Cat says it will take us at least a year to write our book and get a book deal. It might even take us two years. I don't know. But here's what I *do* know: I need to put all my energy into writing. I won't have time for school."

"I can't pretend to understand how all this writing stuff works," Dad sighed. But if you're giving up your schooling for this, you should get something in writing. Have you signed a contract with Cat? Have you met with her agent in person?"

I was about to reply, but Mom had her head in her hands and was still crying, so Dad got distracted from his line of questioning and tried to reassure her. I was glad I didn't have to answer, because I honestly didn't know the details, and I sure as hell didn't have anything in writing. I was trying to think back to anything Cat might have said about pay or contracts or paperwork or meeting her agent, when I was pulled back to the present reality by the sound of my parents shouting at each other.

Dad was arguing that they should help me ("Maybe I should

go up there and meet this Cat and make sure she's not some kind of con artist," he suggested), and Mom argued that I would come back home as soon as I ran out of money ("Which won't take very long," she said confidently). I felt sick to my stomach, afraid that they were both right.

But then I thought about Cat.

Cat had a plan. I had a plan. *We* had a plan.

And Cat had money. Cat was rich. Cat had an agent. Cat knew what she was doing. She wouldn't have told me I could drop out of school and write for her if she didn't know exactly what we were going to do and how we were going to do it.

Technically, I'd be Cat's ghostwriter: she'd tell me ideas she had for short stories, and I'd write them. It would be her name on them instead of mine because she was the one with an agent, experience, and publishing connections. We'd publish the stories and, once they started to get some attention, I'd be able to go and sign with an agent and tell that agent that I had written the stories. Then, assuming this all worked out, I'd be able to get book deals of my own and publish stories and novels and whatever the hell I wanted to write—all in my own name.

Our plan was going to work. It had to.

I stood my ground.

"I've made up my mind," I said. "I'm going to be a writer. I'm going to make this work, and you can't talk me out of it."

This didn't convince them, and I don't even think they heard what I was saying. It didn't matter how many times I told them that my mind was made up—they wouldn't listen to me. They didn't believe me.

I honestly don't get it. Why don't they trust me? Don't they want me to follow my dreams? If this is what I want to do, why don't they support me? They supported me working at Target as a cashier for *five years*—how is *this* not better than *that*? It's not like I'm some screwup who is always making reckless decisions. I was a straight-A student all through high school (and until I got to NYU, for god's sake!). I worked to support myself and pay for my classes. I got into NYU and I got an internship at *ELLE*. It was completely unfair that I had to stand there and defend myself.

I couldn't take it anymore. "I love you guys, I do. But I can't believe you won't support me. I've done nothing to deserve this kind of treatment." I stood up from my chair, went to my bedroom, grabbed my things, and left.

They didn't even try to stop me.

Whatever. When Cat and I publish a book and I have my own book deal, they'll finally get it.

Maybe then they'll finally believe in me.

At least Cat believes in me.

On the drive back to Brooklyn, I called Cat.

"Well?" she asked.

"I told them," I said. I took a deep breath. "I'm in."

I swear I could almost *hear* her smile. She started screaming with excitement so loudly that I had to hold the phone away from my ear.

From: Sophie Bisset
To: Y Combinator
Subject: Runway Fashion Marketplace Subscription Service Startup
Date: August 29, 2017

Bonjour!

My team and I are working on a new online platform (Sidelines Fashion) which brings runway fashion straight to consumers at a discounted price. Instead of a traditional retail platform, we are offering a subscription service. Based on the feedback we've received from early partners, consumers seem more excited about getting their clothing through subscription services than from traditional retailers, which we believe gives us a unique advantage.

My company and I will be featured in a big profile in the October or November issue of *ELLE*. I have over two million followers on Instagram and will be launching an Instagram account for Sidelines as soon as we hit our fundraising goals and are ready to launch the service. We have offices in NYC and Paris, and are working with the largest and most desired fashion labels in the world, including Burberry, The Row, CELINE, etc. I think Sidelines would be a perfect fit for your next batch of companies.

Let me know if we should apply!

xoxo,

Sophie Bisset

The Diary of Lora Ricci

September 2, 2017

Ghostwriting Goals:

1. Work your ass off.
2. Improve your writing.
3. Don't waste time. Don't procrastinate. Don't make excuses for yourself.
4. Learn as much as you can from Cat regarding the things she's good at: character development, plot, etc.
5. Never forget that this is your chance to make it big. Never forget that this might be your *last* chance.
6. Write something really, truly good.

My first day as Cat's ghostwriter is only three days away. I'm trying to get myself mentally prepared for writing, so I've been spending all my time at the library reading a ton of short story collections—as many as I can get my hands on.

Everything is going great except for one thing: my financial situation.

I'm completely broke. I got a credit card when I started at NYU, but I maxed it out halfway through this summer and have no way of making the payments. A few weeks ago, I convinced the credit card company to raise my limit, then maxed it out again as soon as they did.

I get so angry every time I think about it. Angry with myself for not being honest with my parents and for getting into this situation in the first place. Angry with Mom and Dad for being stubborn about it and not supporting me. Whatever happened to *We're so proud of you, Lora!* and *You can do anything you put your mind to, kiddo*??!

Luckily none of my roommates are around to witness my demise—they all went back to school, and I'm the only one left in the apartment. I have a few weeks until my lease is up on the twenty-second. The landlord said I can move to a month-to-month lease—I just have to let him know my plans by the eighteenth. I don't want to live anywhere else, but I don't have money for rent. Without roommates, keeping the apartment seems out of the question, regardless of how much Cat will be paying me.

I have to survive until the fifth. Just a few more days . . .

Jenée Parker | 09–06–2017 2:26 PM
Undercover agent in place at the plaza

Jenée Parker | 09–06–2017 2:27 PM
Working as a housekeeper

Amanda Harris | 09–06–2017 2:31 PM
Anything interesting so far?

Jenée Parker | 09–06–2017 2:33 PM
Other housekeepers told her that there are hidden cameras in the suite

Amanda Harris | 09–06–2017 2:34 PM
Ours????

Jenée Parker | 09–06–2017 2:38 PM
No no no

Jenée Parker | 09–06–2017 2:38 PM
CW installed her own cameras

Amanda Harris | 09–06–2017 2:39 PM
Ah okay

Jenée Parker | 09–06–2017 2:40 PM
Lots of different women coming and going all hours of the day

Jenée Parker | 09–06–2017 2:41 PM
Will know more soon

Amanda Harris | 09–06–2017 2:45 PM
Okay

Amanda Harris | 09–06–2017 2:45 PM
Keep me updated

The Diary of Lora Ricci

September 5, 2017

Today was my first day as Cat Wolff's ghostwriter. It's a strange term, "ghostwriter." I can picture my future résumé: *Lora Elizabeth Ricci. Education: College Dropout. Occupation: Ghostwriter.*

It does have a certain ring to it . . .

I was planning to take the train to The Plaza, but the black SUV was waiting for me as soon as I stepped out of my building. Bob got out and went around to open the door for me.

"Good morning, Lora," he said as I climbed in. "There's a bottle of water and a cup of coffee for you. Cat said you prefer your coffee black."

It was the most he'd ever said to me. "Thanks, this is great," I said. I picked up the coffee and took a sip. It wasn't too hot or too cold—it was just right. "You must have timed this perfectly," I said. "It's the perfect temperature."

I saw him look up and glance at me in the rearview mirror. "I've been doing this my whole life," he said. "Learned a few tricks along the way."

"Do you work full-time for Cat?" I asked.

"Yup. Have for about three, almost four, years now."

"Do you like it?"

"Best job I've ever had."

"What do you think about Cat?" I asked, somewhat nervously.

"I owe her my life. I'd do anything for her." He glanced back at me in the rearview mirror. "Loyalty. That's what she values most. You be loyal to her, she'll take a bullet for you."

Loyalty. *I can do that,* I thought. *I can be loyal to Cat.* I leaned back into the leather seat and sipped my coffee, feeling encouraged and more than a little bit hopeful.

When I got to The Plaza, I went upstairs and found Cat's door propped open. I knocked gently to let her know I was there.

I heard her deep voice echo from the living room. "Come in, come in!"

She was waiting for me at the table, already working. "Am I late?" I asked, hoping I hadn't messed things up on my first day.

She shook her head. "No, not at all. I like to get started early."

We kicked off the morning with room service breakfast and a discussion about some ideas that Cat had for stories. We talked through the ideas until we narrowed the list down to one about a divorce, and decided I would write that one first. "It's definitely not *the one,*" she said, "but it's a good one for you to focus on." I didn't disagree with her. It's not perfect, and I don't think it ever will be, but it's definitely one we might be able to include in a collection somewhere down the line.

Although we had talked about it before, Cat made sure I understood exactly what we need to accomplish. We want a book deal, preferably a two-book deal, with a large advance and a lot of buzz—basically, we want enough money and fame that we can both walk away from our arrangement having laid the groundwork for long-term literary careers. She believes the best way to do this would be to write a short story that is so amazing it goes viral (or as close to viral as one can get with a short story), and then use that to get the attention we need to land a book deal.

The best possible home for our short story would be *The New Yorker,* so that's what we're aiming for. We're going to study old issues of the magazine and figure out the kinds of stories the editors like. "Every editor has a pattern," Cat explained. "They all have certain things they look for, things they want. And *those,*" she said, pointing to a large stack of boxes sitting in the far corner of the living room, "hold all the secrets."

We walked over to the boxes, and she opened them to reveal hundreds of old issues of *The New Yorker.* For the rest of the morning, she sat on the couch reading through issue after issue, tearing out the stories she thought I could learn from, while I sat at the table, writing.

We didn't go out for lunch. Instead, we ordered more room service. My legs had fallen asleep by the time lunch arrived, so, after I ate, I asked if she wanted to join me for a walk in Central Park.

"No thanks," she said. "I already exercised this morning. But you should go."

It was a little warm out—almost too warm—but I didn't mind. I've always loved Central Park, and I fall a little more in love with it every time I'm there. As I walked, I thought about how I was going to write the divorce story, playing it like a movie in my head.

I didn't stay out for long, but when I got back to the suite, the door was locked, and Cat didn't answer when I knocked. I figured she'd gone downstairs or was using the bathroom or something, so I leaned against the wall and waited. I called her, but the call went straight to voicemail. I sent her a text, but she didn't reply.

About half an hour later, a housekeeper showed up to clean the suite. I explained that I was Cat's friend and, after a little coaxing, convinced her to let me follow her inside. Cat wasn't there, though she'd left a hundred-dollar bill for the housekeeper on the arm of the sofa, just like before.

While the housekeeper straightened things up, I sat at the table and worked. Cat didn't return for another three hours, and I didn't hear a peep from her the entire time she was gone. She was pretty apologetic when she returned. There had been some issue with her bank—she'd had to run over immediately to approve a transfer from her father, and she hadn't realized how much time had passed. "I'm *so* glad you were able to get back inside."

I was a little pissed, but decided not to say anything. Whatever. Shit happens.

We worked for another hour or so, and then, around five, she told me she had other things to do. "Solid first day," she said. "Bob is downstairs to take you home. See you tomorrow!" She excused herself, saying she needed to take a shower and get ready for an event, and went to her room. I quickly packed up my things and headed downstairs, where, just as Cat said, Bob was waiting for me.

We drove back to Brooklyn in silence.

It was still pretty early in the evening when I got back to my apartment, so I tried to decide whether or not I should see if my friends wanted to hang out. I kept picking up my phone, wanting so badly to text Katrine or Piper or Maggie, but I couldn't bring myself to do it. I knew they would ask me how classes were going. I knew I'd have to lie. I knew I wouldn't be able to pay when the bill came, and that I'd have to be like *Oops, I forgot my card, silly stupid me, haha, can you cover me this time? I'll pay next time!*

Ugh. I should've asked Cat about my salary today. I don't know why I didn't.

From: Y Combinator
To: Sophie Bisset
Subject: Re: Runway Fashion Marketplace Subscription Service Startup
Date: September 8, 2017

Hi Sophie,

Yes.

Please apply here, the deadline for the winter batch is October 3: https://www.ycombinator.com/apply/

—YC

From: Sophie Bisset
To: Y Combinator
Subject: Re: Re: Runway Fashion Marketplace Subscription Service Startup
Date: September 10, 2017

Merci!

xoxo,

Sophie Bisset

The Diary of Lora Ricci

September 17, 2017

I'm two weeks into my new job, and it's going pretty well so far.

Each day has followed the same basic schedule:

8:00 A.M.: Bob picks me up
9:00 A.M.: Arrive at The Plaza
9:30 A.M.: Room service breakfast
10:00 A.M.: Work
12:30 P.M.: Room service lunch
1:00 P.M.: I take a walk
1:30 P.M.: Work
5:00 P.M.: Bob drives me home

On Friday, I finished up the divorce story and gave it to Cat. She said she'd have some notes for me by the middle of the week, then handed me a big pile of *New Yorker* stories to read over the weekend.

I keep meaning to ask her about pay, but I haven't found a good opportunity to bring it up. I'm embarrassed that I haven't asked by now, and I'm worried the conversation will be even *more* awkward now since we've already been working together for two weeks. She probably has everything already worked out, but at this point I kind of need to know what she's planning...

I'm supposed to tell the landlord my plans tomorrow, but I've been ignoring his texts and emails because I have no freaking clue what I'm going to do about the apartment or my rent. I'm trying really hard not to spiral, but I'm so stressed out and all I can think about is how I'm going to pay for food and where I'm going to be living. I applied for a bunch of credit cards and bank loans and wasn't approved for any of them. Hell, I even went to one of those payday loan places, but they wouldn't give me anything without any proof of income.

I should just ask Cat when I will get paid, since I'm really banking on her coming through.

What if she doesn't?

THE PLAZA HOTEL

Dear Ms. Wolff,

The balance on your account is $61,554.87. Would you please stop by the front desk and pay your bill in full at your earliest convenience?

Warmly,

John

THE PLAZA HOTEL

John:

My wallet was stolen in Greenpoint several days ago, and I had to order replacement cards. My new card is supposed to arrive any day. I will stop by and pay my bill in full as soon as I receive it.

Cat Wolff

The Diary of Lora Ricci

September 20, 2017

My lease is up in two freaking days, and I have no way to pay for next month's rent. If Cat doesn't pay me immediately, I don't know what I'm going to do. Should I try to move back home with my parents? Get another job somewhere in the city? How would I even get a new job *and* get paid in just two days?

I'm completely screwed.

I was in full-on panic mode when I got to Cat's suite this morning. I tried to be calm and collected, and was going to try to bring it up organically, but the second I saw her, I knew I had to ask her right away or else I'd lose my mind. "Is there any paperwork you need me to fill out so I can get paid on Friday?"

She looked at me like I was completely nuts. "What do you mean?"

"You know, paid for the two weeks I've been working for you so far."

"I'm not sure what you're referring to . . ."

"You're paying me to work for you. Right?"

She sighed and sat back in her chair. "Oh, Lora, we don't get paid anything until we get a book deal," she said. "You really didn't know that?"

I lost my shit right then and there. "But how am I supposed to pay my bills?" I shouted. "How am I supposed to pay my rent? How am I supposed to do *anything*? I don't have any money, Cat! I eat peanut butter sandwiches for breakfast, lunch, and dinner when I'm not here!"

She tried to calm me down. “Hey, hey,” she said gently. “It’s okay.”

“No, Cat. This is not okay! Nothing about this is okay!”

“Your parents aren’t paying your living expenses?” she asked, incredulous.

“Of course they aren’t! Are you kidding me?” I shouted. “I thought that you would look out for me! I thought you’d at least pay me minimum wage!”

She sighed as she stood up and walked over to one of the windows that looked out over Fifth Avenue.

“Can you at least give me an advance on whatever we’ll make from the short story?” I begged. My hands were shaking and my voice was trembling. I was such a wreck.

She shook her head. “There’s no money in that. It’s a few thousand dollars at the most.”

“Maybe a few thousand dollars is petty change to you, but it’s a lot to me. That’s my *rent,* Cat.”

She didn’t say anything.

“Okay, then can you give me an advance for the book?” I pleaded. “Please, Cat, you don’t understand. I literally have nothing, okay?” I started to cry, and tried to wipe away my tears before she noticed, but the attempt only made me cry even harder. I walked over to the couch and sat down, put my head in my hands, and sobbed.

Cat walked over and sat next to me, then pulled me in for a hug. “I’m sorry,” she whispered. “I didn’t realize you were in such a tight spot. I didn’t know.”

“Then help me,” I begged. “Please.”

“I will, I will,” she said. “But it’s not that simple. I can’t cut you a check or pay you like a real employee. I wish I could, but I really, truly can't. My father pays all of my bills—the hotel, the driver, my credit cards. I don't have access to the kind of money I would need to pay you a real salary."

I looked up at her. "Can you ask him to pay me?"

She shook her head. "No. God, no. I tried to hire an assistant once. *That* did not go well with him, let me tell you. He cut me off for three months. If I told him I had hired a ghostwriter? He'd cut me off for three *years*. And then you and I would both be broke and homeless. No, no, no—I have to be creative here. I have to think of something special."

She reached for my hands and her eyes met mine. "Lora, I promise you I will figure something out. Just give me a few weeks. Can you do that?"

I was so angry I nearly lost it. "I don't have a few weeks, Cat. I have *two days*. I'm supposed to pay my rent and renew my lease on Friday."

"Two days? You should have told me about your situation earlier. Why did you wait so long? Shit." She bounced her legs up and down anxiously and cracked her knuckles. I could almost see the gears turning in her head as she tried to come up with a plan. "Okay, okay, give me until tomorrow. I promise this will all work out, okay?"

"Okay," I said, wiping my eyes.

She stood up and walked back to her laptop. Then she stopped and looked over at me. "Peanut butter?" she asked. "Every day?"

I nodded.

"Well, we can't have that." She laughed. "Why don't you join me for dinner tonight. We'll go to Paul's, one of my favorite places. Dinner's on me."

Well, technically, dinner was on Paul, the owner of the eponymous restaurant. When we walked through the doors, the chef greeted her, the food was on the house, random people came up to the table to say hello to her, and the waitstaff adored her because she left them a small pile of hundred-dollar bills.

I looked at the tip she left and thought, *Why can't she just give me that money?* For a second, I was tempted to steal it. So, so incredibly tempted. She gives hundred-dollar bills to the housekeepers and the baristas and the waitstaff at restaurants and she doesn't see how giving me a few hundred-dollar bills would literally change my life.

God, I really hope she figures something out. Otherwise, I don't know what I'm going to do. I'm starting to second-guess our whole arrangement. Is she really so out of touch that she thought I could just work for her for free?

Dammit, I should have listened to Dad and gotten something in writing. I could have even typed a contract up myself and said, *This is how much I charge per hour* or something like that. Literally anything would be better than *this*. I'm terrified that she'll come back to me with some insane, nonsensical proposal and I'll have to go running back to my parents, begging them to give me my old bedroom back, admitting they were right all along.

AMERICAN EXPRESS
El Paso, TX 79998

Sidelines Fashion
Attn: Sophie Bisset
c/o Cat Wolff
The Plaza Hotel
1 Central Park South #2040
New York, NY 10019

September 21, 2017

AMERICAN EXPRESS
Blue Business® Plus Credit Card ending in #67891

Welcome, Sidelines Fashion!

We're pleased to tell you that you've been approved for a Blue Business® Plus Credit Card! Congratulations, and thank you for beginning your relationship with American Express.

Set up your online business account today and enjoy the benefits of your card the moment it arrives. You should expect your card to arrive in 2 to 3 business days.

The Diary of Lora Ricci

September 21, 2017

Cat came through for me.

She didn't say anything about the money this morning, and I didn't ask her about it even though it was the only thing I could think about. We focused on coming up with a new story (the divorce one is totally done and in good shape), which led to an idea about two people who meet on a ferry. We workshopped a few different plots and themes and characters and covered the walls of the hallway in Post-it notes, mapping out the possibilities.

When noon rolled around, she suggested we go to the hotel food court for lunch instead of placing our usual room service order. I followed her down to the lobby, to the back of the first floor, and then down an escalator into the hotel's basement. As we walked around the food court, she told me that she had a proposition for me and made me promise I wouldn't interrupt her while she explained.

"So," she said, "I was thinking you could live with me. I have two bedrooms, two and a half bathrooms, and plenty of space for both of us to live comfortably. I have a driver. I can pay for all your food and anything else you need and charge it all to the suite. Anything you wanted would be paid for: clothing, haircuts, dry cleaning, laundry, whatever. All of your needs would be met. My father pays the hotel bill, no questions asked. He'd have no idea that he was paying for both of us, and he'd never need to know. It would just be temporary, of course—as soon as we get our book deal and get an advance, you can walk away with your part of the money and get your own place."

She looked at me nervously. "I know it's not perfect, and I know it's not what you asked for, but it's all I can do right now."

I didn't really know what to think in the moment, and I almost couldn't believe what I was hearing. It sounded great, amazing even. Here she was, telling me that I could live, all expenses paid, in the fanciest hotel in New York. I wouldn't have to move back to Pennsylvania—no old bedroom, no returning to my old job at Target, no running back to my parents and copping to my lies and admitting they were right—and I could keep working as a writer. It sounded too good to be true.

"What's the catch?" I asked.

"Well, the catch is that I can't pay you any money."

Oh, duh. Yeah, that *was* the catch. I'd be completely dependent on Cat. But wasn't I already? I looked over at her and could see that she was nervously awaiting my answer. "Okay," I said. "I'm in."

She let out a huge sigh of relief. "Oh, thank god! I was so worried you'd say no and we'd have to scrap all our writing plans."

We decided on salads for lunch (charged to her room, of course) and headed back to her suite. "I didn't even know you had an extra bedroom," I said as we rode the elevator back up to the twentieth floor.

"Oh, it's upstairs, and it's full of my things right now, but I'll clean it out. What day is your lease up? Sometime next week?"

"No, tomorrow," I said, frustrated she had already forgotten everything I'd told her *literally yesterday*.

She laughed. "Oh shit, I forgot about that. But don't worry, I'll get it all sorted. I'll have housekeeping come up tonight and give the room a deep clean."

We walked into her suite.

"Here," she said, "I'll show you the room."

I followed her up the staircase in the corner of the living room—the one I've always looked at and wondered where it went. There's basically an entire hotel suite on the second floor of her penthouse. At the top of the stairs and to the left of the second floor landing, there was a little office area with a desk and chair—"You can use this, if you ever want to," she said—and, right outside, an enormous rooftop patio. Then she opened another door, and we walked into a huge bedroom filled—no, stuffed—with her things. She seemed embarrassed and didn't seem to want us to stay there very long. "All this will be cleared out," she said. "I'll put it all in my closets downstairs."

She quickly showed me the bathroom, then walked back out onto the second-floor landing. I followed her, and closed the bedroom door behind me. "Do you think the room will be okay?" she asked as we made our way back down the stairs. "Do you like it?"

"I *love* it. It's better than okay, Cat. It's amazing," I said, realizing I hadn't thanked her yet. "You have no idea how grateful I am. Thank you."

She smiled. "I'm so glad we can make it work. It'll be fun to have a roommate. This place is far too big for just one person, don't you think?"

When we reached the main floor of her suite, she sat down

in her chair at the table. "Back to work," she said, and we dove right in.

On the ride back to my apartment, I couldn't help but remember what Bob had said about Cat and loyalty. She barely even knew me, and yet here she was, letting me move into her home. It feels a bit strange to be trusted that much. Like, how does she know I'm not a murderer? How does she know I won't rob her? Why does she trust me so much? (And why do I trust *her* so much?)

It all reminds me of a daydream I had when I was like ten or eleven years old, in which I befriended a new girl at school who was bullied by everyone else. Over the course of our friendship, I learned that the new, unpopular girl was incredibly rich and lived in a huge mansion. After we'd known each other for some time and had become inseparable, she asked me if I wanted to live in the huge mansion with her and her parents. I said yes, her parents adopted me, and I lived the most perfect life imaginable, happily ever after.

That's what this whole situation with Cat feels like.

When I got back to my apartment, my landlord was waiting outside the door. "Well?" he shouted, surprising me and making me jump. "I told you I needed to know by the eighteenth. What is today? Is today the eighteenth?"

"I'm moving out tomorrow," I said. I wished I'd asked Bob to come up to the apartment with me. I turned around and looked back out the door, hoping to see his SUV still parked outside, but he was gone.

"Tomorrow, eh?" he grunted. I was certain he was about to yell at me again, but then he turned around and left. "I better not see you here tomorrow night," he mumbled.

I hurried inside my apartment and locked the door behind me, then called Cat and asked if Bob could pick me and my things up at seven in the morning. I think she could sense the worry in my voice, because she asked me if everything was all right. "It will be," I said.

Time to pack.

The Diary of Lora Ricci

September 23, 2017

Here I am, writing from my new bedroom on the ~~twentieth~~ twenty-first floor of The Plaza Hotel. It's the most beautiful bedroom I've ever seen, and I can't believe *I'm* the one living in it.

There are chandeliers everywhere: one above the bed, two smaller ones framing the TV that's mounted on the wall across from the bed, one in the bathroom, and one in the hallway that leads to my room. Everything is white and accented in gold: the bed frame, the chair, the lamps on the nightstands, the enormous mirror next to my bathroom, and basically the entire bathroom.

And, my god, the bathroom! It's quite a step up from the avocado closet in Park Slope. It has a walk-in shower *and* a separate bathtub. There's even a little room with a toilet *inside* the bathroom. Don't even get me started on the towels, the soaps, the robes, the gorgeous tile . . .

This morning, I stepped out onto the rooftop patio and looked toward Central Park, and it hit me: *This is as good as it gets.* No matter where I am in life, no matter what I do or how successful (or unsuccessful) I am, I will never live like this again. Never. As I stood there, I felt a weird sense of desperation and tried to swallow it down, but it left a bad taste in my mouth.

I went downstairs and found a note from Cat on the table: *Gone to hair appt downstairs, be back at 9, xoxo Cat.* I ordered room service, then headed back upstairs to shower, ready to start my first day as a Plaza resident.

Yesterday, when I moved in, Cat went all out to make me feel welcome. (I suspect that she felt bad about everything and was trying to make it up to me.) Bob pulled up in front of my old apartment at seven A.M. sharp and helped me carry all my things into the SUV. When we got to The Plaza, he told me he'd have one of the bellhops take my things to my new room.

I went up to Cat's suite carrying just my backpack. When I got there, she threw the door open and shouted, "Welcome home!" She was wearing a party hat (one of those birthday ones with the elastic string chinstrap things), and she put one on my head as I stepped inside.

The living room was filled with balloons, and she'd taped a handmade WELCOME HOME LORA banner to the wall above the dining table. A little gift bag that said HAPPY BIRTHDAY was sitting on the table, and Cat picked it up and handed it to me. Inside, I found a room key, a TV remote ("For the upstairs TV," she said), and gift certificates to the hotel spa and boutique. She said I could bill anything and everything I needed at the hotel to the room. "Tell them you're in room 2040, and sign all receipts 'Cat Wolff.'"

I spent the rest of the day working and setting up my room. All my things had been brought up, and I carefully and slowly unpacked them. I didn't have much—mostly just clothes—so it didn't take me very long. We went out for dinner that night to celebrate.

This morning, after Cat came back, we got straight to work. We'd been making jokes all morning about how funny (aka how *not* funny) it would be if I moved in and Cat saddled me with the bill, like, *Hey, come stay with me in my hotel room for free,* and then put it all on my credit card and ran. This gave us an idea for a story, so we went over to the hallway and started writing all the plot points on Post-its and sticking them on the wall. We moved the Post-its around and played with them until a story started to come together.

After lunch, while Cat ran out to do some errands, I wrote a quick (and awful) first draft of the story we'd just plotted. As soon as I was done, I went up to my new room and rearranged my things until I felt like everything was in its right place. I put a photo of me, and Mom, and Dad—my favorite photo of our family, the one my aunt took at my high school graduation party—on one of the nightstands, and tucked my diary under one of the pillows.

Then I decided to explore the hotel a bit. I grabbed my room key and headed down to the lobby, which was busier than I expected, with people walking in and out of the hotel and up the stairs and standing around the elevators. I found the famous Eloise portrait and stared at it for a while, remembering how Mom used to read me the Eloise books. I can't help but wish she was here with me. Maybe when things start to go well for me, I can invite her to stay with us. She'd love it so much—the Palm Court, the spa, the glamour. It would make her so happy.

From: Y Combinator
To: Sophie Bisset
Subject: Your Y Combinator Application
Date: October 8, 2017

We were impressed by your application and would like to meet you in person. Please visit our website to book an interview and learn more about the YC interview process.

We look forward to meeting you.

—YC

From: Olesya Dorokhova
To: Nikolay Dorokhov
Subject: (no subject)
Date: October 12, 2017

Kolya—

Can you alter this passport and driver's license using the attached photo? I need these for future travel.

—Olesya

Attachments: passport.jpg, license.jpg, photo.jpg

From: Nikolay Dorokhov
To: Olesya Dorokhova
Subject: Re:
Date: October 13, 2017

done

Attachments: passport_edited.jpg, license_edited.jpg, photo_edited.jpg

The Diary of Lora Ricci

October 17, 2017

The past few weeks have been so hectic.

Cat is much busier than I expected. I can barely keep up with her. She's in constant motion, always "going somewhere," "dashing off an email," "hopping on a call," "running off to a meeting," going to a dinner or an opening or a gala or a party. Before I moved in, I didn't understand why Bob worked for her full-time, but now I get it.

She's incredibly disciplined and sticks to a very strict schedule. A personal trainer meets her every morning at five thirty and they work out together until six thirty or seven. She eats a quick and very small breakfast (like a granola bar or a banana) when she comes back, then showers and gets dressed, and then has a second (room service) breakfast an hour or two later. Some days, she goes down to the salon and gets a blowout (I think she does this every other day, but I'm not 100 percent sure). She seems to spend a ton of time getting dressed and doing her makeup, and she changes in and out of clothes multiple times each day. She carries a pen and notebook everywhere she goes and is always writing things down.

There have been a few days when she stayed in the suite and worked with me for the entire day, but those days are rare. Most days, she leaves in the morning after her second breakfast and returns in the early afternoon. I try to stay out of her way when she comes and goes, because I think she wants her space. I suspect she sometimes even avoids me on purpose; I realize that sounds paranoid or whatever, but she will just walk in, go straight to her room, and then leave again without me even seeing her (I just hear the front door open and close, then her footsteps, then her bedroom door open and close). She often leaves for dinner and returns late at night; sometimes she asks me to join her, and we go to Paul's or to one of the restaurants downstairs.

Her weekends are more relaxed. She still has places to go, things to do, people to see, etc., etc., but she also sits on the couch and watches TV. Last Saturday, for example, we went downstairs to the Palm Court for brunch, walked around Central Park for an hour, came back to the suite and napped for the rest of the afternoon, then watched TV all night.

I'm starting to understand what it's like to be unbelievably wealthy. You never do anything you don't want to do. You pay someone to clean your apartment, do your laundry, wash your hair, do your makeup, make your food, etc. Every chore is outsourced to someone else. There's a whole schedule to Cat's outsourcing, too—I think she has standing appointments at the hotel salon, with the massage therapist who comes to the apartment every week, with a facialist who *also* comes every week.

It struck me the other day, when her facialist was here, that so many of us do all these "self-care" things that are really just less-fancy versions of the things that rich people take for granted. We put on face masks; they have aestheticians and dermatologists who come to their homes. We use "expensive" skin care from Sephora; they drop $1,500 on a custom anti-aging serum. We take Ubers and Lyfts and taxis; they have their own full-time personal drivers. We order meals through Seamless and Blue Apron; they order room service or have their own personal chefs. We have fitness videos and apps so that we can work out inside our houses; they have their own personal trainers who come right to their doors.

It's funny, but I think if you wanted to start a company that would do really well in New York, all you would have to do is tail a rich person for a few weeks, watch what they pay other people to do for them, and then offer an accessible (i.e., cheaper) version of that on demand in an app. Maybe I'll do that someday, if this writing thing doesn't end up working out—haha.

The thing I can't understand and will probably never understand, though, is how much money it must cost to live this way. I'm guessing a thousand dollars every day, at the very least. I wonder how much money Cat (or, rather, her father) spends each year. It must be a truly horrific amount, an amount so large that I would probably riot against the rich if I knew the actual number. It's probably more than the GDP of a small country.

I'm dying to know more about her family and her father, and how on earth he can possibly afford to pay for her (and, by extension, *me*) to live like this. She's not the only one with this kind of lifestyle, though; the hotel has a few other "Cat Wolffs"—people who seem to live in the hotel, who pay for their laundry and their dry cleaning and their spa treatments, who drink at the Champagne Bar every afternoon and order room service breakfast every morning.

There's one down the hall (I *think* her name is Elyse, but I'm not 100 percent sure), and she's much older than Cat, maybe around seventy-five or eighty if I had to guess. She's a truly lovely person, but she's just like Cat, and even more out of touch. She complains about everything—the carpet, the noise (what noise??), the "clientele," the food, the water, etc. I'm pretty sure if Cat stays here, she'll be exactly like Elyse in forty or fifty years. Or maybe Cat's father will cut her off by then. Although, if we get the book deal, that might not matter.

FEDERAL BUREAU OF INVESTIGATION

DATE OF TRANSCRIPTION: 10/23/2017

JOHN SAMI, a CONCIERGE employee at The Plaza Hotel, was contacted at his employment at 768 Fifth Avenue, New York, New York. Sami was advised as to the nature of this investigation and provided the following information.

SAMI stated that CAT WOLFF has been a full-time resident at The Plaza Hotel since 2013 and that the suite belonging to CAT WOLFF has been reserved by WOLFF HOLDINGS LLC since 2008. He advised that WOLFF HOLDINGS LLC is billed for all regular charges and that CAT WOLFF is responsible for any incidentals.

SAMI stated that CAT WOLFF pays for incidentals using credit cards or checks and rarely pays her bill on time. Sami provided that CAT WOLFF has used credit cards in various names—including "Sophie Bisset," "Jacob Krzyzowski," "Beatrice Black," "Katya Evans," "Inge Wolff," "Cat Wolff," and the names of several businesses that Sami did not recognize or remember—to pay outstanding charges.

SAMI stated that CAT WOLFF has frequent visitors and has requested an additional suite key. Sami provided that hotel staff are often greeted by unfamiliar individuals when they go to the suite reserved by CAT WOLFF.

INVESTIGATION ON: 10/23/2017

At: NEW YORK, NEW YORK

By: SPECIAL AGENT JENÉE PARKER

The Diary of Lora Ricci

October 26, 2017

Weird day.

I was sitting at the table this morning, writing as usual, when there was a knock at the front door. As usual, Cat wasn't here, so I answered the door. It was one of the employees from the front desk, and he asked to speak with Cat. I told him she wasn't here, that she would probably be back later tonight, and he thanked me and walked away.

Well, when she got back tonight, I mentioned it to her. "There was a man at the door today, from the front desk," I said, "and—"

Before I could even finish, she completely freaked out on me. "You can't let anyone know you're here, Lora!" she screamed. "You can't let anyone know, especially not the hotel staff. What if word gets back to my father? What if someone from his bank or his company comes by, and they find you here? Do you have any idea how much I would lose if he found out? How much *you* would lose? We'd have to leave immediately! We'd have nothing!"

I tried to calm her down. I reassured her that it was just one of the guys from the front desk, that I see him all the time, that he has never said anything to anyone—but it was no use.

"Lora, I thought you understood that you need to be discreet. Promise me that you *will never answer that door,*" she insisted.

I promised her that I won't ever answer the door ever again (and I mean it—believe me, I have no interest in being yelled at like this ever again, omfg). I felt bad in the moment, but now I'm just confused. What the hell is going on? Is she really *that* worried about her dad? Why can't she just say, *Oh, this is my friend Lora, we hang out here all the time*?

Like I said: weird.

Not sure what her deal is.

Anyway, Halloween is next week. Cat was invited to a party at the home of one of her artist friends who runs a basement art gallery in Williamsburg, and she's bringing me as her plus-one. She said we have to wear masks, and that "the only rule of the party is that you can't take your mask off and you can't tell anyone who you are." I told her it sounded a little *Eyes Wide Shut,* but she laughed and reassured me that it very much wasn't going to be like that.

Jenée Parker | 10–27–2017 6:31 PM
CW's driver is Bob Mollenkopf

Amanda Harris | 10–27–2017 6:40 PM
Why does that name sound familiar?

Jenée Parker | 10–27–2017 6:42 PM
He pled guilty to federal embezzlement charges

Jenée Parker | 10–27–2017 6:42 PM
In 1998

Jenée Parker | 10–27–2017 6:42 PM
Spent 12 years in prison

Amanda Harris | 10–27–2017 6:45 PM
I wonder what their connection is . . .

The Diary of Lora Ricci

November 1, 2017

I'm so hungover right now, I could barely get out of bed this morning.

We went to that party last night—Cat as the Wicked Witch of the West and me as Dorothy. Bob drove us to the party and waited outside. Cat's friend's "place" turned out to be an enormous four-story town house in Williamsburg, and, by the time we arrived, it was completely packed.

Each floor of the house (*and* the rooftop patio *and* the backyard patio) had an open bar and a unique theme from a movie or TV show, though it wasn't completely clear to me exactly what the themes were (one floor definitely had a *Mad Men* theme). Cat and I made our way up four flights of stairs to the rooftop patio, where we found a DJ and a dance party. We pretty much stayed up there dancing for the rest of the night.

At one point, I took a break and stood in line at the bar. After waiting forever to get my drink, I walked back to the dance floor and looked for Cat.

From beside me a voice asked, in an accent I couldn't place, "So *you're* Cat's new pet, huh?"

I turned to see a tall, thin woman wearing a glittery purple butterfly mask and flapper costume standing beside me. She raised her eyebrows, awaiting my reply. "I work for her," I said. "We met at *ELLE*."

"Well, don't get too close to her," she warned. "She'll chew you up and spit you out and pretend you never meant anything to her. And then you'll spend every day of the rest of your life wondering what you did wrong, wondering why she treats you like you no longer exist." She took a sip of her drink and looked over at me. "I wouldn't have said anything," she added, "but you remind me of myself two years ago, before *she* came into my life. I wish someone would have warned me."

I glanced over at Cat, who was still in the middle of the dance floor. She'd taken off her heels and was dancing in her bare feet with a drink in her hand, lost in the music. She was unmistakable, even in her costume and mask—there was just no one else like her. There *is* no one else like her. For a few moments, I was mesmerized by her. I couldn't look away.

When I turned to respond to the mysterious woman, she was gone. I asked the people around me if they'd seen her, trying to make myself heard over the music. But everyone shrugged—they couldn't hear what I was saying or didn't know who I was talking about. I looked everywhere for her, but she had vanished into thin air.

When I returned to the dance floor, my eyes met Cat's. She danced over to me, smiling, and coaxed me back out to the floor. We danced and danced and danced until our feet were numb and our hearts were full and we couldn't dance anymore.

We left the party around four thirty. As Bob drove us over the Williamsburg Bridge, Cat fell asleep, her head resting on my shoulder. I looked out the window and thought about what that woman had said. Who was she? A model? One of Cat's art friends? An ex-girlfriend, maybe?

It's strange. Some days, I feel like I know Cat pretty well—that even though we've only known each other for a few months, we have a special kind of bond. And I've noticed that there's this trick she has of making the people around her feel like they're her closest friends. It's why everyone is drawn to her. Maybe it's why *I* was drawn to her. I notice it very clearly when she's around other people—how she flatters them, confides in them, flirts with them—but I tell myself that our friendship is based on something real. That she really is my friend, that she truly cares about me. That I *know* her.

But then, on nights like tonight, I realize that I don't really know her at all.

From: Katrine Baker
To: Piper Fenton
Subject: lora??
Date: November 12, 2017

have u heard anything about lora?

From: Piper Fenton
To: Katrine Baker
Subject: Re: lora??
Date: November 12, 2017

No.

From: Katrine Baker
To: Piper Fenton
Subject: Re: Re: lora??
Date: November 12, 2017

i hope shes ok

like i keep thinking maybe i should call her parents and ask them where she is so i can at least check in on her u know?

From: Piper Fenton
To: Katrine Baker
Subject: Re: Re: Re: lora??
Date: November 12, 2017

Yeah

It's kind of hard not to worry.

The Diary of Lora Ricci

November 13, 2017

Living at The Plaza is pretty amazing.

If I wake up early enough, I go to the hotel gym with Cat and join her personal training sessions. After we do some weight training or barre or Pilates or whatever her trainer has on the schedule for the day, she'll hop on one of the treadmills and I'll go for a run in Central Park.

I'd much rather be outside than stuck in the gym. That beautiful New York fall weather is here—the air is crisp and cold and clean, the leaves are changing, and it's absolutely perfect. I'm always a little bit sad when my run is over.

In my free time, I've been doing lots of people-watching. Sometimes Cat and I go to the restaurants and bars in the hotel, look for interesting characters, and guess what their occupations are and what they're doing at the hotel. I always bring a notebook so I can jot down little things I notice and then work them into our stories.

The people who *really* fascinate me are the ones who live in the hotel's private residences. The hotel has two entrances: one for the private residents, who own their suites, and one for the hotel guests. Cat, I was surprised to learn, doesn't own her suite, so we always go through the main hotel guest entrance.

I'm trying to explore the hotel, but I have to be careful not to be too obvious or attract the attention of anyone who might send word back to Cat's father (or Cat). Sometimes, when Cat is out for meetings or errands or whatever she does when she's out of the suite, I sneak out and walk around the hallways. The other day, when I was exploring, I ran into the hotel housekeeper who cleans our suite. She told me that most of the residences (and even many of the hotel rooms that are supposed to be occupied, i.e., are being paid for/reserved) are empty. "You could live in these rooms and nobody would even know," she said. When I asked her if she ever did this, she laughed. "Ah, like I would ever admit to that," she said with a wink.

Last night, when Cat and I were out at dinner, I asked her if she ever got tired of living in The Plaza.

She thought for a moment, then shook her head. "No, never," she said. "I never want to leave. It feels like home to me. It *is* home to me."

I was about to ask her another question, but decided against it, not wanting to offend her or open up a can of worms. She noticed immediately. "What were you about to say?" she asked.

"Nothing," I said, shaking my head. "Really, it's nothing."

She laughed. "You can say anything to me. Anything. To you, I am an open book."

I bit my lip, and then went for it. "What would you do if your father stopped giving you money? If he stopped paying your bills?"

"I think about that all the time," she admitted. "It's one of the reasons we need to write that book. It's one of the reasons I want—no, I *need*—to have a successful career." She sighed and looked off into the distance. "I don't take my life for granted; I really don't," she said. "It can fall apart at any moment. It *will* fall apart—it's only a matter of time."

I nodded.

"The thing is," she continued, "my father communicates his love with money. That's his, what do you call it? His 'love language.'" She laughed softly. "Money is his 'love language.' He doesn't know how else to show me and my brother that he loves us except by supporting us financially. He was very poor as a child, and he grew up resenting his parents for his childhood poverty. He doesn't want me or my brother to ever feel that way about him, I think."

"He's cut you off before, though, hasn't he?"

She laughed. "Oh yes. Many times. When I was a teenager. A few years ago. Earlier this year, too, actually. Whenever I do something he disapproves of or whenever I date someone he doesn't like. It's his way of disciplining me, but it never works as well as he wants it to. He'll cut me off, and then he'll feel guilty about it, worry that I'll resent him or never talk to him again, and then, magically, the money will start coming back into my accounts again."

"Has he ever come out to see you? To visit?"

"Yes, many times. He often does business in New York. He hasn't been back in a while, though—his health hasn't been the best—but he could return any day." At this, she furrowed her brow. "Look, Lora, if he does come to see me, you'll need to pretend you don't live in the suite. You might even need to hide or live somewhere else for a few days. I hope it never comes to that, but we have to be prepared."

I assured her that I would stay out of the way. "We'll figure something out, I promise. Just give me a heads-up."

"I'll try," she said.

From: Olesya Dorokhova
To: Nikolay Dorokhov
Subject: Statements
Date: November 16, 2017

Kolya—

I need some help altering these bank statements. The one that says $652.22 should say $65,222.00 and the other one should say $14,733,653.88, not $1.47.

—Olesya

Attachments: statement1.pdf, statement2.pdf

From: Nikolay Dorokhov
To: Olesya Dorokhova
Subject: Re: Statements
Date: November 16, 2017

done

Attachments: statement1_edited.pdf, statement2_edited.pdf

From: Jason Keebles
To: Cat Wolff
Subject: Regarding Your Personal Loan Application
Date: November 17, 2017

Dear Ms. Wolff,

Thank you for stopping by Banfield this morning to discuss a personal loan. We've looked over your finances, and while we agree with your assessment that you have significant cash on hand (as evidenced by your bank statements), in order to approve a loan for the amount of $950,000, we will require either (1) cash collateral in the amount of $125,000 or (2) someone to cosign your loan.

Sincerely,

Jason Keebles
Senior Loan Officer, Banfield Bank

Jenée Parker | 11–17–2017 2:01 PM
CW is going to every bank in town

Jenée Parker | 11–17–2017 2:05 PM
She's trying to get a loan for around a million

Amanda Harris | 11–17–2017 2:07 PM
Can you send my office a list of every bank

Jenée Parker | 11–17–2017 2:08 PM
Will do

Amanda Harris | 11–17–2017 2:11 PM
Is she having any luck?

Jenée Parker | 11–17–2017 2:15 PM
Not yet

Jenée Parker | 11–17–2017 2:16 PM
She needs a cosigner

Amanda Harris | 11–17–2017 2:17 PM
Hah

Amanda Harris | 11–17–2017 2:20 PM
Good luck finding someone to cosign a million dollar loan

Jenée Parker | 11–17–2017 2:22 PM
Yeah, seriously

From: Cat Wolff
To: Jason Keebles
CC: Franz Wolff
Subject: Re: Regarding Your Personal Loan Application
Date: November 17, 2017

Mr. Keebles:

My father (Franz Wolff) is in town on business, and said he would be more than happy to cosign the loan. He owns a large clean energy conglomerate in Austria, so I believe he would fit your criteria perfectly. He will stop by your office later this afternoon. Unfortunately I have a prior engagement, so I won't be able to join him, but hopefully that won't be a problem.

Cat Wolff

The Diary of Lora Ricci

November 18, 2017

I'm still a bit shaken up about what happened yesterday.

Okay, so remember how in my last entry, I wrote that Cat said she would give me a heads-up if her father ever came into town? Well, he *did,* and she *didn't,* and it was awful and I think I got her in trouble and now I'm freaking out.

Yesterday began just like every other day. We got up, exercised, and I ate my first breakfast while Cat ate her second. Cat left to run some errands while I stayed behind and worked on another story (this one is about a woman who lives in Midtown but wants to pay lower taxes, so she's dating all these people in other states and trying to use their addresses).

When lunchtime rolled around, I put my laptop away and headed down to the Palm Court. I brought a book with me and got so lost in it that before I knew it, several hours had passed. I didn't think anything of it—Cat said she had to run a bunch of errands and wouldn't be home until later, and had encouraged me to take the rest of the day off and go out: "Go see some museums! Go to the zoo! Go on a date!" I should have realized she was trying to keep me away from the hotel, but her hints went right over my head. Why didn't she just *tell* me?

Anyway, I went back up to the room around three and was shocked to find a short, thin old man sitting on the couch. We were both so startled that we jumped at the same time. At first I thought I was in the wrong suite.

"I'm so sorry," I said, slowly backing out of the living room. I walked out and closed the door. Then I looked at the suite number. Nope, this *was* our suite. I paused for a moment, trying to figure out what to do. *Should I go downstairs and tell the front desk that someone is in my room? Should I ask him to leave?*

I summoned up my courage and went back inside. He was still sitting there. "Hi," I said tentatively. "I think you may be in the wrong suite. You see, this is my suite, and—"

"Who are you?" he snapped in a German accent. His voice sounded so familiar, but I couldn't place it.

"Who are *you*?" I snapped back at him.

"*I* am going to call security!" he shouted. He stood up and walked to the phone.

And then it hit me. The German accent. The fact that he looked and sounded almost *exactly* like Cat, if Cat was, you know, a seventy-year-old man. And this stopped me in my tracks. *Oh shit,* I realized. *He's her dad.*

"Wait!" I shouted as he was just about to dial the front desk. "Are you Cat's father? Wait, please, put the phone down. I'm Cat's . . ."

I can't believe I almost said it. I get sick to my stomach thinking about how close I was to giving her secret away. I remembered her telling me how angry her father would be if he found out that she had a ghostwriter who was living with her on *his* dime.

". . . friend! I'm her best friend. My name is Lora! Lora Ricci!"

"Really?" he asked suspiciously.

"Yes, yes, I promise," I lied. "I'm sorry, she didn't tell me you were coming. I just came by to pick up a few things."

"Where is she?" he asked. "I have been waiting for a very long time; she was supposed to take me to the bank."

"I'm really sorry, but I don't know. She said she had a lot of meetings. I can call her, or text her, and . . ."

"No," he said, interrupting me. "Please don't. I will wait here for my daughter. I have several calls to make."

I stood around awkwardly. I didn't know what to do. Should I go up to my room? Should I leave?

As I tried to decide what my next move would be, he walked to the bar area and poured himself a drink. When he turned around, he glared at me. "Why are you still here?" he snarled. "Go!" he shouted.

I apologized and left in a hurry. After I closed the door, I stood in the hallway for a few moments, panicking. My heart was pounding. I couldn't take a deep breath. Shit. I leaned against the wall, closed my eyes, and took a deep breath. Then another one. And another one. Finally, after what felt like an eternity, I gathered my wits and sent Cat a quick text: Your dad is here.

She replied almost immediately: GET OUT OF THERE NOW. Will text you when it's safe to return.

I didn't want to stay in the building in case he ended up wandering around. What if he saw me sitting in the lobby? I figured he'd probably shout at me again. No, I had to leave. I had to stay the hell away until Cat said it was okay to come back.

God, I couldn't believe how nasty Cat's father was. My dad would never, *ever* treat any of my friends like that. Heck, he wouldn't even treat his enemies that way (not that he ever had any). Back when I was in high school, I'd bring friends over to my house and he'd embarrass me in a totally different way. If I left my friends with him for even a few minutes, he'd invite them to have pop and chips with him. When I returned, I'd find out that my dad was now best friends with my friends. Hah, I used to get *so* annoyed with him—I'd roll my eyes and tell him to get his own friends.

As I left the hotel, I couldn't stop thinking about how much I missed my parents. They haven't reached out to me at all in the months since I dropped out. I haven't reached out to them, either. Every time I look at the calendar on my phone, I can't help but notice that Thanksgiving is only a few days away. I've never missed a Thanksgiving with them. Never. Not even once. The thought that I might not see them over the holidays—god, it kills me.

I wonder if they are thinking the same thing. I hope they know how much I love them and miss them. But what if they don't? What if they think I don't love them anymore? What if they think I don't want to spend the holidays with them? I can't even imagine how much that would hurt them. It hurts *me* just thinking about it. Maybe I should go and see them. Maybe I should at least try to mend our relationship, just so that they know how much they mean to me. I don't know. I'll figure it out later.

While I waited to hear from Cat, I walked and walked around Midtown until my legs ached and I started to get cold. I decided to find a place to warm up, but I didn't have any of my things except my wallet and phone, so I couldn't get any work done. I went to a bookstore and picked a random book off the shelf, then sat down in one of the aisles and read until my eyes started to glaze over.

Eventually, I couldn't wait anymore. I texted Cat: Is the coast clear? I was starving and didn't have any cash and all my credit cards had been sent to collections because I never paid them, so I walked back to the hotel and ordered some food and wine at the Champagne Bar and billed it to the room. The wine came first, and I shouldn't have had any of it on an empty stomach, because by the time my food arrived, I was a bit drunk.

I texted Cat a few more times, but she didn't text me back.

I finally decided to go back to the suite. It was dark out, and I was tired, drunk, and angry. The least she could have done was update me. No, no, no, honestly, the least she could have done was what she told me she would do. She should have told me her father was in town. WTF.

When I got back to our suite, she was there, alone, curled up on the couch, watching TV. She didn't even look at me when I walked in. I went straight up to my room and changed into my pajamas. After a few minutes had passed, I took a deep breath and headed back down to the living room.

"You didn't text me back," I said quietly, "to tell me it was safe."

"Sorry," she said, her voice cracking. She cleared her throat. "I'm sorry," she said. "I should have."

She scooted over and made room for me on the couch. I sat down next to her and pulled a blanket over my lap. I was about to say something nasty to her, but I couldn't force the words out. Instead, I asked her if she was okay.

"Yeah," she said. "I'm fine." But she didn't look fine. She looked exhausted. Exhausted and depressed.

"Did you get in trouble?"

"Yeah. But it doesn't have anything to do with you," she said. "He always finds something to fault me for."

"Does he know I'm staying here?"

"He suspects it. I'm pretty sure he thinks you and I are dating, actually. Which, him being who he is, I'm certain he disapproves of." She sighed. "Look, I'm not kidding when I tell you that you have to stay behind the scenes, okay? If word gets back to him that he's paying for you to stay here, we're both out on the street. I need you to understand that. Nobody can know you are staying here. Nobody can know that you work for me. It's for your own good, Lora. It's for your own safety."

"I'm sorry, Cat." I meant it.

"And you've got to stop making friends with everyone here," she said. "I know you're a friendly person, and it's one of the things I love about you. But it's really not good for you to become best buddies with every hotel maid, okay? Do you have any idea how easy it would be for my father to find out from any of the employees here that you're staying with me?"

"You're right, Cat. I'm really sorry. I won't make the same mistake again, I promise."

That seemed to settle it, but I had a hard time sleeping last night. I don't like feeling this way—like I'm a problem or a burden. I never want to feel like this again. The one silver lining of this terrible experience is that I feel a whole new level of motivation to make progress on our writing and get a book deal. I need to be able to stand on my own two feet. I need to not depend on someone else for the roof over my head. Especially someone as complicated as Cat Wolff.

From: Jason Keebles
To: Cat Wolff, Franz Wolff
Subject: Re: Re: Regarding Your Personal Loan Application
Date: November 20, 2017

Dear Ms. Wolff,

You and your father will receive the official loan documents in the mail soon, but I wanted to be the first to let you know that a loan in the amount of $950,000 has been approved.

Thank you for banking with Banfield. We appreciate your business.

Sincerely,

Jason Keebles
Senior Loan Officer, Banfield Bank

Jenée Parker | 11–21-2017 9:59 AM
CW got the loan

Amanda Harris | 11–21-2017 10:01 AM
How

Jenée Parker | 11–21-2017 10:05 AM
Her father cosigned

Jenée Parker | 11–21-2017 10:06 AM
The bank said he signed in person

Amanda Harris | 11–21-2017 10:08 AM
Isn't he from Germany?

Jenée Parker | 11–21-2017 10:15 AM
Austria

Jenée Parker | 11–21-2017 10:15 AM
But get this

Jenée Parker | 11–21-2017 10:16 AM
There's no record of Franz Wolff flying out here

Jenée Parker | 11–21-2017 10:16 AM
At all

Jenée Parker | 11–21-2017 10:16 AM
He hasn't flown to or from the U.S. since 1997

From: Sarah Philips
To: Cat Wolff
Subject: Personal Loan
Date: November 22, 2017

Hello Ms. Wolff,

Following up to let you know that Liberty Financial Services has approved your loan for the amount of $2,500,000. The amount will be disbursed upon confirmation that Liberty has received the wire of the $150,000 collateral as we discussed.

Let me know if you have any further questions.

All the best,

Sarah Philips
Client Specialist | Liberty Financial Services

The Diary of Lora Ricci

November 24, 2017

I don't know why I went home for Thanksgiving. What a stupid idea.

I couldn't afford to rent a car, so I asked Bob to drive me (Cat said it was okay). We left early yesterday morning, before the sun came up, and I got there just in time for Thanksgiving dinner. Mom was shocked to see me, as were Dad and Nana and Papa. "Sure glad you're here, sweet pea," Papa said as we hugged. "It wouldn't have been Thanksgiving without you."

Things were a little awkward at first, but by the time we sat down at the dinner table, it felt just like old times: my favorite food, my favorite people, all of us together and happy and celebrating how thankful we were for one another. And dinner was so, so good. (Honestly, it was strangely refreshing to eat something simple, something without lobster or truffle oil or caviar or quail eggs.)

And then the conversation turned to me.

And everything fell apart.

"So Lora, honey, your Momma tells us that you're working in New York as a writer," Nana said.

"Yeah, I'm writing short stories."

"Is that right?" Papa asked.

"It's really fun. I have a writing partner, so it never gets too lonely."

"And how's school going?" Nana asked.

Mom turned to Nana and gave her a sharp look. "Mom!" she hissed.

"It's a simple question, Carol," Nana said, an innocent look on her face.

I took a deep breath. "I'm taking a break from school to focus on writing. Just for a little while."

"Didn't you have a full scholarship to Columbia?" Papa asked.

"NYU," Dad said, correcting him.

"Sorry, NYU," Papa said.

I nodded. In the back of my head I was saying a little prayer: *Please don't make this stressful, please don't make this stressful, please don't ask any more questions.*

And then Mom jumped in. "You know," she said, "your Dad and I were talking the other day, and we came up with a pretty great idea."

"Oh, what's that?" I asked.

"Well, you can move home and go back to school here."

I put my fork down and felt like I was going to scream. "Mom," I said sharply.

"It doesn't have to be Penn State," Dad said. "You could go to Penn, or Temple, or Bryn Mawr."

Mom nodded. "You can probably get a scholarship just like the one you got from NYU . . ."

I was furious. "Why would I do that? I already have the job and the life I want. Don't you realize how much I've accomplished? Why can't you just be happy for me?"

Nana could tell I was getting angry. She reached out and put her hand on my shoulder. "I'm sure they didn't mean to upset you, dear," she said gently.

I sat there, feeling helpless and attacked, as the discussion at the table devolved into complete chaos.

"I just really don't trust this Cat person," Dad said.

Papa turned to him. "Who's the cat person?"

"The lady who's writing with Lora," Mom explained. "She's some rich girl who lives off a trust fund."

"She has a bunch of cats?" Nana asked me. "How many?"

"Is she in the mob?" Papa asked. "Organized crime?"

"Tom thinks she's a con artist," Mom said.

Nana was lost in her own world. "I always wanted to have a house full of cats. Your Papa here would never let me have more than one . . ."

"What kind of stuff you figure she's done?" Papa asked Dad. "Maybe killed a person?"

Dad shrugged. "I wouldn't be surprised."

"ENOUGH!" I shouted. The table went quiet, and everyone looked at me. "I'm thankful for your concern. I know you just want me to have the best life."

"We just want you to be happy, honey," Nana said.

"Well, I *am* happy," I shouted.

I picked my fork back up and attacked the mashed potatoes. I could tell everyone was looking at one another awkwardly, trying to figure out what to say next.

After a few moments, Papa broke the ice. "Hey, Tom, did you see that old lot on the corner by Phil's place?"

Dad shook his head. "No. Haven't been over there in a while."

"Well, Tom tore that old shed down and put up something new."

I knew Bob was waiting outside and ready to drive me back to New York. When dinner was done, I thanked my family, hugged them, and said goodbye.

I stared out the window the whole drive back to the city.

I feel so alone. So terribly alone.

I don't think I'll ever get used to being estranged from my parents like this. God, "estranged." In a million years, I never would have thought there'd be a day when I wasn't close to them. They have always been the most important people in my life. They have always been my best friends.

I have to believe it will be okay. It *will* be okay. This is just temporary.

All I need to do is work hard, write the story, write the book, and then I can show Mom and Dad that I did the right thing. They'll be proud of me and things will go back to the way they were. Before you know it, I'll be back on my feet and have a new life and find a whole new normal and make everything work. I'll be a writer, and it won't matter that I didn't graduate from school.

The visit home made me realize that not only had I not spoken to my parents in months, I hadn't even really spoken to anyone except Cat and Bob (and the occasional housekeeper) since my internship ended. It's crazy to think about, but it's not all *that* surprising. After all, it's not really possible for me to *go* anywhere, because I don't have any money, so most socializing is out of the question. How would I even begin to explain to anyone that I dropped out of school and moved in with someone I'd just met?

Amanda Harris | 11–29–2017 9:13 AM
CW?

Jenée Parker | 11–29–2017 9:17 AM
Nothing

Jenée Parker | 11–29–2017 9:17 AM
I'm focusing on another case now

Jenée Parker | 11–29–2017 9:18 AM
I'll let you know if I hear anything

Amanda Harris | 11–29–2017 9:20 AM
Okay

FORBES

THE 2017 30 UNDER 30

Sophie Bisset, 27

Founder and C.E.O., Sidelines Fashion

In 2016, Sophie Bisset was working for a fashion designer in New York when she realized there was a business opportunity staring her in the face. "All of these amazing designer clothes were being burned, trashed, or donated once the season ended," she says, "and I thought that instead of destroying them, we could put them directly in the hands of the young women who wanted them the most."

Yes, the young women of the world, who, according to Bisset, often buy clothing from fast-fashion stores—clothing that is based on designer styles from years prior. But designer clothing, according to Bisset, is more humane and sustainable. "Instead of wearing clothing made by sweatshop labor, women could be wearing beautiful runway looks, which aren't made in sweatshops, for a fraction of the price."

The major roadblock was the reluctance of the fashion labels themselves. "Very few of the big labels wanted their clothes to go into the hands of just anyone, so I had to make adjustments to the Sidelines sales model." Instead of an online storefront, Bisset designed a subscription service: customers subscribe to specific designers, and then, at the end of each season, receive the latest runway fashions.

This summer, Bisset founded the company Sidelines Fashion, and has been running it from a small office in Manhattan and a warehouse in Paris ever since. Early next year, she'll temporarily relocate to San Francisco, where she'll be taking the company through the prestigious Y Combinator startup accelerator. After partnering with major fashion labels to sell their clothing on the Sidelines platform, it is predicted the company will reach $15 million in revenue in 2018.

From: Airbnb
To: Cat Wolff
Subject: Your Reservation
Date: December 4, 2017

Customer Receipt

Guest: Cat Wolff

Travel Destination: South Lake Tahoe, California

Travel Property: Cozy Rustic Log Cabin Near the Lake

Accommodation Type: Entire Cabin

Nights: 12

Arrive: Wed, December 20, 2017

View Itinerary

House Rules:

. . .

The Diary of Lora Ricci

December 5, 2017

I'm starting to get a little burned out. I've been writing every single day, but I haven't made much progress. Even though I've written over a dozen short stories, none of them is "the one," and I don't feel like I'm getting any closer to writing it. I'm slowly but surely getting better at writing, but Cat and I just haven't been able to come up with an idea that's actually *good*. And even if we did come up with a good idea and it turned out to be a good story, "good" isn't enough. It needs to be *great*.

Despite the fact that I'm freaking out inside, Cat doesn't seem worried. Every time I hand her a finished draft, she reads it, says "almost," and we repeat our whole process again: we come up with a new idea and plot and theme and set of characters; I go and write a first draft; Cat gives me notes; I revise; Cat gives me notes again; I revise until it's done; and then Cat reads the final draft, says "almost," and we're back to square one all over again.

Speaking of Cat, she just broke some news to me: Sophie Bisset was accepted into Y Combinator and is starting the program in January. *ELLE* agreed to let Cat go to San Francisco and follow Sophie through the program and then write a feature for the magazine about her experience. Cat said she really wanted to do it, and that she'd come back on the weekends whenever she could, but she'd need to be in San Francisco (where she'd already booked a room at the Four Seasons) every weekday from early January until around the second or third week of March.

Then she told me that she's planning to spend Christmas in

Tahoe and, to my surprise, asked me to come with her. "My father's paying for the whole ski trip, and I can use frequent flier miles to get you a ticket. I'd love for you to join," she said. "Just let me know if you're interested."

I told her I wasn't the best skier—I'd only skied twice before. She laughed and said that was totally fine. "I'm not very good, either," she said. "I go for the snow and the fun and the atmosphere. Just come with me—you'll love it."

I haven't made a decision yet, but I think I might go with her instead of going home. Thanksgiving was so uncomfortable, there's no way I can face another parental interrogation, and it would be way too depressing to spend Christmas and New Year's Eve alone.

Part of me wishes Cat would stay here for the holidays, though, because I've always wanted to spend Christmas in New York. The hotel is absolutely gorgeous and so, so perfectly Christmasy. There's a giant tree in the lobby, they have a Santa Claus here that kids can take pictures with (and by "kids," I mean myself, lol), and the whole place is completely decked out with garland and lights and all sorts of wonderful decorations.

On the other hand, I could use an escape. I've been living here for like four months and have barely left the building except to go to Central Park. I should get away, take a break, clear my head.

From: Nikolay Dorokhov
To: Olesya Dorokhova
Subject: (no subject)
Date: December 8, 2017

i'll be in ny next week

i have some business to do

can i stay with you

promise i won't be too much trouble

From: Olesya Dorokhova
To: Nikolay Dorokhov
Subject: Re:
Date: December 8, 2017

Kolya—

Of course.

I can't wait to see you!

—Olesya

From: Nikolay Dorokhov
To: Olesya Dorokhova
Subject: (no subject)
Date: December 10, 2017

jfk at 2:30 tomorrow

meet me at baggage claim

im flying under the name dmitri nemtsev so please call me dmitri when you see me at the airport lol

Jenée Parker | 12-11-2017 4:01 PM
Call me

Jenée Parker | 12-11-2017 4:12 PM
It's urgent

Amanda Harris | 12-11-2017 4:15 PM
In a meeting til 6

Amanda Harris | 12-11-2017 4:15 PM
Can't get out

Amanda Harris | 12-11-2017 4:16 PM
What is it?

Jenée Parker | 12-11-2017 4:17 PM
I know who real CW is

Amanda Harris | 12-11-2017 4:18 PM
No way

Jenée Parker | 12-11-2017 4:19 PM
Olesya Dorokhova

Amanda Harris | 12-11-2017 4:20 PM
Never heard that name before

Jenée Parker | 12-11-2017 4:21 PM
I'm working another case on her brother

Amanda Harris | 12-11-2017 4:22 PM
Who is he?

Jenée Parker | 12-11-2017 4:23 PM
Nikolay Dorokhov

Jenée Parker | 12-11-2017 4:24 PM
Low-level cybercriminal—hacking, bitcoin theft

Jenée Parker | 12-11-2017 4:25 PM
Been following him for years

Jenée Parker | 12–11–2017 4:26 PM
He just arrived here from Moscow

Jenée Parker | 12–11–2017 4:26 PM
Told customs agent he's here visiting his sister

Jenée Parker | 12–11–2017 4:27 PM
Went straight to the plaza

Jenée Parker | 12–11–2017 4:28 PM
And right to Wolff's suite

Amanda Harris | 12–11–2017 4:30 PM
!!!

Amanda Harris | 12–11–2017 4:31 PM
You're sure???

Jenée Parker | 12–11–2017 4:32 PM
Yes

Jenée Parker | 12–11–2017 4:34 PM
Olesya hasn't been seen in 15 years

Jenée Parker | 12–11–2017 4:35 PM
It's her

Jenée Parker | 12–11–2017 4:36 PM
It has to be

The Diary of Lora Ricci

December 14, 2017

Cat's brother, Nikolay, has been here since Monday.

It sounds like the visit was scheduled at the last minute, so Cat didn't really give me much of a heads-up. I was a little anxious about him staying here, but luckily it's actually been really nice. Cat is a completely different person when he's around. She's more relaxed, more carefree, more down to earth. Honestly, even *I'm* happier with Nikolay here. He's the perfect combination of easygoing, confident, and kind.

It was a little shocking how different he is from Cat. First of all, he has a Russian accent and name while she has a mostly German accent and name. Cat explained that their mother was from Russia and their father from Austria. When they were very young, their parents separated and split up the children—their mother took Nikolay, and their father took Cat. So Nikolay grew up in Moscow and Cat in Vienna, and then their parents reconciled when they were older.

"People never believe we are related," Cat said, looking up at her tall, dark-haired younger brother.

Nikolay laughed and shrugged. "It is what it is," he said.

We've been doing a lot of fun things since he got here. He didn't want to just sit around in the hotel all day and night. "You are like a housecat," he said when he figured out my schedule, "all curled up in your cozy spot, your head in the clouds. Go outside, go have fun, go and *live*."

One afternoon, when Cat was busy, Nikolay insisted I give him a tour of Brooklyn. We walked through Prospect Park, got lunch together, and I even showed him my old apartment. It was cold enough that I didn't really want to be outside, but he wouldn't take any excuses. "You think *this* is cold?" he said, laughing. "You should spend some time in Moscow; this would feel like summer to you after that."

The three of us have gone out every night since he arrived. Cat wanted to get wine or cocktails at one of the more upscale restaurants, but Nikolay would have none of that—no, he wanted to go to dive bars and sit and drink beer for hours. So that's what we've been doing. I had forgotten how much fun it is to just go and drink and not think about anything except enjoying the company of the people you're with.

I love seeing Cat so happy. Her father is such an ass, her mother is dead, and, well, I grew up with parents who loved me so much, and I've been feeling sad that she wasn't raised with that. But knowing how wonderful her brother is and seeing how much they love each other—I'm just so glad she has family who cares about her.

I have to admit, though, that seeing them together makes me a little jealous. I never had any siblings or friends who were close enough to feel like siblings. When I look at Cat and Nikolay together, and see all the inside jokes they have and all the weird mannerisms they share, it makes my heart ache, and I wonder what I've missed out on.

Last night, when we were walking back to The Plaza from one of our bar outings, I brought this up. "Seeing you guys together makes me wish I'd had a brother or sister," I said.

Cat raised her eyebrows. "Oh, we didn't always get along."

"You hated me for years," Nikolay remarked. "You thought I was such a pain in the ass. What you really wanted was a sister."

They both laughed. “I *did* hate you for a little while,” Cat said. “And I’m only slightly ashamed to admit I asked our mother if we could trade you in for a sister after you were born.”

Nikolay shook his head and smiled at his sister.

Then Cat leaned over, put her arm around me, and gave me a squeeze. “I found my sister, though. It took me a while, but I found her.” Then she stopped and looked at me with a sentimentality in her eyes that I hadn’t seen before. “That’s what you are to me, Lora,” she said solemnly. “You’re not just my friend, or my writing partner. To me, you are like a sister.”

“There, now you have everything you want!” Nikolay said to Cat. Then he turned to me. “See, this is why she is so happy nowadays: she got what she always wanted.”

I will be sad to see Nikolay go.

Amanda Harris | 12–15–2017 7:48 AM
I think we can get a wiretap

Jenée Parker | 12–15–2017 7:53 AM
Good

Jenée Parker | 12–15–2017 7:54 AM
I think she's planning something hence the visit from her brother

Jenée Parker | 12–15–2017 7:55 AM
And we have no idea what

Jenée Parker | 12–15–2017 8:00 AM
We're running out of time

The Diary of Lora Ricci

December 16, 2017

Yesterday, while Cat was at a meeting, Nikolay and I hung out in the suite waiting for her to get back for lunch. By the time one P.M. rolled around, we were too hungry to keep waiting for her, so we ordered room service. When the food arrived, she still hadn't returned, so we started eating.

Nikolay was saying how much he loved New York, and how different life is here from his life in Moscow. "I think you would like Moscow, though," he said. "You should come visit."

I smiled. "I'd love that. Maybe I'll come with Cat sometime."

"You should. I'll give you a tour."

I couldn't think of anything to say, so naturally I did the dumbest (and rudest?) possible thing: I mentioned their father. "You know, Cat was right: you guys are so similar. And you're nothing like your father."

"My father?" he asked.

"Yeah, your dad. Franz Wolff. I met him a little while ago."

"'Franz Wolff'?" He was looking at me like I was crazy.

"Yeah," I insisted.

"I'm not sure who you met, but I do not believe you met my father. My father is a drunk and a felon."

"He did drink a bit while he was here."

"Franz," he said under his breath. He shook his head.

"He and Cat look so much alike, but he was such an angry person," I said. "He was all pissed at me for being here. He almost called security on me."

Nikolay thought for a moment, then smiled. "That's not

good." He looked over at me. "I'm sorry Franz was mean to you," he said. "I will have to tell Franz to be nicer to you from now on."

"Thanks," I said.

"Can I ask you a strange question?" he asked.

"Sure."

"Does Cat treat you well?" he asked. "Is she nice to you?"

"Oh yeah, she's amazing," I said. "She took a real chance on me. Honestly, she kind of saved me. I was in a really bad place and had nowhere to go, but she believed in me. And now she pays for everything and lets me live with her. But it's just until we get our book deal, you know. I promise I'm not taking advantage of her or anything!"

He nodded solemnly. "Good, good," he said. "I'm glad she's good to you. You seem like a very nice person. I'm sorry you have gotten caught up in all of this."

"It's okay, I know family is complicated," I said. "I don't mind."

Cat returned a few minutes later, and then the three of us went ice-skating at Rockefeller Center. As we whirled around together, laughing and occasionally falling on the ice (I am not the best ice-skater, lol), my heart filled with this heavy nostalgia and sadness. I didn't want the day to end, I didn't want to take even a single moment for granted, and I wanted to hold Cat and Nikolay so tightly and never, ever let them go.

When we got back, I headed up to my bedroom. I lay down in bed, stared at the photo on my nightstand of me, Mom, and Dad, and realized what that heavy feeling was. I miss my parents. I miss my family. I miss my home.

Now that Nikolay is gone, I feel even more alone.

Bob dropped him off at the airport this morning. Cat and I went along for the ride. She started crying when they said goodbye, and promised him that she'd see him again soon. "Next time I see you, it better be in Moscow," he said, then kissed the top of her head.

Cat barely said a word the whole drive back to the hotel. "I really like him," I said. She nodded and kept staring out the window. "Do you think he'll be back soon?" I asked. She shrugged. I could tell she didn't feel like talking, so I gave up on the conversation and pressed my face against the window, watching the city go by.

Jenée Parker | 12–19–2017 5:20 PM

FYI

Jenée Parker | 12–19–2017 5:20 PM

OD is going out of town so the team will go in tomorrow morning

Amanda Harris | 12–19–2017 6:17 PM

Great

Jenée Parker | 12–19–2017 5:20 PM

Thanks for making this happen so quickly 🙏

Amanda Harris | 12–19–2017 6:17 PM

Let's just hope we get something out of it

From: Nikolay Dorokhov
To: Olesya Dorokhova
Subject: (no subject)
Date: December 20, 2017

im worried about you olesya

you're juggling too much

you should come home, before it all falls apart

it will fall apart

please

come home

From: Olesya Dorokhova
To: Nikolay Dorokhov
Subject: Re:
Date: December 20, 2017

Kolya—

I know, I know. I have to get out of here.

But I can't, not yet. I'm so close though. I'm so close.

I will pull it off.

I have to.

—Olesya

PART 3

horse girl

The Diary of Lora Ricci

January 2, 2018

This is going to be a good year. I can feel it. Finally, a year when things actually go right for me.

I forgot to bring my diary on our ski trip, so I didn't get to write about any of the things we did. I'll try to summarize it all here.

Before we left, I called Mom and Dad when I knew they would both be at work, and left a voicemail letting them know I wouldn't make it home for Christmas. They tried to call me back that same night, and every night for a few days afterward, but I couldn't bring myself to get on the phone. Instead, I texted Mom: Sorry, busy with work, can't answer the phone right now. Love you guys! Merry Christmas! She never texted back.

I told Cat about it, and she said I should put it out of my mind, that I should just focus on having fun in Tahoe. She told me I was going to love it and promised that we'd have the vacation we needed and had worked so hard for.

And she was right. God, we had so much fun. We flew into San Francisco and rented a car. The drive to Tahoe was long, but we didn't care—we listened to music and sang along the whole time. It was really late when we arrived, so we didn't get a good look at anything except the interior of the cabin Cat had rented.

We didn't realize how amazing the place was until we got up the next morning. It was like waking up in a fairy tale: perfectly piled snow outside, a frozen lake only a few streets away, and an enormous pine-covered mountain across the street.

We spent the next day shopping for winter gear and exploring. Cat put everything on her credit cards, including ski and snowshoe rentals, and boots, a coat, and pants for me. That night, we went out to a restaurant and made our plans for the next few days while we ate.

The rest of our ski vacation was magical. We skied, or, rather, we tried to ski—turns out we were equally shitty and fell a lot, which isn't that bad when you have someone there with you to laugh about it. After two days of disastrous attempts to ski on the easy slopes, we switched to snowshoeing. We snowshoed every day after that, and ate and drank at the lodge and the other restaurants at the ski resort, then came back to our cabin every night and relaxed in the hot tub.

It went by too fast. Before I knew it, we were driving back to San Francisco and I was dropping her off at her new hotel and then I was on a plane back to New York. I'm back at The Plaza now, and I'm ready to work. I feel like things are going to happen, like my brain is refreshed and ready to get back to work.

I'm going to figure out this story.

I will.

I have to.

Amanda Harris | 01–15–2018 6:40 PM
Where are we on OD?

Jenée Parker | 01–15–2018 6:41 PM
Nowhere

Jenée Parker | 01–15–2018 6:41 PM
We're going in to see if we can find anything else

Jenée Parker | 01–15–2018 6:42 PM
She's traveling back and forth from SF

Jenée Parker | 01–15–2018 6:43 PM
So she's rarely in the suite

Jenée Parker | 01–15–2018 6:44 PM
And when she IS there, she doesn't use the suite phone

Amanda Harris | 01–15–2018 6:48 PM
Anything on her past?

Jenée Parker | 01–15–2018 6:50 PM
We have a few leads

The Diary of Lora Ricci

January 20, 2018

Weird thing that literally just happened:

I'd left the suite and was in the elevator heading downstairs to do some journaling over breakfast, when I realized I'd forgotten my diary. When the elevator reached the lobby, I rode it back up to the twentieth floor. As I stepped off the elevator, I saw some housekeepers going into Cat's room. I was about to follow them inside, when, I swear to god, I saw Aisha.

Yes, Aisha from *ELLE*. In a Plaza housekeeper uniform. Pushing one of those cleaning carts.

I almost stopped her and said something, because . . . ???

But then, at the last minute, I decided against it. What if, like me, she'd had to drop out of school and/or take a side job? I didn't know her well at all. Hell, I'd barely even interacted with her, and almost everything I knew about her was something I'd learned from the other interns. If she had wanted to tell them that she was working as a maid at the hotel, she would have. But she chose not to, just like I chose not to tell them that I was Cat Wolff's ghostwriter. The kind/smart/good thing would be to respect that, right?

I hope she's okay. Dammit, I wish I'd gotten to know her. I wish I'd gotten closer to her and the other interns and stayed in touch with them—at least then I'd have some sort of social life these days. Sometimes I'm tempted to invite people over, or maybe go on a date. But who would I even invite? Who would I even go out with? And how the hell would I even begin to explain why I live at The Plaza Hotel?

FALCONS

ANXIOUS PEOPLE

BEING ANXIOUS

BROOKLYN BRIDGE

CATS

BROOKLYN ARMY TERMINAL

YOUTUBE STARLETS

STARLETS

STARLINGS

PLAZA WIDOWS

DOLPHINS

COLLEGE

HORSE GIRLS (THAT LORA STORY MAYBE?)

DROP-OUTS

BACKYARD CHICKENS

CON ARTISTS

FISHERMEN

FISHERWOMEN?

FERRY

WHALES

The Diary of Lora Ricci

January 24, 2018

I did it.

I really think I did it.

I'm in shock right now because I think I just wrote *the* story.

I think this is it.

This is the one.

Okay, now I have to edit and revise.

No time to journal right now

I'll write about it later!!!

Eeeeeeeeeeee!

Jenée Parker | 01–28–2018 3:12 PM
We finally picked something up

Jenée Parker | 01–28–2018 3:13 PM
A call for a Daphne Rooney

Amanda Harris | 01–28–2018 3:20 PM
Daphne Rooney the writer???

Jenée Parker | 01–28–2018 3:22 PM
Yes

Amanda Harris | 01–28–2018 3:27 PM
Are we looking at stolen identity or . . . ?

Jenée Parker | 01–28–2018 3:28 PM
Call me

The Diary of Lora Ricci

January 28, 2018

After the trip to Tahoe, I completely threw myself into writing. I decided I wouldn't do anything except write and write and write until I finally wrote something that was actually publishable. The first thing I did was go back and comb through all my notes and all the stories I'd written since I started working for Cat. I hoped I'd find something—anything—there that I could use, but none of the ideas were good and none of the stories were good enough.

And then, on Wednesday, I was standing in the living room, staring out the window, when it hit me.

I knew exactly what to do.

I knew the *exact* story I had to write.

I knew because I had already written it.

I ran over to the dining table and opened my laptop. As I looked through all my folders, trying to find it, I was saying a little prayer in my head: *Please let it be as good as I remember.* And there it was, one little Microsoft Word doc named *horsegirlshortstory1FINALFINAL.doc.* I closed my eyes, said, "Please, god," then opened it.

It was *terrible.* Even worse than I'd remembered. As I read it, I realized how much my writing had improved over the past six months. I read it over and over again, trying to figure out how to fix it. And the amazing thing was, I *knew* how to fix it. I knew how to take this thirty-five-hundred-word mess and turn it into something really good. And it turned out that I was right. This was the story. This was *it.* Or, at least, it would be after I completely overhauled it.

By the end of the day, it was done. It was done, and it was perfect. I immediately emailed it to Cat, hoping that she'd agree right away, but she didn't reply.

When she came back Friday night, I asked her if she'd read it yet. "Oh god, Lora, I'm so sorry," she said, "but I really didn't have any time. I'll read it tomorrow, okay?"

I could barely sleep that night. My brain was on fire. I felt like I was sitting on a pile of gold and was just waiting for her to notice it. The next morning, after our breakfast was delivered, I sat down at the table next to her. I couldn't take it anymore. "Cat, I'm losing my mind waiting for you to read this. You have to read it right now."

"Lora, I have so much on my plate right now, you don't even know," she said.

I opened my laptop and put it in front of her. "It will take you a few minutes. You have to read it. Please. Trust me."

She sighed and rolled her eyes. "Fine," she snapped, glaring at me.

I sat there, my heart racing, smiling like the giddy idiot I am, as I waited for her to read it.

Fifteen minutes passed, and each minute felt like an hour. Finally, she closed the laptop. "Holy shit," she said quietly. "That's it. That's the one." She was quiet for another few moments, then opened my laptop again. "There's one thing we need to change," she said as she started typing. "Connor needs to use the 'horse girl' line at the end, not at the beginning."

She was right. OMG. I basically screamed: "Yes! In front of other people! He laughs at her, and he says she's crazy!"

She nodded. "But we still need her to say it in the beginning of the story, to tell him this little detail about herself, so that when he says it, there's some element of truth to it and it doesn't seem out of place."

We sat there for the rest of the day, reading it and rereading it and changing every little thing until it was absolutely perfect. I don't think either of us even got up to use the bathroom. The only thing I remember thinking was that I was so glad we'd written so many stories that *hadn't* worked, because at that moment, when we finally had something that *was* going to work, we were ready. *I* was ready.

Today, I did the final revisions on the story so that Cat can send it to her agent sometime soon. While I've been writing, Cat has been writing, too—she said she's been working on another big feature for *ELLE,* though she hasn't told me anything about it. I asked her if she needed any help, but she shook her head and said that the short story was much more important and she wanted me focused on that, not on an article for the magazine.

I wanted to see how her article was coming along, so this afternoon, when she left the room to take a phone call, I snuck over to the couch to see what she'd been working on. My jaw literally dropped when I saw a Word document open that was three hundred twenty-six pages and seventy-nine thousand words long.

I read the page that was open but couldn't understand much of it. There's a guy who watches an enormous whale breach in the East River and swim beneath the Brooklyn Bridge, but nobody else seems to see it except for him and a woman named Marjorie. It was pretty strange. I'm still not sure exactly what is was (maybe it's a novel?), but it definitely was *not* a feature for *ELLE.*

I was dying to keep reading, but then I heard Cat say goodbye on the phone. I jumped over to my chair as quickly as I could and just barely made it as she walked back into the living room and sat back down at her computer.

The curiosity is *killing* me. I wonder if she'll ask me to rewrite it for her later. From what I could tell, it was really well written, and not at all like the short stories she shared with me last summer. I'm not totally sure *she* wrote it. Maybe someone else is ghostwriting a novel for her? Maybe she's editing a novel for someone else? Maybe it's her secret novel that she doesn't want to show anyone?

PUBLISHERS WEEKLY

BOOK DEALS: Week Of February 12, 2018

By Andy Kirkwood | February 9, 2018

Daphne Rooney's Latest Goes to Little, Brown

Little, Brown's Danica Chapman paid seven figures for **Daphne Rooney's** new novel *The Whale*. The deal was negotiated by **Margot Fletcher** of Fletcher & Ross, who said that *The Whale* "is Daphne Rooney's finest—an unforgettable, bewitching novel."

THE NEW YORK TIMES | BOOKS

Daphne Rooney's Book Announcement Thrills the Literary World

By Jeanine Fox

February 9, 2018

On Sunday, Daphne Rooney, the *New York Times* best selling author of the novels "The Hawk," "Wythe" and "Marigold," announced the publication of a new book. In a cryptic Instagram story, Ms. Rooney wrote, "Surprise: New Book October 16th."

Ms. Rooney's agent, Margot Fletcher of the literary agency Fletcher & Ross, confirmed that a brand-new novel, titled "The Whale," will be published on Oct. 16, 2018, by Little, Brown. "Daphne came to me with a full, lively, perfectly written novel," Ms. Fletcher wrote in an email, adding that the book is a prequel to Ms. Rooney's 2017 bestseller "The Hawk."

The news came as a surprise to the literary world and to Ms. Rooney's fans. After the publication of "The Hawk," the reclusive author stated her intention to take a hiatus from writing. When asked about Ms. Rooney's decision, Ms. Fletcher wrote, "I was just as surprised as everyone else!"

Ms. Rooney declined to comment for this article.

The Diary of Lora Ricci

February 12, 2018

The past two weeks have been absolutely brutal.

I am dying of anticipation.

Literally dying.

Cat said she's going to send the story to Margot Fletcher (her agent), but she wants to have a phone call with her first to get her up to speed and tell her about the story rather than sending it without any context.

We were hoping we could do that a few weeks ago, but it turns out that Margot is totally busy and the soonest they could fit a call in her schedule is tomorrow morning. So we've just been waiting and waiting and waiting, and the anticipation is killing me.

Cat has her work in San Francisco to keep her busy, but me? I've been stuck here in the suite, trying to write yet another story.

The good news is that finally finding *the* story has taken the pressure off, and now I find writing and coming up with ideas a lot easier. We already found *the one,* the one that is supposed to shoot us into literary fame and fortune, so the other stories we write can be merely good, just okay—they don't have to be *incredible.* I wrote two really fun ones that I've been editing and working on. Who knows, maybe we'll be able to put them in a short story collection someday.

From: Cat Wolff
To: Margot Fletcher
BCC: Lora Ricci
Subject: The Story
Date: February 13, 2018

Margot:

As we discussed, here is the short story titled “Horse Girl.” My hope is to place it in one of the more prestigious publications like *The New Yorker.*

I’m eager to hear your thoughts.

Cat Wolff

Attachment: HORSEGIRL.docx

The Diary of Lora Ricci

February 17, 2018

Cat has been gone for almost two months now.

It's been weirdly nice to have the place all to myself on the weekdays. I don't really go anywhere or leave the hotel except on the weekends, when Cat's back from San Francisco and I try to give her some time alone in the suite.

Cat sent the story to her agent earlier this week, and the suspense is killing me. It's hard to think clearly about anything when you're waiting to hear back whether or not you just nailed the short story that will possibly change your life. And I don't know if it was because of the anxiety, boredom, or the need to distract myself, but yesterday morning I snooped through Cat's things. I probably shouldn't have done it, and I'm a little freaked out about the fact that I did, but honestly I'm even more freaked out about what I found.

It all started with the cabinets in the living room. I was standing there, staring at the room service menu for the millionth time and wondering what I should order for lunch, when I looked around and realized I didn't know what was inside all the cabinets. The more I started to think about it, the more I started to wonder why I hadn't looked before. And then, before I could stop myself, I was opening up all the cabinets on the top row. There wasn't much inside—glasses, plates, etc.—so I opened up the bottom cabinets and drawers, which were filled with a bunch of paperwork. Nothing interesting.

I put everything back as carefully as I could, then headed back to my room. As I was walking up the stairs, I realized I'd never actually been inside Cat's room before. Not even once. She's very private about it, and almost always keeps the door closed. I couldn't help but wonder what was inside, and my curiosity got the best of me: before I knew it, I was walking back down the stairs, opening her bedroom door, and stepping inside.

I wasn't very surprised to find that it's almost identical to my bedroom: the same furniture, the same bathroom, gold everywhere. There was a dresser in hers, beneath the TV, and I walked over and opened the drawers. Nothing stood out to me, but as I closed the bottom drawer, I heard something roll around and clink against the side. I reached into the drawer, stuck my hand underneath the folded sweaters, and felt around until I found what was making the noise: a ring of keys.

I stopped for a moment. *What the hell are you doing, Lora?* I asked myself. I almost, *almost,* turned around and went back to my room. But there was a little voice in my head urging me on, telling me that Cat would probably do the same thing and go through my things if she had the chance. (Now that I'm writing this down, yes, I see the self-rationalization, and yes, I feel bad about it, *but*...)

I made up my mind to look around for a few more minutes, but I couldn't find anything that might need a key. There was a rack of clothing by the window, similar to the racks in the fashion closet at *ELLE.* No key needed for that. The nightstand drawers didn't need any keys, nor did the dresser drawers or anything in the bathroom. I walked back out into the living room. Nothing. I went up the stairs, into my room. Again, nothing. I wondered if they were keys to something else—a storage unit? A locker or box somewhere else in the hotel?

I walked back down the stairs, ready to give up and put the keys back where I found them, when I saw it. At the end of the hallway, in the entryway by the door, was a row of closets. All of them had locks. I walked over to one and examined the lock. It didn't take me very long to figure out which key would fit.

My heart was pounding like crazy. The little voice in my head was screaming at me: *Why are you doing this? Cat has been nothing but amazing to you—why would you betray her trust like this?*

I put the key in, then pulled it back out. I couldn't do it—what if she found out that I'd gone through her things?

And then I remembered how she didn't tell me that her father was in town and didn't return my texts. I remembered the woman I'd met at the Halloween party, Cat's obsessive need to keep me hidden away from the hotel employees, and the fact that I was still, ultimately, working for free.

I put the key back in, turned it, and opened the door.

Inside, there were rows and rows of wigs on hangers. I am not kidding when I say there must have been fifty wigs. Some short hair, some long hair, all colors and textures and styles. Wigs that looked like they were toupees made for seventy-year-old men, and neon-colored wigs that looked like they were meant to be worn to a rave. I'd never seen Cat wear any of these. Why does she have so many? It didn't—and doesn't—make any sense. And then my eyes fell on one wig that looked really familiar. It was blonde—the same blonde as her hair—shoulder-length (a little shorter than it is now), and had this wave to it that gave me a sense of déjà vu. I couldn't shake the feeling that I'd seen it before.

I took the wig out of the closet and turned to face the mirror. I pulled my hair up, put the wig on my head, and took off my glasses.

There, staring back at me, was Cat Wolff.

My heart stopped. I closed my eyes, pulled the wig off, put my glasses back on, and looked at myself in the mirror again. It was just boring little nerd me, Lora Elizabeth Ricci. I shook my head, trying to shake out whatever weird feelings were creeping up on me. I'd never realized that we looked so similar before—had she? I put the wig back on.

I walked through Cat's bedroom and into her bathroom. I looked down at my bare feet on the white-and-gold mosaic floor, and then looked up at myself in the mirror. This time, I wasn't as shocked when I saw the woman in the mirror. It was *me,* looking an awful lot like Cat. But it *was* me, and not Cat.

I never realized it until then. How plain Cat's face is and how everything else about her is what *really* catches your eye. She's gorgeous, I'm not trying to say otherwise or anything, but her face isn't what stands out. It's everything else—her hair, her makeup, her voice, her personality, the way she talks and carries herself, the way she puts herself together. As I was standing there, looking at myself, I realized that I couldn't remember her face very well. I felt like I'd never really *seen* her face, as crazy as that sounds—like, I'd never really paid attention to it, and if someone asked me to describe her face, I wouldn't even know what to say.

I was starting to feel really weird and dissociative. I took the wig off, carefully put it back, then closed and locked the closet doors. I was about to leave and put the keys back, but there was one more closet, to the left, right next to the front door of the suite, that I felt pulled to. I stood in front of it with the key hovering in front of the lock. I figured, by this point, I was in so deep that I couldn't *not* look inside. Like, I'd already committed the sin, so would it really make any difference if I continued? (Lol, looking back as I write this, I realize this is like the sunk cost fallacy, except it's about doing bad shit. Way to go, Lora!)

Well, I took a deep breath and opened the final closet. It was just filled with clothes, which was a bit of a letdown after the other closet, to be honest. I didn't recognize anything inside, and there didn't seem to be anything special (except a weird pad thing that I'm a little worried was a fake pregnancy bump but I'm not 100 percent sure—I didn't look very closely).

I locked the closet up and put the keys back. There were a few other keys on the ring that didn't match any locks in the suite, but I wasn't all that interested. I'd had enough of playing Nancy Drew for one day.

When Cat got back this morning, she was excited and in a great mood. She said everything in San Francisco is going so well, and she is so optimistic about the story that she can't think about anything else. The whole day, I've been expecting her to notice that someone had been through her things, but if she did, she didn't seem to care.

From: Margot Fletcher
To: Cat Wolff
Subject: Re: The Story
Date: February 19, 2018

Dear Cat,

It's spectacular. I loved it so much I read it three times in a row.

What an incredibly relevant story for the moment; I suspect it will generate a great deal of discussion around consent and misogyny. And what an ending! I truly felt like someone slammed a door in my face when I reached the final paragraph.

Would you mind if I shared it with my client Daphne Rooney? I think she will enjoy it, and it would be wonderful to have her support.

Could we hop on a call later today to discuss? I am free from 4:30pm onward.

Sincerely,

M.

FEDERAL BUREAU OF INVESTIGATION

DATE OF TRANSCRIPTION: 02/20/2018

CALEB MORROW, A doorman, was contacted at his employment at 750 Park Avenue, New York, New York. Morrow was advised as to the nature of this investigation and provided the following information.

MORROW stated that DAPHNE ROONEY has been a full-time resident of the building since 2010, when she purchased a one-bedroom apartment. Morrow advised that the building's co-op board likely asked DAPHNE ROONEY for her tax returns and financial statements before approving the sale of the apartment.

MORROW stated that guests often come to the building asking to see DAPHNE ROONEY, but that she is rarely in her apartment and does not buzz any guests up to her apartment. Morrow stated that he has not seen DAPHNE ROONEY since August 2017.

INVESTIGATION ON: 02/20/2018

At: NEW YORK CITY, NEW YORK

By: SPECIAL AGENT JENÉE PARKER

Amanda Harris | 02–22-2018 11:37 AM
It's really no wonder she got away with this for so long

Jenée Parker | 02–22-2018 11:40 AM
I know, right?

Jenée Parker | 02–22-2018 11:40 AM
I can't stop looking at these photos

Jenée Parker | 02–22-2018 11:41 AM
She's unrecognizable

Amanda Harris | 02–22-2018 11:42 AM
How do you think she learned this?

Jenée Parker | 02–22-2018 11:43 AM
The makeup skills?

Amanda Harris | 02–22-2018 11:45 AM
Yeah

Jenée Parker | 02–22-2018 11:46 AM
YouTube?

Jenée Parker | 02–22-2018 11:47 AM
Special effects work?

Jenée Parker | 02–22-2018 11:48 AM
I don't know

Amanda Harris | 02–22-2018 11:50 AM
Truly amazing

Amanda Harris | 02–22-2018 11:51 AM
I keep wondering: who else might she be?

From: Cat Wolff
To: Lora Ricci
Subject: (no subject)
Date: March 1, 2018

Lora:

I just got off the phone with Margot. She sent it to *The New Yorker.*

Now we wait . . .

Cat Wolff

The Diary of Lora Ricci

March 13, 2018

It's really happening.

OMFG, it's really happening.

THE NEW YORKER IS GOING TO PUBLISH MY STORY!!!!

I'm FREAKING OUT.

I AM A WRITER.

I AM GOING TO BE PUBLISHED IN *THE NEW YORKER*.

I'm losing my mind right now.

LOSING IT.

AHHHHHHHHHHHHHHHHHHHHHH!!!!

From: Olesya Dorokhova
To: FollowMeNow
Subject: Purchase Page Views and Social Media Shares
Date: March 14, 2018

Hello—

Next week, a short story called “Horse Girl” by “Cat Wolff” will be published in *The New Yorker.* I need to buy approximately two million unique views from around the world, with the majority of them located in North America (New York City, to be precise).

I also need the piece to go viral on social media—Twitter, Facebook, Reddit.

—Olesya

From: FollowMeNow
To: Olesya Dorokhova
Subject: Re: Purchase Page Views and Social Media Shares
Date: March 14, 2018

Regards Miss Dorokhova

Happy to be of assistance. FollowMeNow will provide what you request. Please pay three bitcoins to wallet linked below.

Thank you for your preference in this business.

From: Coinbase
To: Cat Wolff
Subject: Your Bitcoin Purchase
Date: March 14, 2018

Congratulations!

You purchased 3 Bitcoins (BTC) for $27,584.55 USD. Those funds are now available in your account.

Thank you for the purchase.

The Diary of Lora Ricci

March 19, 2018

WE DID IT.

OH MY GOD, I CAN'T BELIEVE WE DID IT.

"Horse Girl" came out today. It's up on *The New Yorker*'s website and it's the most beautiful thing I've ever seen, and it has the most perfect illustration. I pulled it up on my phone and read it over and over and over again.

Then I remembered it was published in an *actual magazine.* I called the concierge and asked to have twenty copies brought up to Cat's suite. After what felt like forever, someone from the front desk delivered the magazines to the front door. And oh my god—it's even more beautiful in print!!

I'd barely finished admiring it when Cat called me. "IT'S BLOWN UP," she shouted over the phone, breathless. "WE'VE GONE VIRAL!"

"What do you mean?" I asked.

"The editor just called me, the editor from *The New Yorker.* She said it's gotten millions of views. She said it's a *phenomenon.* It's all over Twitter; people are going crazy for it. Margot is losing her mind."

What??!

I grabbed my laptop and started looking online.

She was right.

Holy shit, was she right.

It was all over everything, everywhere.

We were famous.

Well, not exactly. *Cat* was famous. The *story* I'd written was famous. But *I* wasn't famous, and I felt a little bit of bitterness and regret, which I tried my best to swallow.

"And I just got a call from Margot," Cat said. "She said I should put together a proposal for a book. Lora, she's been getting calls and emails all day about me. She said I need to sell a book right away."

A book.

I didn't hear anything she said after that. I couldn't stop thinking about a book. A book. *A book.* A book would mean that I could strike out on my own. A book would mean that I would be able to stop ghostwriting soon. It was all coming together. My dream of becoming a writer was going to come true. Holy shit, it was going to come true.

My brain came to a halt.

"Will my name be on the book?"

Cat had still been talking, but now she stopped. "I . . . I . . . don't know, maybe?"

There was an uncomfortable silence.

She finally broke it. "Can we talk about this later? I can ask Margot, see what she says. But, hey, please don't get your hopes up, okay? I haven't really told Margot you're the ghostwriter, and I will, I promise, but that doesn't mean she'll want your name on it or that she'll want to represent you. But if our book does well, then you'll be able to get a book deal on your own, and everyone will see how talented you are. We talked about this, remember?"

"Yeah, okay, no, you're totally right," I said quietly.

"Don't worry, I promise it's all going to work out," she said, and I could hear her smiling through the phone. "I have to follow Sophie to some important meetings—she's pitching her startup to investors today. But I'll get on a plane as soon as she's done and be back in New York tonight and we'll celebrate then, okay?"

After she hung up, I called and placed a room service order for some champagne and dinner that'll be ready when she arrives so that we can celebrate our newfound literary fame. Well, *her* newfound literary fame.

Look, I knew that it was going to be her name on the story. I did, I really did. That was the deal. I made the decision to be her ghostwriter, and I have to live with it. But I was kind of hoping and expecting that she would end up putting my name on it, too, or that she would at least tell her agent that I was the real writer behind it. And to hear her admit that she hadn't told Margot—that really stung, you know? What if she never tells Margot? What if she never tells anyone?

SIDELINES FASHION

Runway fashion, for everyone.

YC DEMO DAY 2018 **(March 19, 2018)**

THE PROBLEMS

WASTE

- Major fashion labels discard used runway and sample clothing, leading to **waste**.
- Consumers buy knock-off fast fashion based on the designs of major fashion labels, and then discard it because of the low quality, leading to **waste**.
- 14 million tons of clothing ends up in landfills each year.

TRUST

- Labels want their clothing to end up in the hands of consumers they **trust**. Consumers want to purchase from exclusive brands and labels they **trust**.

THE SOLUTION

Reduce waste, increase trust.

A subscription service that gives fashion companies a guaranteed home for each season's used and leftover clothing.

A subscription service that gives consumers guaranteed access to trusted designer clothing at an accessible price.

THE SIDELINES SUBSCRIPTION SERVICE

Partner Side

- We partner with major labels across the fashion industry.
- At the end of each season, they sell us whatever they have left.
- No returns, no hassles, no drama.

Customer Side

- Customers sign up for semiannual subscriptions.
- Customers provide their measurements and choose an assortment of labels.
- At the end of each season, they receive a selection of items from their chosen labels.
- No returns, only exchanges for other sizes.

OUR BUSINESS MODEL

- Recurring revenue business
- We charge a $100 curation fee with every subscription
- Built-in 10% commission on each piece

EXAMPLE:

For one box with $2500 worth of clothing:

- $100 curation fee
- $250 commission
- $350 per season x 2 boxes per year = $700 per year per customer

We already have an 8,000-person long waiting list = $5,600,000 in potential ARR without even having done any active marketing or having launched the service.

WHY THIS TEAM?

Sophie Bisset is a 27-year-old international fashion designer and influencer with connections to nearly every major fashion label in France and in the United States. She has been featured in dozens of ad campaigns from major designer brands and has nearly 2 million followers on Instagram. Sophie was featured in *ELLE* magazine and included in the 2017 Forbes *30 Under 30* list.

Sidelines Fashion is already gaining momentum and catching the attention of young fashion consumers.

From: Sophie Bisset
To: Brandon Barnes
Subject: Handshake Deal
Date: March 21, 2018

Bonjour Brandon!

It was *très bien* to meet you at Y Combinator Demo Day. I'm just sending an email to confirm our handshake deal for $250k.

As per YC handshake protocol, this offer is valid for 48 hours. Please confirm acceptance and agree that Barnes Venture Partners will fund this investment within ten business days of offer acceptance.

xoxo,

Sophie

From: Sophie Bisset
To: Henry Fox
Subject: Handshake Deal
Date: March 21, 2018

Bonjour Henry!

It was *très bien* to meet you at Y Combinator Demo Day. I'm just sending an email to confirm our handshake deal for $500k.

As per YC handshake protocol, this offer is valid for 48 hours. Please confirm acceptance and agree that Baylands Capital will fund this investment within ten business days of offer acceptance.

xoxo,

Sophie

From: Sophie Bisset
To: Melanie Chang
Subject: Handshake Deal
Date: March 21, 2018

Bonjour Melanie!

It was *très bien* to meet you at Y Combinator Demo Day. I'm just sending an email to confirm our handshake deal for $100k.

As per YC handshake protocol, this offer is valid for 48 hours. Please confirm acceptance and agree that you will fund this investment within ten business days of offer acceptance.

xoxo,

Sophie

From: Melanie Chang
To: Sophie Bisset
Subject: Re: Handshake Deal
Date: March 22, 2018

Yes.

From: Brandon Barnes
To: Sophie Bisset
Subject: Re: Handshake Deal
Date: March 22, 2018

I'm in.

Let me know how else I can be helpful.

From: Henry Fox
To: Sophie Bisset
Subject: Re: Handshake Deal
Date: March 22, 2018

Yes, Baylands is in.

From: Coinbase
To: Cat Wolff
Subject: Your Bitcoin Purchase
Date: March 23, 2018

Congratulations!

You purchased 103.54 Bitcoins (BTC) for $850,000 USD. Those funds are now available in your account.

Thank you for the purchase.

The Diary of Lora Ricci

April 13, 2018

I've been too busy working on the book to journal.

We are full speed ahead. Margot wants Cat to get a book proposal/manuscript ready ASAP. She already has a bunch of editors at top publishing houses who want to see it right away. The plan is to publish "Horse Girl" as part of a short story collection so we can capitalize on its fame and use it to anchor our book.

My job is to go back to the stories we wrote last fall and improve them while writing a few new ones. As soon as we have a dozen or so ready to go, Cat will send them all to Margot, and then Margot will submit them to the editors.

Cat is back in New York. I'd gotten used to having the place to myself five days a week, so it has been a bit of an adjustment on my end. But it's nice to have her around and it feels good to get back into our old routine. She seems to want more time and space to herself, though—I can tell she doesn't want me hanging around the suite too much. I've been trying to get out and be more social (and by "be more social" I mean "hang out in bookstores").

Earlier this week, I went to a Daphne Rooney book reading. I was way down at McNally Jackson browsing around and looking for inspiration, when I saw their display of Rooney's novel *The Hawk* (apparently the paperback was released last Tuesday). I'd heard great things about it when the hardcover came out but had never read it, so I bought a copy. When I got to the checkout counter, the cashier told me that Daphne was going to be there for a special reading that night, and that tickets came with the book. "Bring the book back with you and you can even get it signed," he said.

When I got back to the suite, I asked Cat if she wanted to come to the event with me, but she said she was way too busy. She even tried to convince me not to go, which was sort of baffling since recently she has been after me to "get out more." "You should really finish editing those stories for the book, Lora—we are running low on time," she said, "and if you don't want to do the work, I'll find someone else who will."

Ouch.

Not wanting to anger her even more, I lied and told her I'd skip the reading and stay at the suite and work.

I'm sorry, but there is no way I am going to work all day *and* all night. If she wants the stories to be done sooner, then why doesn't *she* write them? I'm starting to lose my patience with her—it feels like she is basically expecting me to do all the work while she gets all the credit. And she really does get all the credit—and all the attention. Ever since "Horse Girl" was published, she's been getting nonstop requests for events, interviews, photo shoots, movie deals, television adaptations. Every time she tells me about some new email she got from a Hollywood producer, I want to run up to the rooftop patio and scream, *I WROTE HORSE GIRL!*

I waited until she left for whatever event or meeting or dinner date she was headed to, then snuck out of the suite. By the time I got to the bookstore, the place was completely packed. I had to stand in the very back of the store, where I could barely see Daphne. Luckily I could still hear her. She read from the second chapter of *The Hawk*. It was beautiful. I see why so many people love her books. She's really that fucking good. She sets the story up and makes you think you can see where it's going and then she pulls the rug out from under you—all in one fifteen-page chapter. So amazing. I wish I could write like that, or even just know someone that talented—can you imagine how much I'd learn?

The line for the book signing was at least a hundred people long, and I waited for at least an hour. But by the time I reached the front of the line and was so close I could finally see Daphne, one of the bookstore employees walked up to me and the handful of people standing in line behind me and said, "I'm sorry, but that's all for today. Daphne will no longer be signing books. If you'd like yours signed, you can write your name on a Post-it note, Daphne will sign it later tonight, and you can stop by to pick it up tomorrow."

"But she's *right there,*" I insisted, pointing at the table literally twenty feet away, where Daphne was sitting. She was staring at her phone, avoiding my frustrated glare.

"Sorry," the employee said, and that was that.

I left my book there and went to pick it up the next day. I was a little annoyed, but whatever. I started reading it after I got back from McNally and finished it this morning. It's so fucking good. I can't wait to read her next book, *The Whale,* which is apparently a prequel to *The Hawk* and is coming out later this year.

See, that's the kind of writer I want to be. I want to be Daphne Rooney. I don't know if I'll ever be as good as she is, but that's the level I aspire to. Maybe once this story collection is done and Cat sends it to Margot, I can put my time into writing a novel of my own. Then, when the time comes, I'll have something that's all mine, something that will be published under no one's name but my own. God, how amazing would that be?

From: Cat Wolff
To: Margot Fletcher
BCC: Lora Ricci
Subject: Horse Girl Book
Date: April 17, 2018

Margot:

Here is the draft for my collection of short stories, with "Horse Girl" as the main attraction. I've written nearly a dozen stories in the past year, and I have arranged them in an order that I think makes sense. I will also write two or three new stories. What do you think of *Horse Girl and Other One-Trick Ponies* as a title?

Cat Wolff

Attachment: HORSE_GIRL_AND_OTHER_ONE_TRICK_PONIES_collection.docx

The Diary of Lora Ricci

April 22, 2018

I finished up the proposal and Cat sent it off to Margot. We waited a few days while she read and reviewed it, and getting through those days was pure agony. I know I said I'd try to write a novel or something like that after I finished the collection, but it was basically impossible to focus on anything else with this hanging over my head.

Margot wanted to cut most of the stories in the collection; she said we should only submit the very best ones, which left us with four stories plus "Horse Girl." She's going to send it out to editors first thing tomorrow morning, and she said we should know by the end of the week.

Before we sent it off, I asked Cat if I could put my name on it, and she said that wasn't an option. I knew that's what she would say, but I still had to ask. I get it, and I know that's what we agreed to originally, but it still sucks and I was hoping she'd change her mind.

I've started to resent her. I know I shouldn't, but I do. Her name is on the story. Her name is in the headlines. People are saying she's the next great short story writer. "The voice of a generation." I keep screaming inside: *That's my voice! I did that! I wrote that!*

Do you have any idea what that feels like?

The Diary of Lora Ricci

April 28, 2018

It's almost six in the morning and I've been dancing all night.

We'd been waiting and waiting and waiting, hoping to hear back about the book. And then, yesterday afternoon, Margot called Cat and told her that an editor from Penguin Press loved the proposal and was going to send her an offer by the end of the day. A few hours later, we got it: an offer to publish *Horse Girl and Other One-Trick Ponies,* with an advance of $1.25 million.

It's almost too good to be true. It doesn't even feel real. I still can barely believe it.

We did it.

We fucking did it.

(*I* fucking did it!!!!!)

The first thing we did was scream our lungs out. I was so happy I started to cry. Cat thanked me and hugged me so tight I thought my head was going to pop off. We ordered champagne and drank and laughed and reminisced and went downstairs for an early dinner. When we got back to the suite, Cat dug around in her purse for her checkbook and wrote me a check. "An advance on the advance," she said.

We had originally planned to go out on the town. But by the end of the day, we were so emotionally exhausted from the excitement, we both just really wanted to stay home and chill out and watch a movie instead. We curled up on the couch with our blankets, snacks, and drinks (Cat with her coffee—I don't know how she drinks coffee at night and still sleeps, but she does—and me with my tea).

I turned on the TV and saw that one of the channels was having a musical marathon, and we came in about halfway through *Funny Face*. After we watched Audrey Hepburn and Fred Astaire sing "'S wonderful, 's marvelous, that you should care for me," *Gigi* came on.

"I've never seen this one," Cat said as the opening scene of *Gigi* played.

"Me either," I said. We looked at each other and smiled.

I jumped up, ran to the phone, called room service, and ordered more tea and coffee, then tucked myself back into my corner of the couch.

Gigi turned out to be not that great. By the end, we were a little disappointed and dissatisfied, and we weren't tired enough to sleep—we were still high on the rush of the book deal news.

We tried to read. That lasted for about fifteen minutes, and then Cat threw her book on the floor dramatically. "This will never work," she said in exasperation. "I can't go to sleep like this!"

"Me either!" I shouted.

"We could, you know, see what else is on . . ." Cat said tentatively.

So the TV went back on, and we started up the next musical: *My Fair Lady*. I'd seen it so many times before—it had been one of my favorites when I was a kid—and it seemed that Cat had, too, because we both started singing along with Eliza Doolittle as she twirled around the flower market.

By the time we got to "I Could Have Danced All Night," we were trying to dance along, but the suite was way too small. We peeked our heads out into the hallway and, finding it empty, danced up and down the corridor together, pretending we were at a ball. We got so carried away and were making so much noise that someone complained to the front desk and a hotel employee came up and asked us to keep it down.

We giggled and ran back to our room, out of breath and completely giddy. We sat down by the front door and waited a few minutes for the hotel employee to go back down to the lobby so we could dance again.

As soon as we heard him go down in the elevator, Cat grabbed my hand, opened the door, and led me back into the hallway. "Follow me," she said with a sparkle in her eye. "I know a place we can go—a place where nobody will hear us."

We took the elevator down to the first floor, giggling the whole way. "Now pretend we have something very serious to do," she whispered as the doors opened and we stepped out.

"We're very serious people," I said, before bursting into laughter. Laughing so hard we could barely breathe, we ran through the lobby. When we reached the foot of an enormous marble staircase, she turned to me, offered me an outstretched hand, and led me up the stairs.

The staircase led to a windowed room that was illuminated only by the streetlights outside. Still fighting back our laughter, Cat and I tiptoed across the floor to a pair of doors at the far side of the room. She gently tried the doorknobs, only to find them locked.

"Do you have a bobby pin?" she whispered, pointing to my hair. I always use bobby pins to hold my bangs back when I wash my face at night, and—thank god—I still had them in. I pulled a pin out and handed it to her. She slid it into the lock, jiggled it around, and then, after a satisfying click, opened the door.

The room inside was pitch-black. As my eyes struggled to adjust, I lost track of Cat, and was surprised to hear her voice coming from what sounded like very far away. "Stay there!" she shouted.

A few moments later, the lights turned on, and I found myself standing in the middle of the most incredible ballroom I'd ever seen in my life. Enormous chandeliers hung from the ceiling, and the room was decorated with columns and arches and paintings and gold.

Cat had kicked off her shoes and was running around me in circles on the carpet. I stepped out of my shoes, too, and she ran to me, her arms outstretched, the biggest, most blissful smile on her face.

"Are you sure we're allowed to be in here?" I asked.

"What's the worst they can do?" she asked, smiling. "Tell us to go back to our room?"

I stood on my tiptoes and took a few steps toward her. I reached for her hand, she pulled me in, and together we danced across the floor. I had taken a few years of ballet when I was a teenager, and what I remembered was enough that I could follow her as she danced. And Cat, well, Cat was nothing short of extraordinary. Her dancing took on a life of its own, and she was no longer Cat Wolff, no longer just a person, she was . . . something or someone magical. I've never seen anyone dance so beautifully before in my life. I couldn't look away.

We spun around in circles at one end of the room, then ran back into the center and lay down on the floor, laughing. As soon as we caught our breath, we got back to our feet and started singing songs from *My Fair Lady,* dancing as we sang. We belted out the lyrics, no longer worried that someone would hear. We were completely, utterly lost in the music. And we really, truly, danced all night.

By the time we left the ballroom, it was almost five in the morning. We tiptoed back down the marble staircase and made our way back up to the suite, humming quietly together. When we got home, we went up to the rooftop patio and watched the sun rise.

My heart is so full; my head is ringing.

This is the happiest I have ever been.

I think this was the best night of my life.

THE NEW YORK TIMES | BOOKS

'Horse Girl' Author Cat Wolff Gets 7-Figure Book Deal

By Jeanine Fox

May 4, 2018

In March, the short story "Horse Girl" became a viral phenomenon after being published in *The New Yorker.* According to a person involved in the deal, the story's author Cat Wolff has received a seven-figure book deal.

According to the literary agent Margot Fletcher of Fletcher & Ross, who represented Ms. Wolff in the sale to Penguin Press, "Horse Girl" was the magazine's most-read short story in the past ten years. "Frankly, I think everyone was astounded by the piece's popularity. It's not often that fiction—especially short fiction—goes viral."

The short story, which centers around a brief romantic encounter between Emily, an eighteen-year-old college student, and Connor, a teaching assistant, captured readers' attention and sparked online conversation about drinking, consent and the damaging effects of casual misogyny.

"It was the ending, I think, that resonated so strongly with readers," Ms. Fletcher explained, referring to the final paragraph of the story, in which Connor defends himself against Emily's accusations by telling his friends that Emily is "a horse girl—you know how crazy they are."

"It's an experience every woman has had at one time or another," Ms. Fletcher added. "We face sexism and misogyny and then, when we try to speak up and defend ourselves, are casually and cruelly dismissed."

The collection, "Horse Girl and Other One-Trick Ponies," will be published by Penguin Press in 2019.

The Diary of Lora Ricci

May 9, 2018

It's all over.

I feel like the ground just got pulled out from under me.

Everything fell apart.

And it's all my fault.

On Friday, I had just returned from one of my bookstore trips, and I could tell there was something wrong the second I walked in the door. Cat was there—her shoes were in the hallway, her bag was on the table—but she wasn't anywhere on the first floor of the suite. "Oh my god, you wouldn't believe how busy it was," I shouted as I walked into the living room. "Sorry it took me so long."

"Cat?" I said, hoping she'd hear me. And then I got this weird, sickening feeling in my stomach as I looked at the stairs. Something was wrong. Something was very wrong. I walked up the stairs as slowly as I could, steeling myself for whatever I was about to find.

When I got to the second-floor landing, I saw that the light was on in my bedroom, and the door was slightly ajar. I opened the door, my heart racing, and there she was, sitting on my bed, holding *this* diary. Her face was streaked with tears. She must have been sitting there for some time, reading the whole goddamn thing, because the tears had already dried and on her face there wasn't any sadness, only rage.

"You've been keeping a fucking diary?" she asked, in a cold, angry voice I'd never heard her use before. "You've been keeping a diary this whole time? And writing about me?"

I froze. I didn't know what to say. I couldn't deny it—of course I'd been writing about her. And then my stomach sank. *Oh shit,* I thought, *now she knows I went through her stuff.* "I . . ."

"You fucking bitch," she snarled. And then, still holding my diary, she stormed out onto the patio and headed straight for the edge. I ran after her.

"It's just a stupid diary, Cat," I said. "Nobody is ever going to read it. *You're* not supposed to read it."

"I'm a very private person, Lora. I don't just let people into my life. Especially not people who are going to *write about everything I do.* I can't believe you would betray me like this. After everything I've done for you. After everything I've given you."

I started to get defensive. "Why did you even read my diary? Why were you even going through my things?"

She laughed and shook her head. "You're a fucking hypocrite, Lora," she said, opening the diary. She flipped to a page—I knew the exact page, goddammit—and started reading from it: "'I took the wig out of the closet and turned to face the mirror. I pulled my hair up, put the wig on my head, and took off my glasses. There, staring back at me, was Cat Wolff.'"

She slammed the diary shut. "And you have the audacity to ask me why I'm going through your things? Are you fucking kidding me? You betrayed me, Lora. You used me."

"I'm sorry, Cat," I said, my eyes filling with tears. She was right. I had. I had betrayed her. I had broken her trust. There was no way I could defend myself, not against that. "I'm so sorry. I shouldn't have done it."

"Do you have any idea how much I've done for you?" she screamed. "You would be *nothing* without me! *Nothing!* You would be in Pennsylvania, working at Target, living with your stupid little redneck parents. You would be *nothing*! You *are nothing*!"

With that, she turned and threw my diary off the patio. I screamed and ran to the railing, where I watched my pink notebook fall to the street below. I was in shock for a few moments, then turned back around to face her.

Cat took a deep breath. She couldn't even look at me. "I want you out of here by tomorrow night. I'm not going to let you use me any longer." Without saying another word, she walked back inside, slamming the door shut behind her.

As soon as I knew the coast was clear, I ran across the patio, down the stairs, through the living room and hallway, to the elevator, through the lobby, and out into the busy street. At first, I couldn't find my diary. There were cars and people everywhere, and all I could think about was that all of my most personal, private thoughts could fall into anyone's hands at any moment.

When I finally found it, the cover was water-damaged and nearly ruined, but it was all in one piece. I went back upstairs to my room and carefully set it on the bathroom floor to dry. And, while it dried, I packed my things.

When I'd finished packing, I went back downstairs and tried to talk to her. "Cat, it's me," I said as I stood outside her door and knocked. There was no answer. "Cat," I said again. Desperate to try anything, I opened the door. But the room was empty, and the lights were off. I had no idea where she'd gone.

I had to find an apartment in less than twenty-four hours. I went on Craigslist and called and emailed about every listing. I called hotels. I called brokers. I tried everything I could think of. Against all odds, I found a place in the East Village, and rented it sight unseen. From the photos, I could tell it wasn't the fanciest, and it was a bit more expensive than I could afford, but it's a one-bedroom with an updated kitchen and it's really close to a park.

Cat had given me $15,000 as an advance on the advance, and I would have been completely screwed if she hadn't. Luckily it was just enough to pay for the first month's rent, last month's rent, and security deposit on the new apartment *and* leave me some for bills and groceries.

When I left, I saw Bob standing next to his SUV outside the entrance to The Plaza. As I passed, I waved goodbye. He couldn't even look at me. Cat was still nowhere to be found.

And just like that, it was over.

I didn't even get to say goodbye to the place I'd called home for almost a year. I knew it was all going to end at some point. I had been painfully aware of this underlying uncertainty, painfully aware that it was only temporary, painfully aware that I was at Cat's mercy the whole time—I just never thought it would happen this way. I don't even know how to feel about it all. I'm numb. Completely numb and in shock and wishing that I could go back in time and stop it all from happening.

I don't know what happens next.

From: Coinbase
To: Cat Wolff
Subject: Your Bitcoin Purchase
Date: May 16, 2018

Congratulations!

You purchased 27.87 Bitcoins (BTC) for $250,000 USD. Those funds are now available in your account.

Thank you for the purchase.

The Diary of Lora Ricci

May 23, 2018

I'm so angry. So angry that I'm literally shaking. I don't know why this is happening. I don't understand what went wrong. I don't know what's going on. I don't know what Cat is thinking.

Is she even thinking?

Honestly, it doesn't make any sense. What the hell is wrong with her? What the hell just happened? We got the book deal. We got hundreds of thousands of dollars in cash for the first installment of the advance. We were going to get a *million* more. All we had to do was write a few more stories. That's all we had to do!

Why is she throwing it all away?

I don't understand what happened.

I mean, I understand why she was mad at me, but I really thought she would cool off and that things would somewhat go back to normal. I gave her space. A *lot* of space. Weeks of space. And during that time, I heard nothing.

So, a few days ago, I texted her. She didn't reply.

Then again.

Again, no reply.

Finally, yesterday, I was sick of waiting. I got on the train and headed for The Plaza. At that point, I was willing to do whatever it took to get our work back on track. I'd beg for her forgiveness. I'd offer to write even more things for her. I'd burn my diary. I'd do anything. *Anything.* But I couldn't wait anymore.

When I got to her suite, I rang the doorbell. No answer.

I waited a few minutes and then rang it again.

Nothing.

"Cat?" I yelled. "Cat, it's me, Lora. Let me in!"

Again, nothing.

"Cat!" I yelled again.

A stream of worst-case scenarios flew through my mind. What if something had happened to her? What if she'd taken a bunch of drugs and overdosed? What if she'd gotten drunk and had fallen in the shower? What if someone had robbed her? What if she'd been murdered? What if she was about to die in her room and if I didn't save her in two minutes, she would be gone forever?

I banged my fists against the door, and, to my surprise, it swung open.

I couldn't believe what I saw. There were moving boxes everywhere. So many of them that they completely filled the entryway and the hallway. I pushed my way through, trying to get to her bedroom, and looked through the boxes that were sitting on top of the piles. It was all there—her wigs, her weird costumes, her expensive shoes, the tens of thousands of dollars' worth of handbags, jewelry, books.

"Cat?" I yelled. "Cat!"

I went to her bedroom and opened the door. She was standing there, AirPods in her ears, bobbing her head to the music as she pulled dresses from their hangers and stuffed them into boxes.

"Cat!" I screamed as loud as I could, waving my arms in the air.

She looked up and took one of her AirPods out, then reached into her shirt, pulled her phone out of her bra, and paused the music.

"What do you want?" she asked.

"What's going on?"

"What do you mean?"

"I've been calling you and texting you for weeks, and you've been ignoring me. And now all your stuff is packed . . ."

"Oh, I'm leaving."

"*Leaving?*" I asked, incredulous. "Where are you going? Why didn't you tell me?"

She pulled a drawer out of the dresser and carried it to her bed. "It doesn't concern you."

"But you can't leave! We have a book to finish!"

Cat laughed as she dumped the contents of the drawer into a box. "You're kidding, right?" She threw her head back and laughed so hard it scared me.

"I don't get it," I said quietly.

"We're not writing the book, Lora."

"Is this because of the diary? I'm so sorry, Cat. I'll destroy it. I never meant to—"

"God, you are so self-centered," she said, interrupting me. "It's not about your fucking diary." She threw the drawer against the wall, which startled me so badly I jumped.

"We just signed a contract. We worked so hard to get here. And we got paid, we got paid so much money to write it . . ."

I followed her out of the bedroom, and my jaw dropped when I saw the living room. The place was *trashed.* There was actual garbage everywhere—old moldy food, empty bottles. Cat walked to the dining room table, then pushed a pile of trash off the table and onto the floor as she searched for something. Finally, she found what she was looking for: her checkbook. Then she dug around the trash some more until she found a pen. "Now, how much do I owe you? For the rest of the advance. I already gave you fifteen thousand. How much?"

"Are you on drugs?" I asked.

"Twenty thousand?"

"Are you having, like, a nervous breakdown or something?"

"Fifty thousand?"

"We can get you some help, Cat. It's not a big deal. Everyone needs help. We can call your brother . . ."

Cat laughed. "Oh god, don't tell me you were going to ask for *more* than fifty thousand! Lora, that's just exploitation."

"I . . ."

She wrote out a check. "I can't believe you really thought we were going to write a fucking book. Of course we're not writing a book. God, you are *so naïve* sometimes. You are so goddamn naïve it hurts."

Her words stung. They bit at me so hard I could almost physically feel them tearing at my heart. I started to cry.

She looked down at her checkbook and wrote me a check, then ripped it out and shoved it in my face. "Here," she snarled. "This should be enough for your troubles."

I looked at the check. $65,000.

"Look, I need you to leave now," she said. "I don't have much time, okay? They're after me, and they're going to get me any moment."

"What are you talking about? Who is after you?"

None of it made any sense; nothing was making sense—everything was wrong, so wrong. I looked at her closely. There was something about her, something about the look on her face. Something was going on here. There was something she wasn't telling me.

I stood there, frozen, tears falling down my face.

She pointed to the door. "I said you should go."

"Are you in some kind of trouble?"

She didn't answer. Instead, she grabbed my arm and pulled me to the front door, opened it, and pushed me out into the hallway. Then she grabbed both of my arms, looked me in the eyes, and said, "Whatever happens, don't talk to anyone, and don't you dare come looking for me. You can't know where I am, you can't know where I went, you can't know anything. If anyone asks about me, pretend you don't know what they're talking about. I'm serious, Lora—it's for your own good. Now go. Get the hell out of here. I never want to see your face again."

She slammed the door in my face.

I never want to see your face again.

That was the last thing she said to me.

As I made my way out of the hotel, my brain played everything she'd said on repeat. I felt completely numb. Cat had lost her fucking mind. My life had been turned completely upside down.

Oh, but it gets worse. Much worse.

Early this morning, I walked to the bank and tried to deposit the check. The teller examined the check for a moment, then said she needed to get her supervisor. A few minutes later, she returned with her manager. They whispered to each other for a few moments, and then the supervisor stepped up to the window.

"There's a slight problem with your check, Ms. Ricci," he said.

"Why can't you just deposit it into my account?" I asked. "I don't understand."

He took a deep breath. "I'm afraid we can't do that. The check is fake."

"What?" The alarm bells were going off in my head.

No, no, no, no. This can't be happening . . .

"Yes," he said. "It's a counterfeit check."

"No, my friend wouldn't do that," I insisted. "She's so rich. Her dad is a billionaire. Franz Wolff—that's his name. You can google him."

"I'm sorry, but no."

"Can you try again?"

"Ms. Ricci . . ." I could tell he was losing his patience, but I didn't care. Without that money, I was completely screwed. I *am* completely screwed! I need that money. Cat owes me that money! That money belongs to me!

"Just give it back to me, okay?" I pleaded. "I'll take it elsewhere."

The supervisor shook his head. "I'm sorry, Ms. Ricci, but we can't do that. We need to report it to law enforcement."

"No, no, no," I shouted. "No, you don't get it. That's *my* money. I need it. She owes me that money."

The supervisor and the teller exchanged glances. "The police will be in touch," the supervisor said.

At that point, I knew it was over. And I was furious.

I marched over to The Plaza and tried to go to Cat's room, but the concierge stopped me. "I'm sorry, ma'am," he said, "but she checked out this morning."

Goddammit, Cat.

Goddammit.

From: Nikolay Dorokhov
To: Olesya Dorokhova
Subject: Fwd: Your Reservation
Date: May 24, 2018

here you go

will be waiting for you

From: Airbnb

To: Nikolay Dorokhov

Subject: Your Reservation

Date: May 24, 2018

Customer Receipt

Guest: Kira Leonova

Travel Destination: Moscow, Russia

Travel Property: Cozy Apartment for One

Accommodation Type: Entire Apartment

Nights: 36

Arrive: Wed, July 4, 2018

View Itinerary

House Rules:

. . .

From: Olesya Dorokhova
To: Nikolay Dorokhov
Subject: Re: Fwd: Your Reservation
Date: May 24, 2018

Kolya—

I'm going dark now.

See you on the other side.

—Olesya

Jenée Parker | 05–24–2018 6:01 PM
    She's on the run

Jenée Parker | 05–24–2018 6:03 PM
    Do we have what we need?

Amanda Harris | 05–24–2018 6:15 PM
    I'm getting it all ready now

Amanda Harris | 05–24–2018 6:18 PM
    How much time do we have?

Jenée Parker | 05–24–2018 6:20 PM
    She has a ticket for tomorrow morning

Amanda Harris | 05–24–2018 6:28 PM
    Okay good that gives us enough time

Jenée Parker | 05–24–2018 6:30 PM
    But do we have what we need?

Amanda Harris | 05–24–2018 6:32 PM
    We have enough on IW and SB charges for sure

Amanda Harris | 05–24–2018 6:33 PM
    I'm still finishing DR

Amanda Harris | 05–24–2018 6:34 PM
    So yes

Amanda Harris | 05–24–2018 6:34 PM
    We have what we need

THE NEW YORK TIMES | NEW YORK

Manhattan Con Artist Olesya Dorokhova Arrested

By Jeffrey Blum

May 25, 2018

According to the authorities, for over five years a Russian swindler by the name of Olesya Dorokhova allegedly posed as an Austrian heiress and Manhattan socialite named "Cat Wolff." As Ms. Wolff, Ms. Dorokhova made her way through the worlds of art, fashion, media and literature, working as an editor at *ELLE* magazine, publishing a viral short story in *The New Yorker* and obtaining a book deal with Penguin Press.

Perhaps even more shocking are the allegations that "Cat Wolff" was not Ms. Dorokhova's only alias. According to a statement from Eleanor Wexler, a spokeswoman for the United States attorney's office, Ms. Dorokhova also posed as a fashion designer–turned-entrepreneur named "Sophie Bisset." Ms. Wexler also stated that her office believed Ms. Dorokhova had been operating under several other aliases, but that due to the ongoing nature of the investigation, she would not be releasing those names at this time.

Ms. Dorokhova is alleged to have lied about many details in addition to her name, including her age and nationality. As Cat Wolff, she posed as a 32-year-old woman from Austria. As Sophie Bisset, she posed as a 27-year-old woman from France. But, according to the authorities, Olesya Dorokhova is really 43 years old and was born and raised in Russia.

The FBI arrested Ms. Dorokhova early this morning at Kennedy airport as she attempted to board an Aeroflot flight to Moscow. She has been charged with bank fraud, wire fraud and securities fraud and is awaiting trial.

This is a developing story and will be updated throughout the day.

From: Coinbase
To: Cat Wolff
Subject: Your account has been frozen
Date: May 25, 2018

This is a notification that your account has been frozen and we have restricted your access to the funds in your account.

For more information, please refer to the prohibited use section of our User Agreement.

PART 4

the escape

The Diary of Lora Ricci

May 25, 2018

Holy shit.

Cat was arrested this morning trying to board a flight to Russia, and now her face is plastered all over the news and social media. And that's not even the most shocking thing. Apparently, she's been lying about who she is this whole time. She's not a wealthy Austrian heiress—no, not even close. She's a forty-something-year-old Russian con artist named "Olesya Dorokhova."

What the actual fuck?!

Seriously: what the fuck???????!!!!!!!!!

I'm trying to wrap my head around it all, but I can't. It's too crazy. It's way too crazy.

I don't know what to do.

Should I go to the police? Would they help me get the money Cat owes me? Or—pretty scary thought here—would they suspect me of being involved with her in an illegal way? Would they suspect I was her accomplice??

Without that money, I'm totally screwed. My new apartment costs $3,500 a month. How am I going to pay for rent? The electric bill? Food? There's no way I'll be able to find a job that will pay me enough to cover all this stuff.

Hah, just imagine me trying to sell myself in interviews right now: *Hi, my name is Lora Ricci. I'm a college dropout and the gullible victim of a famous con artist. You'll pay me $100,000 a year, right?*

Like I said: I'm totally screwed.

katrine baker ✨ omg can you believe I knew #manhattanscammer Cat 😼 Wolff aka Olesya Dorokhova??!! We worked at ELLE 💄💅👜 together. She scammed me too, making me believe she was a real heiress. I made a video about my experiences with the #manhattanscammer for my youtube channel. Link in bio. ✨ #ellemagazine #elle #manhattanswindler #manhattanscammer #catwolff #olesyadorokhova #scamartist #fashion #nyc #beauty #youtube

THE NEW YORK TIMES | NEW YORK

Manhattan Con Artist Olesya Dorokhova Escapes From Police

By Teresa Calloway and Jeffrey Blum

May 25, 2018

Olesya Dorokhova, the alleged Russian con artist who went by the alias "Cat Wolff" and pretended to be an Austrian heiress, escaped from the FBI Friday morning. Ms. Dorokhova, who had been arrested by the FBI at John F. Kennedy International Airport, had been charged with bank fraud, wire fraud and securities fraud.

According to an FBI spokeswoman, Ms. Dorokhova escaped before the FBI was able to transport her to Rikers Island. While still at JFK, only minutes after her arrest, Ms. Dorokhova went to the restroom, accompanied by an FBI agent (whose name has not yet been released). When neither Ms. Dorokhova nor the FBI agent returned after fifteen minutes, additional FBI agents entered the restroom, where they discovered the agent blindfolded, gagged and handcuffed with zip ties in a bathroom stall. Ms. Dorokhova was nowhere to be found.

An airport-wide search did not turn up Ms. Dorokhova, and she has not been seen on any airport surveillance footage. Her status and location are still unknown.

This is a developing story and will be updated throughout the day.

The Diary of Lora Ricci

May 27, 2018

Ever since I heard about Cat's escape, I've been sitting in my apartment, staring at the front door, expecting that, at any moment, the police will barge in looking for her.

I keep checking my phone and email to see if she'll reach out to me. I don't know *why* I expect to hear from her, but I don't know who else she would go to. I know she has a lot of acquaintances, but I'm not so sure she has any friends—besides me.

But were we ever really friends? I thought we were. I really did. Even with the arguments and the jealousy and the resentment, I really thought . . . I mean, she's basically the only person I've spoken to for an entire year. I told her all my secrets. She probably knows more about me than anyone else on this earth.

And I thought I knew her, too. Didn't I? Yes, she was closed off and definitely had secrets of her own—secrets she'd never share with me. But there were times she let her guard down, took her armor off, and there was a real, vulnerable person underneath. And maybe I didn't know everything about her, but *that* was the real Cat (or Olesya, or whatever the hell her name is).

I didn't know she was a con artist. I didn't know she was breaking the law. I didn't—I don't—know how many people she scammed, manipulated, and betrayed. And I keep asking myself: Was I one of her victims, or was I an unwitting accomplice? Was she trying to do something real and honest and genuine all this time, or were the story and the book and the ghostwriting job all just a con? But who was she even trying to scam? Me? The literary world? Everyone?

I don't understand any of it, and it makes me feel sick. I mean, just look at everything I did: I dropped out of school, estranged myself from my parents, wrote all these stories and put Cat's name on them. I did those things because I trusted her, but still: *I* did them. Didn't I? Didn't I have free will? Didn't I have the opportunity to choose not to lie to my parents, not to lie to my friends, not to lie to the world?

Was I manipulated? Or did I simply not have any other choice?

I mean, realistically, what else was I going to do? I didn't *want* to lie to my parents. I didn't *want* to use Cat's name to get my writing into the world. It was the only way I could do what I wanted to do—it was the only way I could *write*. And if that meant lying, then so be it. God, I didn't even think twice about it, really. It was either go down this path with Cat, or—or what? I had no other options! I swear, I had no other options!!! It wasn't about ego, it was about *survival*. Wasn't it??? If I'd had any other options, I wouldn't have done those things to begin with. Right?????

But now I'm afraid. Afraid because I might have dug myself into a hole so deep that I can never climb out of it. What if people find out about me and think I'm a criminal? What if the police come after me? What if my parents think I'm a con artist, too?

It never felt right. Remember how angry and resentful I felt about Cat's name going on *my* writing and Cat getting all the praise for what *I* had done? I knew there was something terribly wrong, and I should have paid attention to what my subconscious was basically screaming at me. Why didn't I listen to myself???

And now I'm back to square one. No, it's worse than that. God, I am *way* worse off than I was before I got myself into this whole mess. I have an apartment I can't pay for. I worked for a criminal. I cut myself off from everyone who loved and cared about me: my friends, my parents, my grandparents—everyone. I'm broke and alone and afraid and I don't know how I'm ever going to sleep again.

BUSINESS INSIDER

The founder of Sidelines Fashion lied about her age in an effort to be included in articles about young startup founders

According to reporting by *The New York Times,* "Sophie Bisset" is an alias of Olesya Dorokhova, who apparently lied to investors and reporters about her name and age in an effort to be included in articles about young startup founders and on the *Forbes* 30 Under 30 list.

In 2017, Olesya Dorokhova (aka "Sophie Bisset"), whose company Sidelines Fashion has received a reported $2 million in funding from firms like Y Combinator, Baylands Capital, and Pinpoint Ventures earlier this year, previously reported to *Forbes* and *Fortune* that she was 27. However, according to *The New York Times,* Olesya Dorokhova is actually 43.

From: Brandon Barnes
To: Sophie Bisset
Subject: Circling Back
Date: June 1, 2018

Hello Sophie,

I saw your name trending on Twitter and thought I should circle back with you. Are you looking for someone to lead your next round? I'd love to throw our name into the running.

Let me know how I can be helpful.

All best,

Brandon

From: Mail Delivery Subsystem
To: Brandon Barnes
Subject: Re: Circling Back
Date: June 1, 2018

Your message wasn't delivered to <sophie@sidelines-fashion.com> because the domain sidelines-fashion.com couldn't be found. Check for typos or unnecessary spaces and try again.

The Diary of Lora Ricci

June 4, 2018

I have to do something. I can't just sit around and wait for the police to show up at my door and either evict me or arrest me for helping Cat.

I have to do something.

I have to do something *now.*

God, I don't know what to do.

WHAT SHOULD I DO?!

From: Lora Ricci
To: Margot Fletcher
Subject: Horse Girl Book
Date: June 5, 2018

Hi Margot,

My name is Lora Ricci. I don't know if you've ever heard my name before or even know who I am, but I was Cat Wolff's ghostwriter. We had an arrangement that I would help her write the stories and the book.

I'm guessing you've heard the news about Cat's arrest and escape. Right before she was arrested, she told me we weren't going to publish the book. She then wrote me a bad check for my part of the advance.

I don't know what's happening to the book if Cat isn't going to write it and is on the run from the law, but I still want to write it. I've put so much work into these stories and I care about them so much.

I want to publish them.

Will you help me?

Best,

Lora

From: Margot Fletcher
To: Lora Ricci
Subject: Re: Horse Girl Book
Date: June 5, 2018

Dear Lora,

Thank you for reaching out. I am so sorry to hear of your circumstances.

This is a very delicate and complicated situation, one that will take a great deal of sorting out and that I am not entirely sure I understand. However, I have spoken with Penguin and I believe we can resolve this in a way that will make both you and the publisher happy.

Are you available to meet at my office later today? I can meet any time from 2:00–4:00pm.

Sincerely,

M.

From: Lora Ricci
To: Margot Fletcher
Subject: Re: Re: Horse Girl Book
Date: June 5, 2018

Hi Margot!

Yes, I can be there at 3.

Thank you so much!

See you soon!!

Best,

Lora

The Diary of Lora Ricci

June 5, 2018

I've spent the past week freaking out, unable to sleep, having panic attack after panic attack. I've barely even left my apartment. I can't. What if the police are looking for me? What if the press is trying to find me? I keep watching the news—partly to see if there are any updates about Cat, and partly because I want to know if my name comes up. News about the book is all over TV, but the media doesn't seem to know I was involved. Not yet. It's probably just a matter of time.

In TV shows, whenever there's a scandal, the people involved hire some kind of crisis PR professional, whose advice is always "get ahead of the story." I've been thinking and thinking and thinking about how I can save myself, wondering if there's any way I can get ahead of the story, but I have no idea how to do it.

There was only one thing I knew I could do: reach out to Margot and see if there was any possible way I could publish the story collection. I didn't know how I was going to explain everything and convince her that I was the real author of "Horse Girl." But, to my complete surprise, she didn't seem too skeptical when I told her over email. In fact, she replied right away and invited me to her office. As soon as I got her email, I sat down at my laptop and pulled up everything I'd ever written for Cat. I wanted to walk into that office with evidence that *I* could write and that *I* was the writer behind the whole thing. I printed it all off and put it into an enormous three-ring binder, then got on the train and went up to Midtown.

When I arrived at the Fletcher & Ross office, Margot's assistant asked me to have a seat and wait. I sat there for what seemed like forever, thinking about the book and going over a speech in my head about how I was the real author of "Horse Girl." While I waited, Margot's assistant tried to start up some small talk, but I was too stressed to chat and couldn't manage to eke out anything more complicated than one-syllable answers.

Finally, the door to Margot's office opened. Standing in the doorway was a tall, absolutely gorgeous woman who looked like the kind of character Cate Blanchett would play in a movie. "Lora?" she asked in a rich, warm British accent. I nodded, stood up, and hurried over to her.

"Ms. Fletcher," I said, shaking her hand, "it's so good to finally meet you."

"Call me 'Margot,' please," she said, motioning for me to step into her office.

As we made our way to her desk, she looked at me and stopped for a moment. "Have we met before?"

I shook my head. "No, I don't think so," I said. Of course we hadn't met before—if we had, I would have tried to get her to sign me as a client (and probably would have made a complete fool of myself in the process).

"Do you have any brothers or sisters?"

"No, I'm an only child."

She looked wistful for a moment. "It's strange."

"What is?"

"Oh, it's . . . it's nothing. I haven't really been sleeping. All this terrible, terrible news about Cat. And Daphne . . ." Her glance drifted to a wall in her office where enormous framed reproductions of the covers of Daphne Rooney's books were hanging:

"*WYTHE* BY DAPHNE ROONEY," "*THE HAWK* BY DAPHNE ROONEY," and "*MARIGOLD* BY DAPHNE ROONEY."

"What happened to Daphne?" I asked, bewildered.

"The FBI said . . ." she began, before catching herself midsentence. "Never mind."

She walked to her desk—one of those enormous wooden desks with a dozen drawers—and sat down. I settled into one of the chairs facing the desk, and jumped into the monologue I'd been practicing in my head. "Ms. Fletcher—Margot—I'm so sorry that I emailed you out of the blue. I don't even know how to begin to convince you that what I'm telling you is true, but I've brought this binder filled with evidence. I've been working as Cat's secret ghostwriter—"

"Since last fall," she said, interrupting me. "I know, I know. Look, when I started working with Cat, she couldn't write. She was personable and lovely and so *marketable,* but her writing was in serious need of improvement. I really didn't see a future for her in writing unless she had a ghostwriter, and I told her so. And then she showed up one day with something new she had written—it was sometime in August or September, I believe—and I knew she hadn't written it alone. She didn't want to tell me *who* was writing for her, and we fought about it a little, but, frankly, the magazines didn't give a damn and the publishers weren't going to care and I wasn't going to offer answers to questions nobody was asking. A huge mistake, in retrospect, of course, and one I'll regret for many years to come, but the point is, dear, that I believe you."

She took a deep breath, then continued. "Look, I've already smoothed things over with Penguin Press. They've dropped the book and canceled the contract. Between you and me, they seem relieved to have washed their hands of the whole thing. There are some legal issues with the advance, but you needn't worry about a thing—any and all disagreements are between them and Cat. The important thing is that *you* are free to take the stories elsewhere. I definitely think we can make this work, and quickly. I've already spoken to an editor at HarperCollins—you will *adore* him. He's very excited to read the collection, and I believe he'll make us an offer."

I couldn't believe what I was hearing. "Are you serious? That's . . . that's amazing!"

"Yes, yes, it's really quite amazing indeed. I'm thrilled you're happy with it. There is one small thing, however, that he and I discussed."

"What was that?"

"Look, dear, you and I both know that this collection is wonderful and the world will love it, but the issue, of course, is that nobody knows who you are. You don't have a platform, which means that getting this into the hands of readers will be quite a challenge. To put it bluntly, a collection of short stories on its own is not a very exciting prospect for HarperCollins."

"Oh," I said. It was hard not to sound disappointed.

"The truth is, the world wants more of Cat Wolff. The public is enchanted with her, and they want to know more. Who is this woman? How did she accomplish this deception? What was it like to be part of her world?"

"Okay," I said warily, not sure where she was going with this.

"I think if we went to HarperCollins and said we'd like to do both the story collection *and* a memoir about your time with

Cat Wolff, we would be able to secure a deal right away. They would publish your memoir, you'd have a platform *overnight,* and then we would follow that up with your short stories."

I must have been quiet for a while, because I heard Margot clear her throat and say, "Lora? Is this something you're interested in doing?"

"So we would sell two books?"

"Yes."

"And we would publish them under my name?"

"Yes."

"I wouldn't be a ghostwriter?"

"No, of course not."

I smiled with relief. "Yes," I said. "Yes. I'm in."

She said that the next step is for me to write up a short proposal about the memoir. Nothing too detailed—just a few pages summarizing my experience with Cat/Olesya so that the publisher will know the context of what our relationship was and what I'll write about in the memoir. I promised her I'd start writing it tonight, and she promised she'd schedule a meeting with the HarperCollins editor this Friday.

The complete 180 of going from being broke and thinking that I'll never write again to suddenly having a two-book deal of my own is . . . it's . . . it's so . . . God, I don't even know what to think.

After wallowing in this hell of despair, I finally feel some hope. Maybe I won't just get ahead of the story, but I'll be able to tell the story on my own. Prove my innocence. Let the world see that Cat manipulated me, too. Show everyone how she ruined my life. And I'll be able to write. Yes, I can prove to the world that I'm a writer. And not just about my own life, but about fictional lives, too. God, maybe it's not over for me yet.

When I got back to my apartment, I started to write the book proposal, but quickly got pulled into the rabbit hole of news about Cat. I read an article in *The New York Times* about other people she had swindled over the years, and it made me sick to my stomach. I read about how the "Sophie Bisset" thing had been a fraud, and how there was no "Sophie Bisset"—it was just Cat the whole time. She faked it all: the photo shoot, the interview—everything.

I should have known that there was something going on. I should have picked up on at least one of the messed-up things she was doing, and I should have gotten the hell out of there and gone to the police. Right??

Why didn't I see it? Why didn't I do anything about it?

The thing I keep asking myself, the thing that keeps haunting me, is that, on some level, I wonder if I *did* know, but I was unwilling to see things clearly. I keep thinking back to Thanksgiving dinner, when my parents and grandparents told me that there was obviously something not right about Cat. And what did I do? I snapped at them. I defended her. I told them they were wrong about her. Why on earth did I do that? Why did I choose Cat over my family?

I wonder what Mom and Dad are thinking now—now that her name and face are all over the news, now that they know their daughter worked for a criminal, a con artist, a swindler, a hack. They haven't called me at all. Why haven't they called me?

Do they think *I'm* a criminal?

Jenée Parker | 06–05–2018 7:45 PM
We watched Fletcher's office and the Park Ave apartment all day

Jenée Parker | 06–05–2018 7:46 PM
No sign of her

Amanda Harris | 06–05–2018 7:47 PM
Dammit

Amanda Harris | 06–05–2018 7:48 PM
I thought those would be the first places she'd go

Jenée Parker | 06–05–2018 7:49 PM
Same

Jenée Parker | 06–05–2018 7:50 PM
But get this

Jenée Parker | 06–05–2018 7:51 PM
Fletcher only had one meeting the whole day

Amanda Harris | 06–05–2018 7:54 PM
?

Jenée Parker | 06–05–2018 7:57 PM
A young woman, early/mid 20s, long dark hair, glasses

Jenée Parker | 06–05–2018 7:57 PM
We followed her back to her apartment in east village

Jenée Parker | 06–05–2018 7:58 PM
Name on apt lease is Lora Ricci

Amanda Harris | 06–05–2018 7:59 PM
The same one OD wrote the counterfeit check to?

Jenée Parker | 06–05–2018 8:00 PM
The same

Jenée Parker | 06–05–2018 8:01 PM
And you're not going to believe this

Amanda Harris | 06–05–2018 8:03 PM
?

Amanda Harris | 06–05–2018 8:05 PM
???????????

Jenée Parker | 06–05–2018 8:07 PM
It seems she was an intern at Elle last year

Amanda Harris | 06–05–2018 8:10 PM
No way

Jenée Parker | 06–05–2018 8:11 PM
I think SHE is the assistant we've been looking for

Amanda Harris | 06–05–2018 8:14 PM
Wowowowow

Amanda Harris | 06–05–2018 8:15 PM
What do we know about her??

Jenée Parker | 06–05–2018 8:16 PM
Not much

Jenée Parker | 06–05–2018 8:17 PM
(Yet . . .)

From: Margot Fletcher
To: Lora Ricci
Subject: HarperCollins
Date: June 8, 2018

Dear Lora,

I just heard from Mike Eppman at HarperCollins. He was very impressed with you in today's meeting and will be sharing HORSE GIRL AND OTHER ONE-TRICK PONIES and the UNTITLED MEMOIR proposal with his colleagues next week. We should expect to hear from him by Monday evening at the very latest.

In the meantime, I wonder if we shouldn't publish an essay about your experiences with Cat to set the stage for the book news. Perhaps a short op-ed in the *Times* or something in *New York Magazine.* Why don't you call me tomorrow morning and we'll talk it through.

Sincerely,

M.

The Diary of Lora Ricci

June 10, 2018

First, the bad news: I haven't paid my rent, so I'm officially going to be evicted. I think I have some time before they can actually kick me out, so at this point I'm just waiting for it to happen. I've basically given up. I don't think there's anything I can do about it. Not at this point.

And now, finally, some good news: I met with my new editor. It went well. It went really, really, *really* well. He loves the idea of doing the memoir and following it up with the short story collection. I think it's all going to happen—it's just a matter of time. I'm trying not to get *too* excited, though—not until it's all in writing and the contract is signed and the advance is in my bank account.

I had a dream about Cat last night. In it, I was going to meet with a cop or lawyer or someone like that. I got into a cab, and the cabdriver went right past where we were supposed to go and just kept driving. When I started to freak out, the cabdriver turned around and—surprise!—was really Cat in disguise. We drove all the way to the Canadian border, where we abandoned the taxi in the woods and walked for miles and miles until we crossed the border. Once we got there, dream-Lora thought that she and Cat were going to do things together, that they'd be a team, but Cat didn't need Lora anymore. "I just wanted a companion for the journey," she said. "Now get the hell away from me. I never want to see you again."

I woke up in a cold sweat.

I wish I knew where she was. By now, she has probably already left the country. If she was able to scam and scheme for so many years, there's no way she didn't have an exit plan in place. If she could escape from the police, she can escape from anyone.

After my dream, I finally broke down and called Mom and Dad.

I prepared myself for the worst, knowing there was a good chance they'd tell me not to come home, and gave myself a pep talk.

You have done nothing wrong, I told the girl in the bathroom mirror. *Okay, that's not true. You made some mistakes, but you are a good person. You got caught in someone else's web. You are young, you have your whole life ahead of you, and you want it to be a good life. You want your parents to be in your life. You don't want to be alone in the world. You don't want to be like Cat. You want to go home on the weekends and hug your mom and BBQ in the backyard with your dad.*

As the phone rang, I paced in small circles around my bedroom. *Pick up, pick up, pick up,* I pleaded.

It went to voicemail.

I threw my phone down onto my bed and nearly burst into tears, but I swallowed my anger and sadness and managed to calm myself down. Then I sat down on the bed and waited. I must have waited a whole hour. Not a single notification came through.

Finally, I got up to get a glass of water. As soon as I left the room, I heard the phone ring. I sprinted back to my bedroom and answered without even looking at the caller ID.

"Oh my god, I'm so glad you called me back," I said into the phone, feeling a wave of relief wash over me.

"I didn't think you'd want to talk to me." The voice was deeper than the one I'd been expecting. Deeper, and with a fake German accent. My German Scarlett Johansson.

I immediately felt sick to my stomach.

"I'm waiting for a call from my parents," I said.

"Lora, I need you to do something for me," she said. "Please. It's very important. I promise I won't ask you to do anything ever again. But there's a safe in an apartment, on the Upper East Side, and I need to get into it. It's my apartment; it's not like I'm asking you to steal from someone. Now, look, if you go there and open it, I need you to bring me the—"

I was so angry I was shaking. "Go to hell, Cat!" I shouted. Then I hung up the phone.

I looked back at the call log to see where she had called from. The phone said it was an unknown number.

"I'm not going to break into an apartment for you!" I shouted at my phone. "I'm not going to do anything for you—not ever again!"

My eyes filled with tears. Dammit. I'd been trying to be so confident and composed before calling my parents. I wiped my eyes and tried to breathe.

The phone rang again.

This time, I looked at the caller ID. It said MOM.

Thank god.

I burst into tears as soon as I heard her voice.

"Lora," she said gently. "Lora, oh honey, what's going on?"

I couldn't get a word out. I just kept crying, my body shaking from how hard I was sobbing.

Dad was on the call, too. "Hey, kiddo, we heard the news about that Russian lady. Awful stuff, just awful."

"We were going to call you, but we didn't know if you wanted us to," Mom added. "We've been going nuts over here, wondering if you were okay."

"Tell us what happened," Dad said.

"Just give her a minute," Mom said quietly.

When I finally stopped crying, I told them everything. The whole story. This was my chance to come clean. To prove to them—and to myself—that I was *not* like Cat.

I didn't leave a single thing out.

I told them about how I basically failed my classes. How I lost my scholarship. How I alienated my friends at school because I was so ashamed. How I met Cat at *ELLE* and how even though she used me to help with her schemes, I also kind of used her to help me get out of my situation. I told them about the book deal, and how she never intended to write the book. I told them about the wigs, about her father, her brother, about how she'd called me only a few minutes ago and tried to get me to help her get something out of a safe.

I must have been talking for three hours straight before I finally reached the end of the whole story. It felt like the hugest weight had finally been lifted from my shoulders. I could breathe again.

After a few moments of silence, I heard Dad's voice. "We're here for you, kiddo. Tell us what you need."

I looked around the apartment. "I want to come home," I said. "I just want to come home."

"You know, I could really use an extra pair of hands in the garden," Dad said. I could hear him grinning through the phone. "You should see how big some of these veggies are now. We've really got a lot growing."

We came up with a plan. I'll move home around the Fourth of July (or sooner, if I get evicted before then). Dad will take the third off work and drive out here to help me. I'll move back into my old room and I'll finish writing the stories and memoir there. Then I'll figure out what's next. Maybe I'll go back to school. Maybe I won't. It doesn't matter. I don't have to decide right now.

I'm going to be okay.

FEDERAL BUREAU OF INVESTIGATION

DATE OF TRANSCRIPTION: 6/11/2018

LORA E. RICCI was approached while she was walking through Tompkins Square Park in New York, New York. Ricci was advised as to the nature of this investigation and provided the following information.

RICCI stated that she worked with OLESYA DOROKHOVA AKA CAT WOLFF at *ELLE* magazine in the summer of 2017. She advised that OLESYA DOROKHOVA AKA CAT WOLFF approached her and requested her help with research. Ricci provided that OLESYA DOROKHOVA AKA CAT WOLFF told her that she was an Austrian heiress.

RICCI stated that in September, 2017, she began working for OLESYA DOROKHOVA AKA CAT WOLFF as a ghostwriter. Ricci provided that instead of hourly wages or a salary, OLESYA DOROKHOVA AKA CAT WOLFF offered her a room in her suite at The Plaza Hotel in New York, New York. Ricci stated that in September 2017 she moved into The Plaza Hotel with OLESYA DOROKHOVA AKA CAT WOLFF and that she worked for OLESYA DOROKHOVA AKA CAT WOLFF until May 2018.

RICCI advised that as part of her work for OLESYA DOROKHOVA AKA CAT WOLFF, she was the ghostwriter of a short story OLESYA DOROKHOVA AKA CAT WOLFF published in *The New Yorker*. Ricci further stated that after the short story was published, OLESYA DOROKHOVA AKA CAT WOLFF had a book deal and Ricci had the understanding that she would ghostwrite the book. Ricci provided that after the publisher paid OLESYA DOROKHOVA AKA CAT WOLFF for the book, OLESYA DOROKHOVA AKA CAT WOLFF stated to Ricci that there was never any intention to write the book, only to take the money.

RICCI provided that she has not heard from OLESYA DOROKHOVA AKA CAT WOLFF since her arrest. Ricci stated that she will assist in an investigation into OLESYA DOROKHOVA AKA CAT WOLFF.

INVESTIGATION ON: 6/11/2018

At: NEW YORK CITY, NEW YORK

By: SUPERVISORY SPECIAL AGENT JENÉE PARKER

The Diary of Lora Ricci

June 11, 2018

Today was the worst day of my life.

I finally left my apartment to pick up takeout from a restaurant down the street, and as I was walking there, a woman wearing a suit approached me in the park.

"Ms. Ricci?" she asked.

I nodded.

"My name is Jenée Parker. I'm a special agent with the Federal Bureau of Investigation."

Time stopped, and the ground fell out from under me. I couldn't think clearly, I wasn't sure what was happening. I seriously couldn't think of anything to say. The only thing that came out of my mouth was the dumbest possible question: "Am I under arrest?"

"No," she said. She looked around and pointed at some benches in the park. "Why don't we go sit down? I need to ask you some questions."

As I followed her, I felt a wave of anxiety wash over me. *Oh shit. I'm going to be in trouble for not reporting Cat to the police. They think I'm her accomplice. Now I'm going to jail. I'm never going home. I'm never writing a book. What if I end up in prison? Oh my god, what if my parents can't bail me out? What if I get a life sentence? I want to do this all over. I made a mistake, a stupid mistake. I want to start again. I want a second chance. Please, give me a second chance.*

We sat down on a bench in the park.

"Now, I know that you worked with Olesya Dorokhova at *ELLE*. Is that correct?"

"Yes."

"And you were close to her?"

"Yeah, well, sort of. She was hard to really *know*. She was really manipulative, and I don't know how much of what she told me was real or fake, you know?" I was tripping over the words as they came out. "I was her assistant, sort of, more of like her ghostwriter, and I worked with her for a while, but she just lied to me the whole time. I had no idea about any of this stuff in the news, none of it, I just can't believe it's all true, I really don't know what to think about it . . ."

I looked up at the FBI agent.

"Why don't you start from the beginning," she said.

And so, as I'd done with my parents yesterday, I told her everything. *Everything.* This was the universe giving me a second (third? fourth?) chance, and I wasn't going to mess it up this time.

She asked me *so* many questions. I answered as many as I could, but toward the end, the questions were unanswerable. She wanted to know where Cat went, how she escaped, where she could have gone. I kept saying that I didn't know. That I had no idea where she'd be.

Even though it was terrifying to be questioned by the freaking FBI, strangely enough, the whole time I was sitting there, I felt safe. The more I spoke, the more convinced I became of my own innocence, the more I believed that I *had* been scammed and I *had* been a victim and I *had* done nothing wrong.

But then everything went downhill.

The FBI agent had just written down her last note, and then

she turned to me. "Now, if you cooperate with our investigation and agree to testify against Olesya in court, there's a chance you could be granted immunity from prosecution."

My heart stopped.

Shit.

"Immunity from what?"

"Prosecution."

"What prosecution?" I asked, feeling my face grow beet red. My palms got so clammy I had to wipe them on my pants, leaving streaks of sweat where my hands had been. "But I didn't know . . ."

"Ignorance of the law isn't an excuse," the FBI agent said, without a shred of pity or mercy or understanding in her voice. I could tell she'd had this conversation a thousand times before. "But if you testify . . ."

"I can't do that," I insisted, shaking my head. "No, I can't testify in court, I'm sorry. I promise I'll help you, but I can't do *that.*"

"You'd rather risk facing federal criminal charges?"

What was I supposed to say?

The whole walk back to my apartment, I felt like I was going to throw up. Yes, Cat had scammed people, but could I really stand up in front of everyone and *in front of her* and say she was a terrible person? Even worse, did this mean *I had to admit that I had scammed people, too*? Was I a criminal? Was I *really* her accomplice? Would my parents think I was a criminal? Would testifying and being part of the whole case announce to the world that I was a criminal??

The headlines flashed in front of me:

ASSISTANT TURNS ON DOROKHOVA, TELLS ALL.

IN EXCHANGE FOR IMMUNITY, DOROKHOVA ACCOMPLICE TURNS ON RUSSIAN CON ARTIST.

When I got home, I lay down in my bed and cried until I didn't have any tears left. I tried to fall asleep, but I couldn't. I can't.

From: Lora Ricci
To: Cat Wolff
Subject: GO TO HELL CAT
Date: June 12, 2018

The FBI told me I have to testify against you or else I'LL GO TO JAIL.

JAIL, CAT. JAIL.

WHY DID YOU DO THIS TO ME?

I'M ONLY TWENTY-THREE YEARS OLD.

I DON'T DESERVE THIS.

YOU RUINED MY WHOLE LIFE!!!

You turned me into a criminal and I didn't even know it. But YOU knew it. I bet you knew it the whole time. You just didn't care. You never cared. You lied to me. That's all you know how to do: *lie*.

I can't believe I ever thought you were my friend.

I'm so fucking done with you, Cat.

I'm going to tell the whole world what you did.

From: Cat Wolff
To: Lora Ricci
Subject: Re: GO TO HELL CAT
Date: June 12, 2018

Lora:

You've done absolutely nothing wrong, and neither have I. The FBI is just trying to rattle you. Don't listen to them. Don't talk to them, either.

This is all just a terrible misunderstanding, I promise. I'll explain everything later.

Cat Wolff

From: Lora Ricci
To: Jenée Parker (FBI)
Subject: Fwd: Re: GO TO HELL CAT
Date: June 12, 2018

OMG she just lies and lies and deflects and lies some more. It's like she is PHYSICALLY INCAPABLE of telling the truth!

I'll testify against her. I don't care. I just want her to stop lying and stop hurting people.

Everyone will know tomorrow. I'll tell the whole world.

. . .

[Show forwarded content]

From: Jenée Parker (FBI)
To: Lora Ricci
BCC: Amanda Harris
Subject: Re: Fwd: Re: GO TO HELL CAT
Date: June 12, 2018

It's critically important that you don't email Ms. Dorokhova again without first consulting with me.

She's facing federal criminal charges okay?

All the best,

Jenée
SSA Jenée Parker

Amanda Harris | 06–12–2018 10:03 PM
What on earth is Ricci talking about?

Amanda Harris | 06–12–2018 10:03 PM
"tell the whole world"???

Jenée Parker | 06–12–2018 10:04 PM
Unclear

Jenée Parker | 06–12–2018 10:05 PM
I'll find out

From: Jenée Parker (FBI)
To: Lora Ricci
BCC: Amanda Harris
Subject: Re: Re: Fwd: Re: GO TO HELL CAT
Date: June 12, 2018

Hi Ms. Ricci,

Could you please clarify: what do you mean by "Everyone will know tomorrow"?

All the best,

Jenée
SSA Jenée Parker

Amanda Harris | 06-12-2018 10:31 PM

??????????

Jenée Parker | 06-12-2018 10:37 PM

NEW YORK MAGAZINE

I Wrote "Horse Girl"

By Lora Ricci

June 13, 2018

On May 25, Olesya Dorokhova was arrested by the FBI and charged with bank fraud, wire fraud, and securities fraud. Her name and face were plastered all over the news, accompanied by a wide range of stories about the thefts and scams she had perpetuated. According to the FBI, she had spent her entire adult life using myriad aliases and posing as everything from a fashion designer to a wealthy heiress. Some people knew her as Olesya Dorokhova. Others knew her as Sophie Bisset. I knew her as Cat Wolff. And I was her ghostwriter.

We met the summer I was an intern at *ELLE*, when she worked there as a contributing editor. Before we met, I had heard of—and about—her from the other interns. She was fashionable, unfathomably wealthy, the heir to an immense clean energy fortune, and everyone wanted to work with her. Even more than that, everyone wanted to *be* her. She was magnetic; she was distant and cool in a way that made everyone want to get close to her. But she wouldn't let anyone get close to her—until she met me.

At the time, I believed she chose me because she thought we were kindred spirits. Little did I know, she had chosen me as an unwitting accomplice in her newest scam because I was young, impressionable, naïve, and desperate to become a writer. At the time, I had no idea she wasn't who she said she was, or that "Cat Wolff" wasn't her real name.

One day, she asked me to help her with research for a piece, and as we worked together over the next several months, she spun an intricate web of lies about the work she was doing and the people she was interviewing. She pretended to interview a fashion designer–turned-entrepreneur named Sophie Bisset, and even recorded fake interviews of the two of them talking—Cat in her deep German accent, Sophie speaking in her high-pitched French accent. "Sophie Bisset," of course, was just another one of Olesya Dorokhova's aliases.

I was studying English and journalism at NYU, about to start my senior year in the fall. While working together, I told Cat about my dreams of becoming a writer. Along the way, we discovered that we made a great writing team. Cat was creative in the way that only came from time and experience, and I could write in a way that didn't come to her naturally. "Together," Cat said, we made "a great writer." And so, when my internship came to an end, Cat approached me with an offer she knew I couldn't refuse.

It was her dream, she said, to publish fiction. She wanted to write short stories, novels, screenplays; she had so many ideas, she said, but she needed someone who could translate the visions in her head into stories on the page.

And so we struck a deal: I would write a short story, we would publish it under her name, and then we would use that short story to land a book deal. The book, she said, would be published in her name. There was just one catch, however. Cat insisted it was a full-time job, so if I wanted to write with her, I would have to drop out of school. And not just for a semester, or for a year, but indefinitely.

I shouldn't have agreed. I shouldn't have dropped out of school. I should have registered for classes, finished my degree, and applied to MFA programs. But I wanted to be a writer so badly that I couldn't see past my own short-term dreams or my own short-term fears. The trouble was, I had a secret of my own, one that I had let her in on. One that only she knew.

I'd been a straight-A student my whole life. School had always been easy for me, and I'd never really had to work to prove myself—until my junior year of college, when I transferred to NYU. I wasn't ready for the difficult upper-level classes, and my grades betrayed my lack of preparation. Surrounded by competitive, high-performing classmates, I was deeply embarrassed and isolated myself from everyone—my friends, my teachers, and my family. In retrospect, it was a very minor problem, and all I had to do to fix it was return to school in the fall and ask for help. But my problem felt insurmountable. Cat was offering me a way out, and I took it.

Before I realized what was happening, I was drawn into her world. It would have felt like a fairy tale if it hadn't been so jarring. I moved into the famous Plaza Hotel with her, where we lived like royalty. I ate at fancy restaurants with her every day, never paying for a single meal. At five in the morning, Cat's personal trainer did a 1.5-hour-long personal class with her, and she had psychiatrists, massage therapists, doctors, dermatologists, hairstylists, and makeup artists on call 24/7.

And the money—the money was everywhere, though I never really understood where it came from or why there was so much of it. Cat carried a thick pile of $100 bills with her, which she left everywhere and gave to everyone: the hotel maids, the bartenders, the coffee shop baristas, the wait-staff, the people who delivered her Seamless orders. There was never any doubt in my mind that she was unbelievably wealthy, because her wealth was constantly on display—as were clues to her secrets.

There were strange calls on the three different phones she carried with her at all times. Meetings at odd times, even in the middle of the night. Then there were her closets, filled with dozens of wigs of all colors and styles, outfits of every size, and even what appeared to be fake noses, a fake pregnancy bodysuit, and more.

The whole time I was living at The Plaza, I was writing. Cat would send me her ideas, and then I'd work day and night to turn them into something good. I must have written thirty stories before I wrote "the one." I wrote about an incident that had happened to me, and wrote it as fiction. I added much more drama to it, raised the stakes, and invented an ending, but the basic plot was what I'd experienced the summer after my freshman year at community college.

Cat loved it, and so did the rest of the world. The piece went viral—with Cat's name on it—and before I knew it, we had a book deal. I couldn't believe my luck. I daydreamed about the book, about seeing it on bookshelves everywhere, about it turning out so well that eventually people would learn that

I had written it and that I would finally get to publish a book under my own name.

When I took my book ideas to Cat, she laughed in my face and broke the news to me: she had no intention of us actually writing the book. She gave me a check—my portion of the advance—and then told me to get out of her life. When I tried to cash the check, the bank told me it was fraudulent. Everything, it turned out, was a scam, a way to drive up interest in the book and get the highest advance possible so she could take the cash and run. And run she did, as fast as she could, but it wasn't fast enough. She was arrested a few days after I last saw her.

I was scammed the same way she scammed so many others all over the world, and she preyed upon me because she knew that I was desperate and weak and isolated and insecure. I felt numb, shell-shocked, horrified—I still do. I lost a year of my life, I dropped out of school, I gave up everything. I'll never get that time back. My entire future is incredibly uncertain. All I can do now is use my own words to tell my own story.

I certainly wasn't the first person she scammed, but I hope I was the last.

katrine baker ✨ Reading this brought such a rush of emotions. I interned with Lora at Elle the summer when she met #manhattanswindler Cat 🙀 Wolff aka Olesya Dorokhova. She completely dropped off the face of the 🌎. I thought she had gotten in a car accident or something, but it turns out she actually left school to be a ghostwriter 👻 and write Cat's book 📖 New video on my youtube channel about my experiences with Lora and Cat. Link in bio. ✨ #friends #ellemagazine #elle #manhattanscammer #catwolff #olesyadorokhova #loraricci #scam #fashion #nyc #beauty

PUBLISHERS WEEKLY

DEAL OF THE WEEK

Ricci Double Debut Lands at Harper for Seven Figures

By Andy Kirkwood | June 15, 2018

Short story collection *Horse Girl and Other One-Trick Ponies* and an untitled memoir by **Lora Ricci** sold to HarperCollins for a sum rumored to be in the seven-figure range. The same short story collection had previously been sold to Penguin Press by **Cat Wolff**, but the deal was canceled after it was revealed that "Cat Wolff" was an alias for the con artist Olesya Dorokhova, and that "Horse Girl," the viral *New Yorker* short story that inspired the collection, had been ghostwritten by New York University undergraduate student Lora Ricci. The author was represented by **Margot Fletcher** of Fletcher & Ross, who sold North American rights, in a two-book deal, to **Michael Eppman**, senior editor at Harper.

From: Lora Ricci
To: Cat Wolff
Subject: (no subject)
Date: June 16, 2018

Hi Cat,

By now you've probably read my essay.

Look, I talked to the FBI, and they said if you turn yourself in now, things will be a lot better than if they have to come find you.

They said you can cut a deal with the prosecutor or something.

Please let them help you.

Please.

Best,

Lora

From: Lora Ricci
To: Cat Wolff
Subject: Re:
Date: June 18, 2018

Please, Cat. Please turn yourself in.

I don't want anything bad to happen to you. I know you want to have a normal life. I know you don't want to spend the rest of your life in jail. The FBI say they can still make that happen.

Please call me. I'm here, I can help you. Please let me help you!!

From: Lora Ricci
To: Cat Wolff
Subject: Re: Re:
Date: June 20, 2018

CAT YOU HAVE TO TURN YOURSELF IN!!!!

PLEASE!!!!

BEFORE IT'S TOO LATE!!!!!!

The Diary of Lora Ricci

June 21, 2018

I knew Cat must have read the article. I knew she would feel betrayed, and that my betrayal must have cut her to the core. At this point, she knew that the police were after her and that I'd been talking to the FBI. But what choice had she given me?

I'd been staying up late every night, reading the articles that kept coming out about all of the people she swindled. I hoped that they would make me angry at her all over again, that I'd stop feeling bad for ratting her out, that I'd stop feeling sick to my stomach whenever I pictured her reading my essay. But with every new piece I read, I just felt worse. Each tale about some terrible thing she'd done just made me miss her more and hate her less, because I know she's probably going to spend the rest of her life in prison.

I kept emailing her. I begged her to call me, I begged her to turn herself in. She never replied.

I wanted to tell her that we could find a way to get her out of this mess, and that I was going to help her. But she has to make it right. She can't keep scamming and swindling and lying. She has to make up for what she did and pay it all back.

I was absolutely sure I would never see her again. Even so, my head was filled with daydreams about confronting her. I rehearsed what I would say, exactly how I would say it, how I would try to make her *see* how much she had hurt me. I wanted her to feel bad, and in some of the daydreams, I succeeded: she'd cry and tell me how sorry she was, and we'd call the FBI together and she'd turn herself in. In others, I'd fail: she'd laugh in my face and walk out the door.

Then, last night, I was sitting on my bed with my laptop, working on my memoir, when I heard someone buzz my apartment. At first, I thought it was food delivery, but then I remembered I hadn't ordered anything. I walked to the intercom, half expecting it to be the FBI.

And then I heard her voice.

"Lora! It's me. It's Olesya. Please, let me in. I need to see you. Please."

Olesya.

My heart stopped for a moment and I froze. I didn't know what to do. Pretend I wasn't home? Call the police? Let her up and hide her in here until they stopped looking for her?

Before I could make up my mind, I heard her voice again.

"Lora, *please.*"

I buzzed her in.

The three or four minutes it took her to walk up the stairs felt like an eternity. I unlocked the door, sat down on my couch, and stared at the doorknob, waiting for it to turn. I'd had so much I'd wanted to say to her, but now that she was on her way up, now that I'd soon be face-to-face with her, my mind was completely blank.

She knocked.

"It's open," I said, but she didn't hear me. "It's open!" I shouted.

The door opened, and she came in, smelling awful and looking like a complete mess. Her clothes were filthy, her hair was greasy and tangled, and her mascara was running down her face in small black streams. At first, I thought that her mascara was just running because she'd been caught in rain or something, but the moment she said my name, I realized she was crying.

"Lora, I . . ." she began. There was no ambiguous accent, there was no fake deep raspy voice. It was the first time I'd ever heard her real voice, with its thick Russian accent. It was also the first time I'd ever actually seen her cry.

I tried to open my mouth to speak, tried to force some—*any*—words out, but my mind was still blank. Instead, I walked to her and helped her out of her clothes. I went to my closet and pulled out some pajamas, underwear, socks, and a towel. Without saying a word, I led her to the bathroom and turned on the shower.

As she started to undress, she turned to me and begged me not to leave. "I can't be alone right now," she said, trying to fight back her tears. I wrapped my arms around her and hugged her tight, then closed the lid on the toilet and sat down. "I'll stay right here, I promise," I said, finally finding my words again.

While she showered, I tried to remember all the things I'd wanted to say to her, all the things I'd rehearsed. But for some reason I couldn't explain, everything I'd wanted to say seemed hollow, empty, *fake*. Just like her. Fake.

I started to get angry. I couldn't let myself get caught in her psychotic web again. I couldn't let myself be manipulated, and god, she was so good at manipulating me. I had to keep my head straight. I had to remember who she was and what she had done.

When she was done showering, I went to the kitchen and made us some tea. She walked out of the bathroom, wearing my pajamas, and asked if I had anything she could eat. "I haven't eaten in days," she said. I believed her. She was skin and bones. She must have lost fifteen pounds since the last time I saw her.

And then we sat on my bed with crackers and cheese and it all came out at once, her whole story. She'd been telling lies for so long, I was surprised she even remembered the truth (if it really *was* the truth—the crazy thing is, I have no way of knowing).

She told me about her childhood in Moscow, about her (English—not Russian) mother's depression, and her father's failed attempt to become a writer. At a young age, she wanted to follow in her father's footsteps, but she was determined to achieve the success he never could and become the next great Russian novelist. She read voraciously and wrote whenever she could. Everything was going as planned, but it all fell apart when her mother committed suicide. Her father turned to alcohol, became increasingly violent, and eventually lost his job. And Olesya? Well, Olesya had no choice but to drop out of school and take care of her little brother.

"I was fourteen years old," she explained, "and the amount of money anyone would pay a teenage girl to do anything was nowhere close to the amount of money I needed to support me and Nikolay." The only jobs she could get at the time, without any high school diploma or college degree, were low-wage manual labor jobs. "And there was always prostitution," she said, grimacing. She started lying about her age, making fake IDs so that she could pass as a twenty-two-year-old college graduate.

"I made a fake high school diploma, and then I faked a college degree." It worked, but only for so long. A year later, she was caught when she applied for an office job and the hiring manager called the university to verify her degree. "He called me back and yelled at me afterward, but then he gave me a little piece of advice. He said, *If you're going to fake a college degree, at least use the name of someone who actually graduated from the university.*"

She then spent months looking for people who had done things—graduated from college, worked various jobs, written things—but who were complete nobodies. "I needed people who I could masquerade as, people who weren't on anyone's radar, people who had the degrees and résumés that I needed." The best victims of her identity theft scheme, she quickly discovered, were young women who were hospitalized or in long-term psychiatric care, women who'd been in accidents or overdosed on drugs and were in comas.

She watched makeup tutorials on YouTube and learned how to make herself look almost identical to the women she impersonated. She became a pro at using things like fake ears, fake noses, fake eyebrows, special contact lenses, and the wigs I'd seen in her hotel suite. She already spoke Russian and English, but she knew that wouldn't be enough. To get an ear for different accents, she watched movies and recorded herself speaking in a variety of fake voices, practicing over and over again until she had perfected them.

At first, she only perpetuated the lies and used the stolen identities so that she could financially support herself and her younger brother. Using one of the names, she got a job in public relations at a big firm in Moscow and worked her way up the corporate ladder. But after Nikolay graduated from high school, she wanted to do things right.

"I decided I was done with the lies," she said. She applied to universities, wrote a novel and several short stories—all under her own name, without embellishing her résumé—and thought that everything would fall into place. But every college that she applied to rejected her, and she couldn't get any agents or publishers to read what she'd written. "They didn't want any of it. They didn't want *me,*" she said, "and I couldn't figure out *why.* Nothing was different, nothing had changed, except my name and background." Still determined to obtain work legitimately and not fall back into her old identity theft game again, she worked low-paying jobs in Moscow for a few years while she tried to get her life started, but she couldn't get anyone to take her seriously.

"I started to get angry, resentful. I knew I could write. I knew I was smart. I knew that if someone—*anyone*—just gave me a chance, they'd see how amazing I was. But that chance never came, and I wasn't going to sit around and waste my life and my talent. I knew that if I stopped playing by the rules, I could go anywhere, be anyone. The whole world would be open to me."

So that's what she did. "I bought a stolen passport belonging to an Englishwoman and moved to London. A few weeks later, I was Felicity Frankman, stockbroker and graduate of Cambridge University." When she said this last part, she said it in the most perfect English accent I'd ever heard.

Her adventure in England only lasted so long. After two years, the real Felicity was released from the hospital, realized that her passport and identity had been stolen, and reported it to the authorities. Olesya had to give up that alias, and quickly.

Just as Scotland Yard was closing in on her ("At one point, they were *right* outside the door of my flat, and I jumped out the window and ran across the rooftops until I was safely far, far away," she laughed), she stole a passport from an Irishwoman in her building, who was leaving society and "going off the grid" with her wealthy musician boyfriend.

"I took one look at the name on her passport, and I knew exactly who I was going to be next. She had such a literary name, the novels practically wrote themselves," she said. And that's how Daphne Rooney came to be.

Olesya went back to the novel she'd written as a teenager and revised it until it was perfect. And then she found a woman named Margot Fletcher, who had just started a literary agency in New York, Fletcher & Ross, with her partner, Amy Ross.

According to rumors Olesya had heard, Margot had recently been fired from her job at an art gallery in London and was running from an enormous scandal. The move to New York and the complete switch in professions were parts of her attempt at a fresh start. "The family who owned the gallery wanted to keep the whole thing quiet, but *I* knew. I suspected Margot would be eager to sign clients quickly and knew I could use the scandal as leverage over her if she ever figured out who I was and decided to turn me in."

So, one Friday afternoon, she emailed Margot, introduced herself as Daphne Rooney, and sent her the draft of *Marigold*. Margot signed her the following Monday and, six months later, Olesya had a book deal with a major publisher.

They worked this way for a while—Margot in New York, Olesya posing as Daphne in London—but Olesya was running on borrowed time. "Scotland Yard was still searching for me, and I knew I'd always be looking over my shoulder until I got the hell out of there. So I—as Daphne, of course—told Margot I wanted to move to New York, and she helped me get an apartment, a visa, and everything else I needed."

The moment she arrived in New York, she felt at home. "I can't describe how much I fell in love with the city. It was where I was meant to be."

But the advance for *Marigold* was small—too small to live on. So Olesya stole other identities. For a few years, she was "Sophie Bisset"—a persona that was only useful for a few years, when Olesya could still pass as a twentysomething aspiring fashion designer from Paris. Sophie brought Olesya some money, but it wasn't much more than minimum wage.

"I was barely eking by. I didn't realize how little money novelists and amateur fashion designers made, even when they were doing well and doing everything right. I tried to figure out how others were surviving in New York, and found that they almost all had trust funds, were still living with their parents, or were crammed into studio apartments with multiple roommates."

And then, at a party in SoHo one fateful, magical night, she met Inge Wolff. "Inge was perfect. An Austrian heiress, rebelling against her parents, living with a boyfriend her parents absolutely hated. She casually boasted that her father paid for a suite at The Plaza, but that she 'hated the stuffy place' and never went there, and her father owned a place uptown, so he didn't use the suite, either."

While they were at the party, Olesya stole Inge's driver's license and headed straight for The Plaza. "When I arrived,

I told them my father was paying for a room and I would be staying for the foreseeable future. I expected them to kick me out then and there, but they didn't. Instead, they asked if my name was 'Inge Catherine Wolff,' I said, 'Yes, but call me 'Cat,' without so much as blinking, and they led me up to suite 2040.

"Nikolay made me a fake copy of Inge's passport and that was that. I never saw Inge again; the last I heard, she ran away to Buenos Aires with her boyfriend and they secretly eloped. I've been Cat for almost five years now," she said, her ambiguous Russian-mixed-with-a-tinge-of-German-with-a-bit-of-English accent returning. She didn't tell me all the other schemes she'd run since becoming Cat, and she didn't have to—after all of the news clippings I'd read, I knew them all. Or, at least, I knew the ones that had been discovered.

I had so many questions, but one bothered me more than the others. "So you lied to me? The whole time I've known you, you've just been *lying*?"

"I wanted to protect you."

"Protect me? How is lying to me *protecting* me? You *used* me."

"I didn't use you."

"Yes, yes you did."

"I thought of you as my friend."

"We are *not* friends!" I shouted. "Friendship is built on honesty and trust. Friends don't lie to each other. They don't drag each other into schemes and scams, and they certainly don't make them commit, what is this, *fraud*? I don't even know how many terrible things you've done. No, Olesya. I am not your friend. And you have never been mine. You're just a con artist and a liar and a scammer!"

She looked at me with fire in her eyes. "You're no better than me, Lora, and you know it."

"That's not true," I said, shaking my head.

"Look at us. We both came from nothing. We've both been underestimated and trampled and ignored. We've both had to lie to get what we want—what we deserve—in this world."

"No, no, no, I would never."

"Yes, you would. And you did. You lied to your parents. You lied to the world. You even lied to *me*. And I never judged you for it—not for a single moment, Lora—because I have been there myself. I know what you're up against, and that's why I befriended you. That's why I let you live with me; that's why I helped you. You're me, twenty years ago."

Her words left me reeling.

We sat in silence for a few minutes.

I don't know how much time passed before she spoke again, but the sound of her voice cut through the silence in the room like a knife. "Listen, I need to stay here for a few days," she said, her German accent returning as she went back to her fake deep voice.

Against my better judgment, I told her she could stay as long as she liked, but that she'd have to stay inside the apartment. "If anyone sees you around here, if the police find out you're staying with me we'll be in *serious* trouble."

She agreed to keep a low profile. I didn't tell her that I was about to be evicted. I didn't tell her that I was planning to leave for my parents' house in a week and a half.

It was three in the morning when we finally crawled into bed. As I turned off the lights, I thought of one last question I had to ask. "What are you going to do now?"

She was quiet for a moment. "I don't know," she said, her voice cracking. "I can't stop running. I can't stop, because if I do, I'll spend the rest of my life in prison. I don't want to go to prison, Lora. I can't go to prison."

I was just beginning to drift off when I heard her say quietly, "You're my only friend in New York." I pretended I didn't hear her, but I fought back tears. I didn't tell her that she was my only friend here, too. My only friend anywhere.

I couldn't sleep. I kept thinking about what she had said, and I couldn't help but wonder if she was right. Was I really not that different from her? If she hadn't been arrested, and everything hadn't come crashing down with the book deal, would I have been on the path to becoming just another Cat Wolff? Would I have had a choice? Did she?

I did know one thing, however: I *did* have a choice now.

As soon as the sun rose, I carefully crawled out of bed. As I got dressed, I worried that she'd hear me and wake up, but she was completely out, sound asleep. From the way she looked, she probably hadn't had a good night's sleep in quite some time. I wrote a quick note and left it on the nightstand by the bed.

I snuck out the door, taking my laptop, diary, and backpack with me. As I closed the door, I paused for a moment, debating if I should leave the door unlocked or locked.

I locked it. I wanted to give her a fighting chance.

As soon as I stepped out of my building, I called the FBI and told Agent Parker that Cat was in my apartment. I wasn't sure if Cat would hear the sirens, or if the FBI would even use sirens at all, so I buzzed the intercom a few times, hoping that the loud noise would wake her up.

I ran down the street as fast as I could, tears streaming down my face, and saw police cars rushing down the street, headed straight for my apartment.

Olesya,

RUN.

Best Love, Lora

(P.S. I didn't have a choice. I'm so sorry. Please forgive me)

THE NEW YORK TIMES | NEW YORK

'Cat Wolff,' Manhattan Swindler, Steals Yacht and Escapes From Police

Olesya Dorokhova, who called herself 'Cat Wolff,' stole a private yacht and remains a fugitive.

By Teresa Calloway and Jeffrey Blum

June 22, 2018

With warrants out for her arrest in two states and active extradition orders from four different countries, Olesya Dorokhova is no ordinary fugitive. According to the authorities, Ms. Dorokhova, who for several years has gone by a number of aliases including "Cat Wolff" and "Sophie Bisset," conned and schemed her way through Paris, London, San Francisco and New York.

Ms. Dorokhova was arrested last month, but escaped only minutes after her arrest. The FBI had been unable to determine Ms. Dorokhova's whereabouts after her escape. But yesterday, the FBI received a tip from a source that Ms. Dorokhova was staying in an apartment in the East Village.

When the FBI arrived at the apartment, which is believed to belong to a friend of Ms. Dorokhova, they found the apartment empty. Soon after, the New York Police Department received a report that a vacant charter yacht had been stolen from a pier on the East River—only a few blocks away from the apartment.

In the widely televised chase, the FBI and officers from the NYPD followed the yacht, which is reported to belong to

Prestige Yacht Charters, a private yacht charter service, across the East River to Hunter's Point, where they were able to board the yacht. Ms. Dorokhova was nowhere to be found.

NYPD searched the yacht and the surrounding area for the suspect but were unable to locate her. She is believed to have jumped into the river. Authorities have not been able to confirm that Ms. Dorokhova survived the jump. A mission is underway to find the body, but authorities caution that it could take days, even weeks, to recover.

RELATED

Read more about Olesya Dorokhova:

How 'Cat Wolff' Conned New York

Opinion | The Manhattan Con Artist's Only Crime Was Showing Us Who We Really Are

Who Is 'Cat Wolff'? A Look at the Life of the Manhattan Swindler

"We have assured the public that, while the Manhattan Swindler is a fugitive, we do not believe she is violent or poses any danger," NYPD spokesman Don Rattingly said in a press conference Thursday afternoon. "We believe there is no immediate threat, and we aren't even sure she is still alive at this point, but we do encourage members of the public to be on the lookout for Ms. Dorokhova."

A reward of up to $500,000 for information leading to the capture of the fugitive is being offered.

The FBI and NYPD said that inquiries on the matter should be directed to the U.S. Attorney's Office for the Southern District of New York, which did not immediately respond to a request for comment.

The Diary of Lora Ricci

June 22, 2018

She did it.

I don't know *how* she did it, or where she went, but ~~Cat~~ Olesya got away. Again.

Agent Parker called me back a few hours after I called the FBI. She said that they chased Cat through the city, across the East River, and lost track of her near Long Island City when she jumped off a stolen yacht.

She was shouting at me over the phone and sounded so angry at me: "Where is she? Where did she go? Can she swim? Was someone waiting for her? Why did you leave her a note? Why did you warn her? Why didn't you call us earlier? Are you *trying* to go to prison?"

I was freaking out so hard. I thought I had done everything right. I didn't know what else I should have done. Should I have called the FBI the second Cat got to the door? Will I go to jail for the note I left, for telling her to run?

The only thing I could do was tell the FBI the truth, and make sure I didn't leave anything out. So I told Agent Parker what happened, but she wasn't satisfied. She wanted to know where Cat was. I started to get frustrated, because why would *I* know where she went? It was the FBI that followed Cat, for god's sake, not me!

Agent Parker told me I needed to go to the U.S. Attorney's Office *right now* or else she'd have me arrested. Then she hung up. Going to that office was pretty much the last thing in the world I wanted to do, but I didn't have a choice.

I walked back to my apartment. The FBI and the police were still there. I wanted to be alone, so I waited outside until they left, then went inside and took off my clothes, and had a long hot shower. When I got out, I sat on the bed for a few minutes before bursting into tears for what felt like the millionth time. My head was spinning.

I felt weird about feeling relieved that Cat got away, and guilty for feeling relieved when Agent Parker told me they weren't sure she had even survived the jump. *If she's dead, I won't have to testify against her,* I thought for a split second, *and nobody will ever know that I was involved.* I pushed the thought out of my head as quickly as possible. I don't know why I thought that. I don't wish bad on anyone—I know how those thoughts can come back to haunt you.

What if she did get hurt? What if she really did drown when she jumped in the water? I have no idea if she can swim. If she did survive the jump, I have no idea where she might have gone, where she might be hiding. What if she has nowhere to go?

While I was getting ready to leave my apartment to go down to the U.S. Attorney's Office, I kept imagining these awful nightmare scenarios in which her body was found at the bottom of the river. And then I saw myself getting thrown into jail, destined to rot away in prison for the rest of my life, and my mom and dad coming to visit me and finding me in an orange jumpsuit. For a few minutes, I even thought about running away. I could rent a car, drive away, and just keep driving until I couldn't go any farther. Maybe I'd go down to Mexico. Maybe I'd find Olesya and we'd run away together and start brand-new lives. I'd be the Bonnie to her Clyde. We'd rob banks or make fake checks or go somewhere nobody knew our names and would do the same things she did here in New York until the authorities caught on to our schemes.

But even if I wanted to do that (which I really *didn't,* I swear—it was just ~~a fantasy~~ an intrusive thought that popped into my head in the moment), there was no way it could ever happen. I didn't know where she was. And there was no way in hell she'd come back to see me after I'd set the police on her trail. Not now. Not ever.

I finally pulled myself together and headed downtown. The moment I walked through the doors of the U.S. Attorney's Office I could feel this anger and aggression in the air. I was so scared. I honestly didn't even know if I would ever see the outside world again.

I found myself in a room with Agent Parker and Amanda Harris, the Assistant U.S. Attorney who was working on Cat's case. Apparently, the FBI and NYPD had combed "every fucking inch" of Brooklyn and Long Island City, yet there was no trace of Cat. "She just disappeared!" Agent Parker shouted. "Into thin air! It's like she's fucking invisible!"

The crazy thing was, it seemed like she really *had* disappeared. They had knocked on every door, searched every building, watched every CCTV feed. They even sent divers into the river to find her body in case she'd drowned (they haven't found anything, not yet, which is a relief to me—it means she might not be dead; I don't like her, but I really, really don't want her to die).

Agent Parker and Amanda grilled me about everything that happened, again and again and again. I told them everything I remembered, but it wasn't enough. They threatened to have me arrested if I didn't tell them the truth.

"How do we know you haven't been lying to us the whole time?" Agent Parker asked. "How do we know you haven't been running around with Olesya, scamming everyone in New York?" She turned to the prosecutor and said that they should arrest me. "There's no deal," she said, shaking her head. "You helped her, and you're going down with her."

"I swear I didn't do anything wrong!" I shouted, tears streaming down my face. "All I did was write her book. I was just her ghostwriter. I didn't do anything illegal! I swear! You can read my diary—it's all in there!"

This caught her attention. She turned around and both she and Amanda stared at me. Their jaws dropped.

"Um, what diary?" Amanda asked.

"I have a diary, okay? I started writing in it when I started working at *ELLE,* before I met Cat. I wrote about everything we did, about our writing and our friendship and her brother—everything."

"And you've, um, been withholding this from us?"

"It's my diary. It's private. It's personal. I didn't think it was important. I'll give it to you, I'll show you, it'll prove I didn't do anything wrong."

They told me to bring it in. I made them promise that they wouldn't give it to my parents or show it to anybody, but I don't know how well they'll keep that promise. If they use it in their case against Cat, it'll probably become public record and the whole world will get to read it. Goddammit. But I guess it doesn't matter anymore. I'll take public humiliation over jail. Not that I really have a choice at this point.

From: Olesya Dorokhova
To: Nikolay Dorokhov
Subject: (no subject)
Date: June 29, 2018

Kolya—

Wednesday. Sheremetyevo. Flight SU 123.

I'm coming home.

—Olesya

The Diary of Lora Ricci

July 2, 2018

This is the very last diary entry I'll ever write.

Tomorrow morning, I'm going to hand a copy of this diary over to the FBI and the Assistant U.S. Attorney, who will use it as evidence in the case against Cat. I don't want to give it to them, but I don't really have a choice. This diary is the only way I can prove my innocence, the only way they will let me walk free.

After I drop off the diary, I'm going to HarperCollins to drop off the signed contract for my memoir and pick up my first advance payment. Mike Eppman, my new editor, said it would be fine to return the contract and get the check in person.

For now, I'm going to move back in with my parents and write my memoir and the rest of *Horse Girl and Other One-Trick Ponies* from my old bedroom. Thanks to my advance for the two books, I'll have enough money that I won't have to work anywhere for a while. I'm not sure what I'll do next. Maybe I'll find a job in journalism. Or maybe I'll go back to school, somewhere like Penn or Temple or (more likely) back to Penn State.

I don't think I'll move back to New York. Maybe not ever. I know that I'll have to come back and testify against Cat when—or really, *if*—they catch her, but I don't think I could ever call this city "home" again.

When I moved to New York, I hoped that studying at NYU would open doors for me. I thought that I would really, *really* learn how to write, that everything would fall into place, that I would be accepted and mentored and appreciated. Instead, everything fell apart. I wasn't the perfect student. I didn't belong. I wasn't good enough.

And then I met Cat.

She danced into my world and took me on a wild, crazy adventure that completely changed my life. I've resented her so much in the past few months—for turning me into her unwitting accomplice, lying to me, using me, tricking me into helping her scam the world. God, there have been so many times when I thought that meeting her was the worst thing that had ever happened to me. I thought that she had ruined my life.

I feel like I can only say this in retrospect, now that she's gone, but the truth is, I'm so grateful for her. She believed in me. She taught me how to write. She gave me something to write about. She gave me a life worth writing about. She showed me the ways the deck was stacked against people like us, and taught me how to find my way in a world that insisted I didn't belong.

The only thing I wanted in life was to become a writer. That was *it*. That was the big dream.

And now look at me!

I'm a writer, *a real writer,* with something to say, who has a deal with a great publisher to write two books.

Cat made all my dreams come true.

From: Michael Eppman
To: Lora Ricci
Subject: Manuscript
Date: July 2, 2018

Hi Lora,

Thank you for taking the time to chat tonight.

Per our conversation, please bring the signed contract to my office first thing tomorrow morning. My assistant will be there to make sure it gets to the right place.

I'm glad to hear you will be staying with your parents in Pennsylvania for a while. You've had quite the adventure here in New York. Have a wonderful break away from the city, and let me know when you are back.

Let's plan to have a call sometime toward the beginning of August, after you've had some time to settle in and put together an outline.

Best,

Mike

P.S. My assistant will be able to give you your first advance payment when you get here. As per your request, the $300,000 check is made out in your name. We don't usually bifurcate the advance money or royalties—we usually send the checks to the agents, who then send the appropriate amounts to the writers—but Margot has assured me this is fine.

Jenée Parker | 07–03–2018 9:56 AM
I have Lora Ricci's diary

Amanda Harris | 07–03–2018 9:59 AM
Did you remind her re: deal terms?

Jenée Parker | 07–03–2018 10:02 AM
Yeah

Jenée Parker | 07–03–2018 10:03 AM
She knows her diary will be used as evidence

Jenée Parker | 07–03–2018 10:04 AM
And agrees to testify against Dorokhova

Amanda Harris | 07–03–2018 10:04 AM
👍

Amanda Harris | 07–03–2018 10:05 AM
Is she still there with you?

Jenée Parker | 07–03–2018 10:06 AM
No she just left

Jenée Parker | 07–03–2018 10:07 AM
She's moving back in with her parents in PA

Jenée Parker | 07–03–2018 10:09 AM
She asked if there were any travel restrictions

Jenée Parker | 07–03–2018 10:10 AM
I told her no, she's okay as we discussed before

Amanda Harris | 07–03–2018 10:12 AM
Yeah that's right

Amanda Harris | 07–03–2018 10:13 AM
Why did she ask? Is she flying somewhere?

Jenée Parker | 07–03–2018 10:14 AM
I think she's taking the train to Philadelphia

Amanda Harris | 07–03–2018 10:14 AM
Okay

Jenée Parker | 07–03–2018 10:15 AM
She seems traumatized by the whole situation

Amanda Harris | 07–03–2018 10:16 AM
Yeah I bet. I feel bad for her

Jenée Parker | 07–03–2018 10:18 AM
Same

Jenée Parker | 07–03–2018 10:18 AM
She really got taken for a ride

From: Coinbase
To: Lora Ricci
Subject: Your Bitcoin Purchase
Date: July 3, 2018

Congratulations!

You purchased 45.94 Bitcoins (BTC) for $300,000 USD. Those funds are now available in your account.

Thank you for your purchase.

From: Lyft Ride Receipt
To: Lora Ricci
Subject: Your ride with Lovepreet on July 3rd, 2018
Date: July 3, 2018

Lyft

Thanks for riding with Lovepreet!

Lyft fare: $28.24

Congestion Surcharge: $2.75

Tolls: $7.00

Black Car Fund Surcharge: $0.71

New York Sales Tax: $2.51

Apple Pay (American Express): $41.21

Pickup 11:09 AM

HarperCollins Publishers

Drop-off 11:47 AM

JFK TERMINAL

Have a good ride? ADD TIP

NEW YORK MAGAZINE

Letters to the Editor

Horse Girl

We were surprised to find our daughter listed as the author of “I Wrote ‘Horse Girl.’” Like the young woman in the story, our daughter, Lora, was also an English major at NYU and an intern at *ELLE*. But, unlike the young woman in the story, our daughter was seriously injured in a tragic car accident last year and has been in a coma ever since; she is currently hospitalized at the Hospital of the University of Pennsylvania. According to the NYU registrar’s office, only one Lora Ricci has ever been a student at the school: our own Lora Elizabeth. We believe there must be a mix-up or, even worse, that someone has stolen our comatose daughter’s identity. Please issue a correction at once—our friends and relatives have been calling to congratulate us on our daughter’s miraculous (and, frankly, highly unlikely) recovery.

—Tom and Carol Ricci, *Allentown, PA*

Aeroflot Russian Airlines Boarding Pass

BOARDING PASS / посадочный талон

ISSUED BY / выдан: AEROFLOT RUSSIAN AIRLINES

NAME OF PASSENGER / фамилия пассажира:
RICCI / LORAELIZABETH

FROM / от: NEW YORK JFK / JFK

TO / До: MOSCOW SHEREM / SVO

FLIGHT / рейс: SU 123

DATE / Дата: 03JUL

TIME / время: 12:20

TERMINAL 1

GATE: TBA

BOARDING TIME: 11:40

SEAT: 15A

HAVE A NICE TRIP! / Счастливого пути!

Gate closes **20 minutes** before departure / посадка заканчивается **за 20 минут** до времени вылета

Acknowledgments

I would like to thank: Liz Parker, the greatest literary agent on the planet, for everything she does to make all of my wildest writing dreams come true; Liz Stein, my wonderful editor, for believing in me and this book and helping me make it so much better; Ariana Sinclair, Holly Rice, Amelia Wood, and everyone at William Morrow and HarperCollins, for all of their remarkable work; Sara Nestor, my incredible film and TV agent; Ken Kamins, my amazing manager; my brilliant publicist, Rebecca Taylor; Bill Weinstein, Chris Lupo, Haley Haltom, Tiana Coles, and everyone at Verve; Sopan Deb, who read drafts, gave me fantastic notes, and talked me through all the hard times; Jessica Powell, Lindsey Schwoeri, and Sara Fowler, who gave me invaluable feedback on early drafts and gave me the encouragement I needed to keep going; Aisha Harris, Jen Parker, Jenée Desmond-Harris, and Eleanor Barkhorn, for being such wonderful colleagues and friends; the FBI's Office of Public Affairs, for generously spending so much time answering all of my questions (anything that's not realistic in this book is completely my fault); Faran Krentcil and all of the amazing editors, reporters, and interns who helped me understand what it's like to work in the world of fashion journalism; Julie Satow, whose book *The Plaza* served as my tour guide when I couldn't visit The Plaza

Hotel during the pandemic; and, above all, my husband, Chad, for supporting me and loving me and also for laughing with me every time I came up with a new joke to work into the book, and our two beautiful children, Seymour and Boaz, who spent a lot of time in my office cuddling with me while I wrote and edited. To all of you, I owe this book.